The

KINGDOM

of

BROOKLYN

MERRILL JOAN GERBER

LONGSTREET PRESS

Atlanta, Georgia

The
KINGDOM
of
BROOKLYN

Published by LONGSTREET PRESS, INC.
A subsidiary of Cox Newspapers, Inc.
2140 Newmarket Parkway
Suite 118
Marietta, Georgia 30067

Printed in the United States of America

1st printing, 1992

Library of Congress Catalog Number 91-71785

ISBN: 1-56352-022-2

This book was printed by R. R. Donnelley & Sons, Harrisonburg,
Virginia. The text was set in Sabon.
Book design by Jill Dible.
Jacket design by Tonya Beach.

For my daughters,
Becky
Joanna
Susanna

The

KINGDOM

of

BROOKLYN

1

There Issa is. There, faltering on the top of the front stoop, wearing a red plaid dress with a white lace collar. (Since it is March, and cold, how did I ever escape without a sweater?) A customer of Gilda's is coming up the walk to the house. She is here to get a haircut upstairs. She shocks me by saying, "Issa dear, what a big girl you are!"

I am three years old today and the one truth I know about myself is that I am a very small girl, very little, hardly a person yet. Grownups can be wrong and grownups can be stupid. I am shocked but deeply satisfied by this idea. I feel stronger, knowing it.

Upstairs in the beauty shop is where real life is: the clip, clip of Gilda's silver scissors, the sizzle of the little sausages of brown paper as she dips them in hot water, their sudden squish as she presses them into the rubber tubes. The tubes are part of the metal holders that Gilda clips over the cylinders of the women's rolled hair. Their hair fries and smells terrible, but afterward gets curly and beautiful. Gilda, my aunt, is a magician.

Gilda announces to all her ladies, "My little angel has natural curls. She'll never have to come to me." She presents me, holding out her arm as if I am coming on stage (I have already been to a movie where dancing girls kick their legs high) but what she says isn't true. I'll always have to come to Gilda. I'll always want to. I wish she were my mother and not my aunt because an aunt can't have me whenever she wants.

My mother owns me and says so. "You're mine, you're not hers. And she better not forget it." Sometimes when Gilda wants to take me shopping on Avenue P, my mother says, "No, you cannot go with her to the bakery. She wants you to? So what? She wants lots of things. She'd like to have your father, too, if she could. She'd probably like to do away with me. No, darling, it's too bad if she wants to take you to the bakery. You stay right here with me."

I don't know why it has to be too bad, my mother has no plans. I could be with Gilda without hurting anyone, without having to stay in this house where someone, possibly myself, will die soon. This is the house where my grandmother is busy clutching her chest and putting small white pills under her tongue, where my mother has to squint her eyes shut against the pain in her head. Something terrible is definitely going to happen in this house.

Outside, with Gilda, if I could go shopping with her, I would hold onto the black wicker stroller (I don't ride in it anymore) as we walk down 4th Street to Avenue P, past the three playgrounds strung out across 3rd, 4th and 5th Streets, to the fish store and the bakery, past the Claridge Theater (where I first met Pinocchio), into the drugstore where Mr. Bass always gives me a Cocilana cough drop. With Gilda I am important; Gilda holds back her arm and presents me joyfully to the world.

When my mother drags me shopping (I feel dragged; I hold onto the stroller and she races along with it so that I am pulled) she never talks to the bakery lady, she only buys bread, buys it fast, is annoyed when the bakery lady gives me a cookie. She's annoyed that the bakery lady knows all about me from my trips with Gilda (bends down to talk to me, asks me about my doll, Margaret—Peggy for short—by name); my mother doesn't see the sense of wasting time on chatter with unimportant people. For Gilda talking to people is the whole point of shopping.

* * *

My mother has to put up with a lot; that's what my father tells me when she has her fits. My mother has to have three things besides cooking every day: her fits, her headaches, and her piano playing. The fits come the instant I don't eat my food. She thinks I will die if I don't eat whatever she cooks for me, and the meals are endless. Hardly do I manage to get up from the hard kitchen chair after one meal when she begins chopping and peeling for the next. She hates grease on her hands, the smell of onions on her fingertips, but she cooks so I can stay alive.

Why does she think I could die at any moment? I have come to believe, I am *certain*, this is a real possibility. When I think it, my heart loops loose like the chains of the swing when I pump too hard; also something snaps shut in my throat.

As soon as she's done cooking and I don't eat it all, she gets her headache. Her headaches started when The Tree Trunk didn't want her to name me Issa. The Tree Trunk is the secret name she calls the other grandmother, my father's mother, because of her thick ankles. The Tree Trunk told my mother Issa was no name for a girl. My mother said, "She's my baby and I'll name her what I please!"

Issa sounds like a secret, like the steam escaping from the pressure cooker so it won't explode and kill us all. *Issa* is me. Part of me comes from my mother's dead father, Isaac, who died on my birthday ten years before I was born.

The Tree Trunk argued with her, and then pulled me bodily out of my mother's arms. At that moment my mother got her first blinding headache. Maybe it was also the moment my own heart tore loose and began its wild flying about in my chest. Who knows? Everything has the moment of its beginning; my mother is certain of it. Usually someone is to blame.

Bring me a wet cloth, darling.

I know how to do this very well, I am the family expert when the headaches come. I wring out the washcloth so it doesn't drip, but isn't too dry. I make sure the shades are pulled down before I take the cloth to her bed and lay it over her forehead. There is a blue wing-shape beating above her eye. I have checked my own forehead to see if I have one, but the only blue in my face is the color of my eyes. ("Like little bluebells," Gilda described my eyes to one of her ladies. "Blue eyes, yellow curls, pink cheeks. This child is the rainbow of my life.")

"Keep everyone out," my mother tells me when the washcloth is in place. She means my grandmother and the ladies, who like to offer their wishes for her to feel better. In the next room we can hear the clip of Gilda's scissors and the dull roar of the standing hair dryer. I am turned into a policeman for my mother, which stiffens my mind. It means I cannot get deeply into my games with my doll and her cradle, with my forcing Peggy to eat unless she wants to die, with my punishing her for not eating and giving me headaches.

Being given authority means I have to be alert and pay attention so that no one peeks into the bedroom and bothers my mother. I feel important but under pressure, limited in my freedom.

My mother is bothered by so many things. I understand that it's possible to see the whole world as a bother; I begin to practice thinking this. It's very satisfying. Instead of being bored and obedient, I begin to have tantrums almost as wild as my mother's. I can tell she admires me for this. I carry on about the unfairness of having to eat when I don't want to, of having to take a bath and shiver till my teeth bang together.

Being cold is my horror: each night I dread getting out of my warm clothes and into cold pajamas, sliding into a bed as hard and cold as whatever it is we all fear will happen in this house. Then—each morning there is a worse threat: the furnace in the cellar shudders and bellows. Every radiator in the house begins to clank as if there is a monster in there with a great hammer. One day the pipes will burst and we will all be engulfed in flames. I have seen the furnace; I know. When the door of it is opened, I understand what it must be like to die by fire.

My father watches me change. His forehead creases. I know he's worried that I am not enjoying myself. He points out to me the beauty of icicles hanging from the eaves. He warms my cold sheets with a hot frying pan before I slide into bed, he holds the wedge of an orange inside his lips to make me laugh (I don't), he sees me sitting on the toilet with a stomach ache, and he sticks his head in the doorway, making horrible faces while using his own hand to grab his own hair and pull his head away.

I protect my stomach ache, keep it with me, double over with it, and throw him a look of disgust. I am catching on: *look what I have to go through!* My mother is extremely pleased I have learned her important lesson.

She invites me to join her in bed, wring out a washcloth for myself as well as for her. We lie there in the dim bedroom, hearing the whirr of the electric clock and the hum of the standing hairdryer from the next room. I wish she would hold my hand, but she doesn't. We could both die at any moment. Won't my grandmother be upset? Won't Gilda? And won't Daddy? We will have their complete attention if we die. We can almost never get it during regular time. My grandmother is busy holding her heart, and Gilda is absorbed cutting hair and my father is determined to make endless, silly jokes. They are all so stupid. My mother wants me to see this. I do, it's true. Stupid, stupid. I discover this myself, in grownups, even before she points it out to me. But could it be my mother is wrong some of the time, lying in the dark, sighing angrily? Aren't there also things that are wonderful? Beautiful? Isn't the snow beautiful? Isn't Gilda's dog, Bingo, beautiful, lying with his nose between his paws, his sad eyes watching Gilda cut hair?

My mother is surely beautiful, resting there. If I could roll over and press my cheek against her, my heart's swinging chain would slow down and hook back into rhythm, the gate in my throat would open. I might even become hungry. But she keeps her profile to me, her nose toward heaven, waiting for something to save her.

* * *

On certain nights my father goes on "calls." On these nights he could be robbed because he carries rolls of money in his pocket. He goes up long stairways in strange houses to attics, or down long stairways in strange houses to cellars to buy antiques which he needs for his store. Anyone might be waiting to knock him over the head with a gun; strangers call and he goes to whatever house they ask him to go to and he takes rolls of cash. Is he really that stupid? Would he *be* that stupid, that he would let himself be knocked over the head and die? What would we do without him?

No one seems to know. They all watch out the front windows of the house, taking turns. Gilda and my mother peek out from behind the curtains every few minutes, but my grandmother opens the front door and lets blasts of icy wind come in. On the street, cars swish through the slush; I can see the snow falling against the street lamp. The place where my father would park his car, just in front of the wishbone tree, is empty. I begin to imagine how the scene will look as his car pulls up, its headlights shining on the hedges along the street. Please let it pull up, let him be in it, let him come into the house shaking snow from his hat, let him put his huge freezing fingers on my cheeks, let me have him back!

Now I know why everyone in this house is afraid to die. We would be gone forever. It is the worst thing that can happen to you, and it is the worst thing you can do to someone else, be gone forever.

Knowing this gives me a new bad feeling, different from all other bad feelings, and it is the worst. Absolutely the worst. I watch with them, I keep my eyes at the window, I press my hot, damp palms against the cold glass, making paw prints, where is he? *Where is he? Daddy, I want you, want you, want you!*

Sometimes I am forced to go to bed, but sometimes I am awake when he comes in, in a blast of cold, a cloud of smoke coming out of his mouth. He is alive! The women dance around him, taking his coat, his scarf, his hat. They don't even ask if someone hit him over the head and took his money. They just surround him, and then Gilda makes him hot chocolate, and my mother brings him his pipe, and my grandmother smiles with her big white teeth while she lays his scarf on the radiator. Even though it's late at night, very late, and the whole world is sleeping, my mother—just before we all go upstairs to bed—sometimes plays a few chords on the piano, not sitting down, but with her head bowed over the keys, chords that are deep and thrilling, but are also wonderful and calming. They reverberate through the house, they make the curtains shiver. When she raises her head, we all smile at each other. For this night we are safely here, all of us together.

* * *

The piano is the one place my mother can get calm. The piano sits, unafraid of her, square in the living room downstairs. Its legs are also like tree trunks, but these she admires, down on her knees, dusting and polishing them, standing to caress the shiny black lid above them. When my mother plays, I know she is not thinking about any-thing but music. She has forgotten me by the time her pretty legs move about under the bench. One is tucked back, and one taps here and there on the pedals, those lit-tle rounded gold feet I like to rub with my finger. They are cold and smooth to my touch. She doesn't mind if I lie under the piano while she plays. She doesn't care about me at all, or about anything, then.

I love her music because—when she plays it—I am safe from her fury and she is happy.

* * *

There comes a day I simply cannot swallow little squares of liver. They have things in them, secret pock-marks, rubber knots that will not be chewed or swal-lowed. My mother has broiled them on a wire grate.

Flames have shot into the air, nearly catching her hair on fire. (Her hair has gone white. Worry has turned her hair white. *I* have turned her hair white.) On the plate are lima beans, grainy as mashed chalk. And spinach, which has iron in it, that Popeye eats for strength, but it's sandy in my mouth. I cannot ever eat enough to please my mother.

"Eat it," she says. "Chew and swallow it or I'll kill you." It's very simple. Either I will die from not eating, or I will die while eating, or—if I don't eat—she will see to it that I die by her own hand. My stomach ache comes back, my old friend that now lives with me. I know this pain. It swirls and swishes like the washing machine in the cellar. I double over with it—it's wonderful, it will get me to the bathroom where I can spit out the liver.

"No you don't," my mother says. She has left the burner on and blue flames form a star on the top of the stove. "You will not get away with that. Do you know what the butcher charges for liver? Your father works his heart out to pay the butcher."

I gag. I didn't plan it, but I gag.

"All right," she says. "I'm calling the Peter Pan Nursery." We both know what happens there. Even though she knows I know, she tells me again. "When they take bad girls like you away to live there, they give you black stockings to wear. If you don't eat, they make you sit at the table till you do. And if you throw up, they make you eat the vomit from the floor."

This is the moment when my mother goes to the phone. Black and cold, it sits in the living room. When she picks it up, I become a giant ear. I freeze as she begins to dial. I count. She is proud that I can count and have not yet begun kindergarten. I count: one, two, three, four, five, six! Only six! I am saved! Six is not a phone number. Only seven dials of her forefinger is a phone number. Only seven dials will bring the black van from the Peter Pan Nursery. Only seven swings around the circle of the dial will bring my tongue to floor to lap up liver vomit.

She is warning me, that's all.

I rush to my seat at the table. Gratefully, I shove little

cubes of cold liver into my mouth. I set my teeth to grinding. Gag all you want, I tell the snake moving up and down in my throat. I will get this down. I love her! She isn't going to send me there tonight. Tonight I get to slide between my freezing sheets and live till morning.

* * *

In the morning we do rhymes sitting on her bed. I want to help Gilda with the ladies, but my mother insists that rhymes are very important, more important than *hair*.

"Star!"

"Far!"

"Cat!"

"Hat!"

"Another!"

"Mother!"

"No—another word that rhymes with hat."

"Bat! Fat! Rat!"

She kisses me. I glow, there is a hot spot at the point her kiss meets my cheek.

"Tomato!" she cries out.

"Potato!"

Now she hugs me. Hugs and kisses. For this!

"Candy!"

"Sandy!"

"Jacket!"

"Racket!"

We both laugh in triumph.

"Olive."

"Bolive."

"Don't be silly," she says. "We can't afford to be silly about this."

"Why can't we?"

"Because if you do this right, you are going to be a very important person."

"Really?" I have her attention now.

"You are already brilliant," she says. "Just wait and see, Issa. You are going to be someone *important*."

How to behave when I go to school is what we talk about. I am not going to school for a long, long time. I am still too small, but my mother wants me to be prepared. I didn't know there could be so many situations to cause trouble, but my mother paints them for me in varieties of difficulty so convoluted that my stomach reaches a new level of agitation. If children make fun of me (why would they?) I must remember that I'm important and they are nothing. If a bad boy hits me (why would he?) I must tell the teacher at once. And above all, I must always listen to what the teacher says. Teachers know important things, they aren't like Gilda, who only cuts hair and chatters all day with big-mouth women. (None of Gilda's customers have bigger mouths than anyone else. I check to see.) But after these sessions with my mother, waves, bigger than those I have seen at Coney Island, wrench the flat surface of my belly, and now I can see, as well as feel, the grinding avalanches of pain.

"Butterflies," Gilda says to me, as—more than ever—I have to hog the toilet, keeping her from bringing her ladies inside for their shampoos. "Everyone gets butter- flies when they worry. But your mother is getting you into a state for nothing and she shouldn't be doing this."

An alarm goes off in my head. This is what I have been

warned that Gilda should never do: talk against my mother.

While I clutch my stomach, Gilda tells her lady to wait in the beauty parlor for a few minutes and read a magazine. Then she gets a wire pull from the milk bottle cap and begins forming it into a flower for me. She sits on the tile floor of the bathroom while I hunch over her on the toilet and feel the wild animals (not butterflies) roaring in my stomach. Gilda is so patient with me, I want to stroke her pitted face.

"There. One petal, two petals, three petals." Gilda leans on the round curve of her hip with her legs out to the side. Everything about her is dainty. Her auburn hair, twisted like a challah, shines in the light. She forms a flower for me out of the silver wire.

"I have to get in there," my mother says at the door.

"Issa is in here. Her stomach again."

"Do *you* have to be in there, too? Do the two of you have to have a party in there? Let me get in there to throw up."

My mother comes in and Gilda goes out fast. My mother heaves and gags over the sink, violently pushing away the shampoo tray on a stand that the ladies fit their necks into. She doesn't really vomit. I watch though I don't want to see it come out, but nothing does. She tries and tries. What makes her want to vomit? She isn't even trying to chew and swallow liver. My mother eats only chocolate malteds and sliced tomatoes.

"Look at this!" she screams to me. I slide off the toilet seat and pull up my pants. I look in the sink where little black hairs from the ladies' shampoos lie curled like worms along the edges of the porcelain.

"I can't take it! I'm through putting up with this!" my mother cries. "I can't take it another minute. I wish to God your father were home. I'd like him to have to stick *his* face in this sink."

* * *

What my mother can't take is not having privacy. She talks about privacy as if it were an object, like a glass statue of an angel, something my father once bought on a call, something hard to find, hard to get, valuable and rare, but to which she is entitled. She enumerates to me the damages done to her daily: how my grandmother comes into the bedroom *while she and my father are still in bed* to gather laundry for the wash. The endless appearance of Gilda's customers up and down the front walk, their chatter in the bedroom Gilda uses for a beauty shop, their hairs, their *disgusting* hairs, in the sink in the bathroom. There is more—how for years *she* has been taking care of Gilda and Grandma and enough is enough. Let Gilda get a job out in the world. Let her get married. Let someone else put a roof over her head. Let her take my grandmother with her and *disappear*.

Later that night she tells all this again to my father. He holds me on his lap on the green chair while she rages around the bedroom. I'm fine when he is holding me, balancing the center of my behind on his thigh. His thick arms around my waist will keep her from hitting me even if she wants to. He doesn't like her to hit me, ever. She doesn't really hurt me when she hits; it's just that the sound of her screams gets deafening when she swings her hand at me and I think the roof will come down and the walls fall in.

When my father tries to defend Gilda, take her side, remind my mother that Gilda isn't beautiful like my mother is, that she doesn't do well out in the world, my mother screams: "So you want her here forever? Then divorce me and marry her!"

This idea gives me a horrific, wonderful thrill. Gilda—now my mother—making wire flowers for me. My father—now Gilda's husband—warming my bed with a hot frying pan. It will be quiet and peaceful with just the three of us. Maybe even my grandmother can stay. I will never have to count the turns of the dial to the Peter Pan Nursery.

* * *

The next time I can't swallow, when the three-minute egg, with all its slime and mucous, won't go down my throat, my mother lifts me straight out of my chair. The gate in my throat has simply locked shut, there is nothing I can do to get the white slime to move from my tongue down my throat. It has slipped back out into the spoon.

"I have no choice," she tells me. "You have forced me to this." She runs upstairs and I follow in terror. I beg God (he is the same man as "The Lord" in the prayer I have to say at night) behind my closed eyes for a lady to be in the bathroom having a shampoo. But no one is there. Only Bingo is in the hall, his ears laid back, his dark fur moving as he breathes heavily.

She has already taken from the medicine cabinet the bottle of iodine—the torture of my life, the dreaded liquid fire she applies to my cuts to kill the germs, the red-black poison she spreads with its glass tube over my bleeding flesh. The pain from it is much worse than the scrape of the roughest cement on my knees. Glass tubes are terrible instruments; mothers take your temperature with them, mothers run them along open wounds. (If the glass breaks, it can kill you.)

The iodine label has a skull on it to remind me—and anyone else: "Never swallow this." (Did she think, after what it did to my knees, that I would ever take it into my mouth?)

But now she plans to swallow it herself because the egg was too soft, because I have driven her to it.

"Please, don't!" I tug on her skirt. I wrap my arms around her hips. "Mommy! Please don't!"

Gilda comes running down the hall, her silver scissors held aloft. "What's happening here? Why is Issa crying?"

"Mind your own business! Issa is mine."

"I couldn't swallow my egg," I try to explain.

"Ruth, you're out of your mind!" Gilda cries. "You're going to destroy this child."

"She's none of your business," my mother screams.

Then she flings the iodine bottle into the bathtub, where it shatters. The red poison drips down the porcelain side and forms a row of zig-zag teeth.

"You belong in an insane asylum like Mrs. Disic next door. They need to come and take you away in a strait jacket."

My mother glows blue like the liver flaring in its grate on the stove.

"Keep your claws off my child and off my husband," she warns Gilda. Her eyes have something wild in them. I don't even recognize her.

"He won't be your husband much longer if you keep this up," Gilda hisses. "No man can take this forever." Gilda's face is white. "You're crazy, Ruth. Look what you're doing to this precious child."

I am sobbing and pulling toilet paper off the roll in long strands, shredding it and pushing it into my eyes.

"Go down to the kitchen and help Grandma make mandelbrot," Gilda whispers to me. "Or go play with your doll."

I wipe my eyes on her apron. I run out of the bathroom to my room and jerk Margaret/Peggy from her cradle. She has a painted-on, blank stupid face. Stupid! They're all so stupid. They all ought to take iodine and leave me alone.

* * *

I am Jewish. Being Jewish means I am entitled to wear a blue star around my neck instead of a gold cross. The person who teaches me this is Mrs. Esposito, who lives on a farm on the corner—with chickens in a cage and two goats in the backyard. She grows grapes and tomatoes and big cabbages. Two men live with her, Tommy and Joe; one is her brother and one is her husband, but I can't tell them apart. Gilda takes me there to collect money for the Red Cross and Mrs. Esposito invites us in, gives us sour balls to suck, and puts strangely shaped tomatoes in a bag for me to take home.

One day she gives me a teeny blue six-pointed star,

rimmed in gold. She fastens it around my neck, bending so close I can smell her hair. I feel something important has happened to me, although I don't know why. Kneeling in front of me, she holds out the chain of her gold cross and I hold out my blue star. We let them touch. Then we smile and she kisses me. I am proud to be Jewish, it seems to be a good thing. Gilda is proud of me, too. She hugs me. Anything that happens away from the house is good. Anything that happens in the house gives me terrible stomach pains.

* * *

A war is going on across the sea, men are killing one another although their bullets can't get to me.

"They are fighting across the ocean and the ocean is this big," my father says, "as big as the world." He is stretched out on the floor of the living room and I am sitting on his chest with my shoes tucked under each of his armpits and my palms pressing over his beating heart. My mother is playing the piano, something she laughs at called boogie-woogie. Her bottom, which is heart-shaped, jiggles on the piano bench as she rocks from side to side, playing. When she thumps on the low keys, my father bumps me up on his chest and I ride along, laughing. My grandmother passes through the room and stops because we are all laughing. She laughs, too—her teeth are big and white and even. I've seen them both in and out of her mouth. She's very nice, but not too interesting.

Gilda comes downstairs and my mother starts to play "White Christmas." Gilda leans into the curve of the piano and sings along—she has a voice like the thinnest end of an icicle, very sharp and cold and high. It drips with music, but it could crack, break. My father admires her voice. His eyes are bright, watching her. The war, luckily, has made us all sing and laugh. We have had to draw the black curtains closed and pin them together so the airplanes can't bomb our house. Even though we are safe, I don't feel safe. The bombs could hit; the planes

could come across the sea (they fly fast), they could see
the light through the curtains, the bombs could hit right in
the center of the piano. Bingo seems to understand this
because the louder the music gets, the flatter his ears get,
till finally he runs off to the kitchen with his tail bent
under. His tail and his ears are flat. I know never to pet
him when he's that way.

When it's time to go to bed, my father gets the frying
pan hot for me. It looks like cooking, but it isn't. The pan
is empty of food, which looks wrong but makes me very
happy. He carries me upstairs sitting on his shoulders, his
neck between my legs. His one hand holds my ankle and
one the frying pan.

He knows I hate my cold pajamas, so he says, "Let's
not tell anyone you're going to sleep in your clothes. We'll
just cover you way up to your nose! No one will ever
know. And in the morning you'll be dressed already!"

He zips the hot pan over my sheets, he zips me under
the blanket, he rubs noses with me.

The next thing is the prayer my mother taught me
because she likes the rhymes in it: *Now I lay me down to
sleep, I pray the Lord my soul to keep . . .* but there is
something wrong with this, according to my father.

"We don't have a Lord, not that one," he says. "Don't
say that anymore," he tells me. "Even if she wants you
to."

It's hard to remember what I shouldn't say in front of
certain people because other people don't want me to. It's
like not letting Gilda talk about my mother. I have to
watch my lips, my ears. Soon I will have to not see what I
see.

I don't want to stop feeling good. My father kisses me
goodnight and goes downstairs. The instant he leaves my
room, the face appears at the window. It's always there,
I'm used to it, it's the little man who hangs onto the window sill with his fingertips and stares in at me. He doesn't
try to come in, but he watches me and makes my heart
flip. If I am brave enough, I can turn my back on him, but
sometimes I have to scream out, into the hall, down the

stairs, scream for a drink of water.

Sometimes my mother comes up, or my father. Sometimes my grandmother, but she's very slow. Best, of course, is Gilda, who knows it isn't water I want, but herself, in my bed, next to me, till I go to sleep. In the morning, the man at the window is always gone.

CHAPTER

3

Although my father does not wear a six-pointed star, he is also Jewish. One night he stands in the corner of his bedroom facing the wall, wearing a white shawl around his shoulders, a small round black hat on his head, and he bends forward and back, forward and back, mumbling over a book he holds in both hands. I have come in to get a puzzle I left on the bed earlier in the day, when my mother and I were both lying there like twins with washcloths on our foreheads.

His rounded shoulders alarm me, since he looks weak, not strong as he always is. I am glad my mother doesn't see him in this posture, because it would make her more powerful to know he could be reduced in this way to a small man.

What is he doing? It is not a song he is singing, but it rises and falls like music. It is not a lesson he is learning because, though he holds the book, his eyes are closed. I know he would not want to be disturbed; this is very serious, very private. I back out the door, and ask no one, not even Gilda, what he is doing.

* * *

The shul is another place to be Jewish. In the fall of the

year, Gilda closes the doors of her beauty shop and she and my father walk to the Avenue N shul. He wears the same white shawl and carries the black book; Gilda is dressed in a dark blue dress, a blue coat and a black hat. We pass by all the familiar houses on 4th Street—some of Gilda's customers live here; also some old ladies my grandmother knows, who come and sit with her on the bench in front of our house.

My mother cannot be with us on this walk to shul; she has been arguing with my father, and her headache is so bad she is nearly blind. The argument made my grandmother run to the couch, clutching her chest. Now the two sick women are resting, one with her little bottle of pills, one with her washcloth.

I crunch my shoes in the dry maple leaves blown in piles against the garden hedges and watch Gilda's heels click in tune to the rhythm of my father's big walking feet. How nice to smell the leaves and be out of the house. How lucky I feel for no special reason.

Because he is Jewish, my father has to pray all day today. He can't eat. He can't shave. He can't laugh. He goes downstairs in the shul, and Gilda takes me upstairs, where the women are. When I get tired, she lets me walk around outside. I can look into a basement window and see the men below, all of them round-shouldered, hunched forward and rocking in their white shawls the way my father rocked in the corner. They are all humming, but not exactly a song. They are singing words, but not the same words. They all look a little weak, not strong the way men are. They all look like my father, but not the father I am used to.

Gilda's black hat has a veil that covers her face. She looks quite beautiful, with the little black squares covering her eyes and her nose. When she breathes, the veil quivers. Outside we meet some of her ladies, but they don't chatter and tell stories the way they do in the beauty parlor, they look very serious, almost on the verge of tears. Not one of them looks as if she has ever had her hair fried or her nails painted; in fact, they all wear dark gloves, like Gilda. Something is going on and it's very important. I am honored to be part of it.

Gilda takes me home and I take a nap with my mother. Much later, my father comes home. He speaks to me and his breath smells bad. His face is gray with growing beard. I hope he will not rub his cheek against mine and scratch me. My grandmother is busy in the kitchen. She prepares food very calmly, not like my mother. She moves slowly, she won't care if I eat it or not, she isn't going to kill me if I don't swallow something. Something is flat about her—as if, if I pushed my finger against her pale skin, it would stay pushed in. Her skin is like flour dough. She is my white, soft, old grandmother.

I like the cold food she is preparing, nothing meaty, nothing greasy, nothing slimy about what she is putting on the table. Smoked white fish, and bagels and lox and cream cheese—nothing that will get stuck in my throat. I love challah, fluffy bread that tears apart and tastes sweet and wonderful. I especially love food that no one watches me eat.

For once, on this special night, no one is watching me chew and swallow. My mother eats sullenly—not what's on the table, but her own meal: tomatoes and a chocolate malted. Gilda and my father are in very good spirits. "To the new year," my father says and lifts his glass. "To the new year and health and happiness," Gilda says, and lifts hers. She offers me a sip of her wine, sweet grape wine. It burns my throat but goes down easily. I like it! I ask for more. My father gives me a sip of his. My mother flies up from her chair and goes into the living room to play the piano.

Boogie-woogie comes out.

"Please, not that music, not now, Ruthie," my father calls to her.

She plays louder.

Gilda and my father look at each other.

"You should take her on a vacation," my grandmother says. "She's no good this way."

* * *

Because we leave Brooklyn and ride the train for days and nights, we are going to get that thing my mother needs so badly—privacy—and we will get it in Miami Beach. We will get coconuts and hot air. We will get soldiers in our hotel. The war is closer here, because we are right on the edge of the ocean; no one tells me, but I know, that just on the other side of the water is where the fighting and bombing go on.

For once there are just the three of us: Mommy, Daddy and Issa. We live in one room with three flowered couch-beds. Why does Mommy still have to throw up? There are no customers, no hairs in the sink, no hair frying, no liver cooking. Why is Issa still getting stomach aches? There is no more talk of kindergarten—that is still nearly a whole year away. Why has Daddy left his white shawl at home? Why are we in this hot place where I never get cold and there is no furnace?

Gilda isn't here, Bingo isn't here, Grandma isn't here. That means there's nowhere to run if Mommy gets wild. The good facts are that there's no iodine here, no telephone (except the one in the lobby), and no Peter Pan Nursery.

* * *

This is not a vacation. This is serious business. We may be able to stay here forever. Another person is coming, too. My brother or my sister. All this is revealed to me on the day I am given a matching spoon and fork set in a little box. The utensils have pearly handles; one has a shiny bowl, one has shiny, sharp prongs.

Out on the street we can hear the soldiers marching, *Hup*, two, three, four, *hup*, two, three, four. I count *one* when they say *hup*, but it's close to what I know. Their legs open and close like scissors, they have guns over their shoulders, but they are not going to shoot them here, only across the sea.

My father goes out every day to find a business. Grandma and Gilda don't know about this, it is a big secret. My mother puts her finger across her red lips and smiles. *A secret.* If Daddy finds the business, we can stay here forever where it's warm. We will never have to hear the radiator pipes bang again. She and I stay on the flowered beds all day, my mother resting or eating sliced cold tomatoes, and I playing with Margaret/Peggy, or cutting heads of ladies out of the newspaper (when I cut out ladies' heads, I pretend I am Gilda, and also cut their hair. I cut some of them bald so they have no hair at all).

When my mother and I walk on the beach, we discover it is covered with soldiers. They spread out like a brown rug all over the sand. They stand in line or lean against palm trees or sit in circles till the mess hall opens and they can go in to eat. (I ask myself why they call food "mess." I have many ideas that seem like good answers.) My mother's cheeks get red when the soldiers stop and talk to me. Her hair is long at the sides and her bangs are frizzed at the front. Just before we left Brooklyn, Gilda convinced her to sit down in the beauty parlor chair and "get some curls around that puss of yours."

My mother agreed, which surprised me. But she said, "Just as long as you don't take my eyes out or stab me in the back with your scissors." Gilda dipped the sausages in hot water herself, she did her magic quietly, and my mother didn't chat like one of the regular ladies. After she finished my mother's bangs, my mother said, "That's enough. I don't need curls all over, I don't want you making me into some kind of movie star."

"You're no movie star," Gilda said, "believe me."

What happens on the beach is that the soldiers don't talk to my mother at first, they always talk to me. Then, after they learn my name, they begin to talk with her. They forget me and they make her smile, even laugh. She blushes when she laughs. She casts her eyes down to the sand. Her shorts flare out over her hips like a tiny skirt. She has dimples in her knees.

Day after day I play in the sand at the edge of the water

till only the bottoms of my feet are white while the rest of me has turned brown. I have a new pinafore in the shape of a blue-and-white butterfly. My mother takes dozens of pictures of me because I am so beautiful. She hasn't had one headache in Miami Beach; I am afraid to tell her this, in case it will remind them to come back.

* * *

Where my father finds a business, or how, I never know. But we go there the next day and we see him in a store, which is now his. He sells—not bread, not cough drops, not fish—but the voices of soldiers. In his store they can write letters without a pen, or sing a song to send directly home to their mothers or wives.

There's not much in this store, it's tiny, all there is is a little booth with a curtain around it (like at the doctor's office) and a machine that turns a record around and spins out black thread. He lets me stand next to the recording machine, lets me collect the springy strands of warm black plastic. He sings to show me how it works: *"You are my sunshine, my only sunshine, you make me haaaaapy, when skies are gray, you'll never know dear, how much I love you, please don't take my sunshine away."* Then he plays the record for me on the record player and there it is, my father's wavery familiar, golden voice, telling me how much he loves me.

"See? See?" he says joyfully. "Every soldier can send his voice home, captured forever on a record."

"In case he dies in the war," my mother says. She hates the war, just like she hates shul, and chatting in the bakery, and Gilda's ladies. But the war is interesting to me—there are the soldiers marching, and the soldiers counting and the soldiers singing: *"Off we go into the wild blue yonder, flying high, into the sun . . . ."* One soldier has given me a Hershey bar on the beach, after asking my mother's permission. Another let me ride on his shoulders and touch the golden wings pinned to the front of his hat.

This is a wonderful place, this beach, this sunny place,

without trouble, without liver, without . . . I have almost forgotten my grandmother and Gilda. I feel a shock of shame.

But my father is showing us the business next door, where a fake palm tree is against the wall, and where the soldiers have pictures taken of themselves to send home to their mothers and wives. He already has a friend there, Eddie, who offers to take a picture of the three of us. So there we are, I in my blue-and-white pinafore, with my brown legs and white soles, and my mother with her frizzy bangs and round tummy, and my father, with his sweet face, his wild curly hair, his wonderful smile. I love the way we are, all of us happy, none of us sick.

"A paradise on earth," my father tells my mother at night, when the three of us are in our flowered beds. "All we need to do now is kill Hitler."

CHAPTER

4

There is no upstairs or downstairs here, no backyard or front yard, no Bingo, no ladies who tell stories about their operations or about husbands who won't ask for a raise even after they have worked twenty years selling clothes at Macy's. There is only "Let's Pretend" and "The White Rabbit Bus" on the radio, "Sing this song with your Uncle Don," and news about the war.

In the daytime, on the beach, I collect baby coconuts, which at night I peel away leaf by leaf, layer by layer, imagining that at the core I will find a tiny crystal doll-baby, or a miniature white rabbit.

Something is beginning to happen between my mother and father; it's a buzzing noise that rises between them like the hiss of the mosquitoes that come near my head at night. Their sounds have changed since Brooklyn. I never used to hear my mother's laughter (the new sound she makes on the beach in the daytime, with soldiers, never with my father), or her soft tears (as she cries at night on her flowered bed when she thinks I am asleep). My father's sounds have changed, too. His round strong funny words have changed to zigzag, loud, sharp responses that make me afraid. This sound is worse after the radio news, or when, at the end of the day, my father brings home the newspaper and my mother snaps back the last page and reads to him a list of dead soldiers' names, soldiers killed on the other side of the ocean. She keeps saying, "Let it not be Marty Goldstone." I know him, he's my father's cousin, he always gives me chewing gum when I see him. He is in the war. My father says he's like a kid brother to him. Everyone is in the war. My father says he would join up, too. These are the words that always start my mother's tears.

Living in this one room is too friendly. It's true my mother has got her privacy with Daddy and me, away from Gilda and Grandma, but now we're too private in this one room. She says she needs air. She opens the windows but the sound of soldiers marching, hup two three four, makes her cry softly, and the sound of mosquitoes buzzing makes her throw her bathrobe over her face.

I get busy snipping the heads off the ladies in the newspaper. My parents notice the rows of heads on the faded flowered rug and the next day they buy me a toy, a green segmented snake with red eyes and a black diamond on his forehead. I am allowed to keep him in the bathtub and pretend to fish for him with a safety pin on the end of a string tied to a long stick.

When they set me up to fish and then go out of the bathroom, I prefer to put water in the tub, just a little, and watch my snake/fish melt away into green blots, with drops of red, like blood, swirling into the water. He gets pale, little by little, as if he is dying. I know I am ruining him, but it gives me a great deal of satisfaction.

One night my father and I have dinner of fried eggs that my mother makes on a hot plate in the room, while she eats sardines with the spines and tails and fins because my father says she needs the calcium for the baby's bones. She gags, but she swallows it. I wonder how she likes eating something she hates. Sometimes she throws up in the bathroom sink. It's too bad I don't know the number for the Miami Beach Peter Pan Nursery if there is one. I could threaten her with it, or go out to the lobby and pretend to dial their numbers, but I'm really too afraid. I'm always afraid of her.

These days she's not paying much attention to me; we never nap on the same bed anymore, I never squeeze out a washcloth for her here, and on the beach she takes the soldiers' attention away even though they start out talking to me. She steals them from me and then they see only her, with her flared shorts, instead of me in my butterfly pinafore. She's not even that pretty now. When I see her naked, I realize her stomach is getting very big, as if she has swallowed an enormous coconut. It occurs to me that because Gilda isn't here to want me, she doesn't want me, either.

After dinner my father picks up the bag of garbage and I go with him as he carries it to the cans in the back alley.

A man—a soldier—jumps out of a doorway and points a rifle at us. "Halt! Who goes there?" he shouts. My heart stops beating, then begins again, as if a bird were flapping its wings in my chest.

"Just a civilian!" my father cries, dropping the garbage and grabbing me up in his arms. I can feel his heart thumping against the bones of my chest. The thing in his chest feels like a giant bird, bigger than a pelican. "I'm just a civilian, this is my child."

"Here on vacation?" the soldier asks.

"No, I have a business here."

"Your business is *over there*," the soldier says.

"I have a wife and child," my father answers apologetically. "And another on the way."

"Isn't that convenient? You look fit enough to heft a rifle. It doesn't take more muscle than that garbage there."

"I know," my father says. He sounds sad. He sounds almost sick, as if he might cry. He asks the soldier for permission to pick up the garbage. Then he carries it back to our room.

My mother is on her flowered bed with a small plate balanced on her chest.

"I *have* to join up," he says to her. "I'm a strong man. They need me."

"You want the telegram boy to ride up to my door

some day?" She throws something with all her strength across the room—a quarter of an orange. "You want me to be a widow?" She flings another piece and this one hits the wall.

"Don't start anything, please! Of course I don't want that!"

"Do you want Issa to grow up without a father?" She *is* starting. I can tell from her voice. "After I jump off the roof, she'll have no mother, either! Maybe you'd like Gilda to raise her."

"Ruth—they need men over there."

"I need you more here. Anyway—you're doing your part," she says. "You make the recordings. That's all some poor women will have left of their men someday."

"The records aren't making us enough money. The antique business was better; maybe we ought to go back to Brooklyn."

"I'll never go back," my mother says. "Never." She looks to me for confirmation. Her eyes don't really see me. She's deep in her own head. Now that I often do that myself, I know how it feels. You pretend to be paying attention, but you're not. "You never want to go back, do you, Issa? To that freezing snow? To that crowded house?"

I am thinking that it's better here: I have not seen the little man looking in my bedroom window for a long time. Or heard the terrible clanging threat of the furnace monster. I shake my head in agreement. No, I don't want to go back.

* * *

We are going out to dinner and I am getting dressed up. This is unusual because restaurants cost too much, and my mother eats only tomato slices, anyway. But we are celebrating something, I don't know what. I am allowed to wear my red plaid dress (although by now it's too short and the waist is too high) and my black strap shoes. While my mother is in the bathroom, I ask my father to fasten my Jewish star around my neck. To see him hold it so gently in his huge hand, that tiny blue star with the gold rim, makes me think he is holding a tiny, tiny animal that he loves.

We walk in the warm dark air to the restaurant. My father wants to order me my own dinner, and my mother won't let him.

"She'll never eat the whole thing."

"But she's a person, she ought to get her own plate and choose her own food. Just this one time."

"What are you having?" she asks my father.

"Lamb chops."

"She can have some of yours."

He wants his own, I know. He's a very hungry man. When she fries him his sunnyside-up eggs, he stabs them with his fork, in a hurry to get the food into his mouth. He wipes up the yolk with his bread as if he is trying to clean the plate so it won't have to be washed. I like to see him hungry; eating fast makes him happy.

So when the lamb chops come and she takes one off his plate to cut it up for me, in little pieces, I know he's sorry to see it go. She takes a big blob of his mashed potatoes, too. Why doesn't she give me what's on her plate? I'm not sure what it is—we never had it in Brooklyn. They look like fat white worms, with pink lines on them. My father, who likes to taste things off her plate, doesn't touch them.

He holds up his wine glass to celebrate the reason for this dinner out: "To our coming new member," he says, reaching across the table to bang her glass, but she bangs too hard and he tips the glass and spills some wine on his pants.

"Wash it out or it will stain," my mother says; then, when he leaves the table, she quickly takes a pat of butter from the bread dish and drops it on top of his mashed potatoes. As it begins to melt, she leans across the table and mashes it in till it disappears.

"Don't breathe a word," she says. "This is an experiment." I don't know what she is experimenting with, but I agree to keep her secret. Her eyes are sparkling in a way I never see. She looks alert and cheerful.

When my father comes back with a dark wet spot on his pants, right in front, as if he has made in his pants, he starts eating his food in great shovelfuls. His lamb chop and his green beans and his mashed potatoes.

My mother laughs out loud. He looks up and smiles because she is laughing. She looks so pretty; we almost never see her teeth. She throws back her head and laughs.

"What is it?" he says, still smiling. He is almost laughing himself.

"You can't even tell," she says.

"Tell what?"

"You can't tell what's in your mashed potatoes!"

"What?" he says. He looks down. His potatoes are gone. He puts his fork down. "What do you mean?"

"Tell him, Issa."

They both look at me.

"Mommy put butter in your potatoes."

He stares at her.

"And you didn't even know the difference!" she says. She leans forward and stares at him. "All that nonsense," she adds. "You can just forget about it."

I know what this is about now. Being Jewish. Milk and meat can't go together. Milk is like butter, like ice cream, like cream cheese. There is some kind of rule he has that causes her trouble, or did, when she was cooking at home. She always had to keep his potatoes separate from mine, in which she put butter.

I touch my Jewish star and realize at once that's a mistake. She didn't even know I was wearing it and now she's looking at it, getting ready to start something. She never liked Gilda to take me to see Mrs. Esposito and she wouldn't let me wear the star after I got it, saying that jewelry was for special occasions, not for playing in the sandbox.

I never tried to wear it on the beach where I had to play in the sand every single day. But now I'm worried.

"*You* can forget about that nonsense, too!" she says to me. She reaches behind my neck and tries to open the clasp with one hand, but she can't.

"Do it," she says to my father. "I don't want her wearing that nonsense."

"It's hers," he says. "It belongs to Issa."

"What does she know? She's a baby. I don't want her head filled with that dovening baloney, all those old guys in beards doing a hocus-pocus act, don't do this, don't do that, eat this, eat that."

He is getting angry that she's doing this. I wonder why she is, especially at a restaurant on a special night when we are all dressed up and looking beautiful.

She tells me to eat, not to waste this expensive food.

Now? She shoves a forkful between my lips. Again, I have little squares of meat in my mouth that won't go down. My father hasn't finished his lamb chop, but he's certainly done eating.

"Leave her alone, Ruth," he says. "Don't get worked up. It's not good for you."

I think he's wrong, she likes it. It's not good for *us*; we hate it.

Then suddenly she pulls my Jewish star hard. I feel a pinch on my neck till the chain snaps, and she throws my star on top of my mashed potatoes.

I don't know what to think. My father's face is ugly and I don't like him. I don't like her either. What will happen to me if I hate them both? I wish Gilda were here; I wish I could run somewhere. I burst into tears and my father lifts me in his arms, puts some money on the table, and carries me out of the restaurant.

He jerks along the sidewalk very fast. Over his shoulder I can see my mother coming after us. But not too fast. She is watching us carefully, she looks almost cheerful. In the hotel he puts me to bed. When she comes in, they say nothing to each other. Even after they get into their beds, they say nothing. For the first time I realize that silence can be louder than noise.

My mother and I are walking along the street near the ocean wall. The breeze is blowing the palm fronds, the sky is bluer than my bluebell eyes, there are troop ships on the horizon. Pelicans perch on the jetty rocks; their hanging beak-pouches are round and taut like my mother's stomach. No one is holding my hand. We are going to get wafer cookies at the store. When the wafers are fresh, they are perfect: crunchy outside and sweet and white inside. I eat one cookie in two bites, never more, never less. I can eat as many as I want; I am always hungry for these cookies. Even when I can't eat one more bite of hard-boiled egg, I could eat ten cookies. We have not had any meat since the restaurant. I begin to hope I will be free of meat, especially of liver, for the rest of my life. I even hope we will never have a kitchen again. That is my most urgent hope.

Three men come running out of a hotel; they run into my mother and knock her down. She falls right on her stomach; she rolls on it, this way and that, as if she is a seesaw balanced on a ball, head down, feet up. Head up, feet down. I see this happen as if I am on a swing, going up and down myself, because I feel dizzy. They aren't ordinary men, they are soldiers. I can tell from their sharply creased brown pants.

They help my mother stand up, they look down at her belly. She looks down. She bends her knees and looks between her legs, at her white shorts. There is nothing to see.

The men help her to the beach wall. She sits there. That's all she does: sit there—but I am more frightened now than I have ever been, more afraid of having seen her flailing on the sidewalk than I ever was of the furnace catching fire or the monster in the pipes in Brooklyn exploding into my room. More afraid of this than of my stomach aches, than of having to eat my own vomit.

What will this seesaw rocking do to the baby inside her? Will the baby be hurt? Will the baby need iodine? Will my mother have to drink it to get it to the baby? Who is this baby, anyway, and why does it have to come? There is hardly room for the three of us.

I don't know what we will do next. Do I get my cookies? Do we walk home? Do we call my father? All I see is my mother rocking on her round stomach like a seesaw.

* * *

"Buy me a newspaper," my mother says as soon as my father walks in the door. The soldiers have walked her back to the hotel, holding her between them (and one holding my hand), and my father has been called home from his recording store. The wife of the owner of the hotel has given my mother an aspirin. The soldiers have left. The owner's wife has left.

My mother is lying on the flowered bed, looking quite regular, as if she has forgotten that she was knocked down to the ground.

"Get the paper. I want to see the casualty list today."

"You don't need to read it every day. You don't need to get upset. You've had enough excitement for one day."

"Get it," she orders my father, "go down to the drug store and buy it right now."

He hesitates, but he has to take her orders. Everyone does. He goes out. He seems glad to leave. While he is gone, I get some eggshells out of the garbage and take them to feed to my dead snake in the bathtub. I stir the mess with the long fishing-stick till my father comes back.

I watch from behind the bathroom door as she snaps open the paper. "I knew it!" my mother screams. "See? It's Marty Goldstone! There it is. It's Marty's name, right there!" My mother screams louder. She throws the news-paper in the air and it flutters down heavily, like a pelican with a pouch full of fish. "Missing in action! Missing in action!" She gags right there, on the bed. She sobs and talks as she gags. I push open the bathroom door in case she needs to use the sink. "This is insane! Who made war? Who needs it? What is it FOR?"

My father knocks on his own head. "Marty, my cute kid cousin," he says. "That cute kid who used to drink sarsaparilla soda all the time."

Is my father *crying*? Does my father have tears in his eyes? *Does* he? That is scarier than anything I have *ever* seen.

"Where will this end?" my mother shouts. She screams it at my father, as if he knows but won't tell her.

He goes and sits on her flowered bed and puts his arm around her. Then he sees me and motions me to jump into his lap. The three of us hug each other hard. We are suf-fering, it's true, but it is wonderful to hold onto one another so tight.

* * *

Bad things often give you good feelings, but no one is allowed to say this. Bad things force you to be excited, to push yourself out in a new way, to get busy, then get tired, then be happy to rest, too tired to be afraid. There is so much happening, there is no time to turn on the radio, or to get me wafer cookies. My parents don't even remember that I need them.

I go over my bad list. The soldier who pointed his gun at us. My snake, who fell apart in the bathtub, whose head fell right off and crumbled to mush. The butter in the mashed potatoes. My Jewish star left buried in them. The soldiers knocking my mother down. Marty Goldstone, who disappeared in the war.

Even more bad things had to go on the list after my mother called Gilda in Brooklyn. My grandmother had a bad fall. Mr. Carp, one of the ladies' husbands, died of a heart attack right in the fish market. And the biggest bad thing: my father has to rush back to Brooklyn right away or be drafted into the army.

Talk, talk, talk. My mother and father talk and I listen, sitting on the floor, peeling the layers off baby coconuts very fast. I have a huge collection of these small green coconuts with yellow-pointed tips. I gather them whenever we go out. We have big ones, too, full-sized, grownup coconuts with hairy heads and little holes for eyes, nose and mouth. My father collects the big ones and takes me out in the alley behind the hotel to crack them. He smashes them down on the ground, over and over. He hammers on them, he pries them open with a screwdriver. His face gets red and he grunts as he tears the shells off. It's hard to believe these soft little green ones that I love turn into those huge, tough, hairy coconuts that he collects. I suppose it happens if they hang on the tree long enough.

When he finally gets one open, we're supposed to drink the coconut milk. He pretends it's delicious, but it tastes thin and warm and hairy to me. The coconut meat is a wonderful white color, but it's hard to chew. And it has a scaly brown skin. My father says it's good for you, it makes you strong.

Once, in the alley, a piece of coconut got stuck in my throat and I choked. He got it out of me by turning me upside down and banging me on the back, but we never told my mother. He reminded me, "If we tell her, there'll be no end to it."

That seems to be an important difference between them—she never lets things go, she pulls them back when they've almost disappeared and make fights out of them. My father lives through things and forgets them. Or, if he remembers them, and if they're bad, he doesn't add them on to everything else bad that ever happened. My mother's way lets her scream and get started anytime she wants to, which I understand. I sometimes want to get started but I have no new reason to; if I held onto everything bad, I could just get going with no new reason. I practice doing this, but my memory is not as good as hers. Maybe I haven't lived long enough, and therefore I don't have as many bad things to remember. Going to school seems to be a bad thing, but I haven't even gone yet! It seems as if I have, as if bad boys have made fun of me and hit me already. I am just waiting to tell them I'm important and they're nothing. When will I finally be able to do all the things I have practiced to do?

Talk, talk, talk. We have to go back to Brooklyn because my father has got his draft notice. The army is taking older men. They are taking men with wives and children. But he has one way out: if he goes to work in a defense plant, he doesn't have to go over the ocean to the war.

He *wants* to go over the ocean.

My mother wants him to work in a defense plant.

What kind of plant could that be? I imagine a plant with big green leaves, with bombs growing out of it. Bombs are on posters all over the city. A man called Uncle Sam, who wears a tall hat with stars on it, is also on the posters. He wants my father. My father wants to go and "take care of" whoever shot down Marty Goldstone's airplane.

Thinking that Marty is dead makes my father Jewish again, even if it's dangerous with my mother there. He opens his little black book from Brooklyn. He doesn't have his white shawl at the hotel, but he takes a towel and drapes it over his shoulders. He puts a washcloth over his head and stands in the corner and mumbles.

My mother laughs at him. He ignores her till she comes and tries to pull the towel off his shoulders. Then he snarls at her, like Bingo snarls at me when he's eating and I try to pinch his back. They bark at each other; they look as if they will kill each other.

I wish I had my snake/fish to jerk around in the tub, to bleed the green blood out of and kill him again. I have no one to be my enemy here, while my mother and father have each other.

* * *

We say goodbye to all the coconuts, big and small, except for one baby coconut I am allowed to take back to Brooklyn with me. We say goodbye to the palm trees, the pelicans, the blue sky and ocean waves, the flowered room, the soldiers on the beach. We say goodbye to my father, who has packed up his recording machines and sent them back to Brooklyn. There are no friends to say goodbye to. I never met one child in all of Miami Beach. My mother says I don't need children anyway; they are bad and will hurt me. And they are all stupid. She says I will see for myself when I get out in the world.

The biggest exciting thing of the bad things is the airplane we have to fly on. Just my mother and I get to fly on this plane, a troop plane going to Brooklyn. My mother has to be on it because the doctor said the train ride would kill the baby. Even the plane ride might. I hope it will, because if children are bad and stupid, why should this one get to live in our house?

My father kisses us over and over. I push him away. He's blocking my view of the plane, a big black thing, just like in the newspaper. My mother hugs him and whimpers and whines till my father turns us over to a soldier and leaves us under the wing of the plane. The minute he disappears, she gets happy. She laughs and her dimple pops in and out. She has dimples on her cheeks and her knees, and I don't have one anywhere. If she loves my father so much, why does she cry when he's there, and laugh when he's not?

I have to hang on to my mother now; there's no one else here, no one at all. I pull her down to me and give her a big kiss, right on the lips. She's surprised, but she likes it. She's proud of me. When we get on the plane, I get to sit on the knees of one soldier after another. The propeller noise is terrible and my mother has to vomit at least three times. But the soldiers bring her wet washcloths and drinks and one strokes her hair the way my father does, very softly and gently, and I am jealous. I know something new now: I will always want to be just like my mother.

6

Luckily, the baby dies. Gilda says it's just as well because it wouldn't have been any good after all the shaking it got on the plane. "I hope she's learned her lesson," Gilda says, as if all this were my mother's fault. I don't think it's fair of Gilda to blame her, but in no time another baby is growing, and another big fuss starts up and this time I do blame my mother. There must be a way to stop things like this from happening; I just don't know yet what they are.

Do I like being home again? No. I miss coconuts and soldiers; I miss living where there is no kitchen. And Bingo smells bad out of both ends. He drags his rear part along the runner in the upstairs hall as if he is using it for toilet paper. My mother tells Gilda: "Your dog is disgusting." I used to love Bingo, but now I don't like to watch him squat to make because he stares at me even while his duty is coming out. I know that when I'm on the toilet with my stomach aches I can't look at anyone when the actual thing is happening. Body secrets give me deep, breathless feelings, but no one talks about them. Body secrets are things grownups keep to themselves.

When I watch my grandmother put her teeth in and out, I want to ask her, *how does it feel to have those, why do you have them, will I have them?* But I know my grandmother has very few words—she would rather smile or cook than talk. My father has words, but I automatically know he wouldn't like me to ask: *why do you have those balls and that tube in the front of your body? Do they itch that much? Are they so heavy they make a hole in one certain place in all your underpants?*

Gilda could be asked anything, I'm never afraid of her, but I am afraid it's possible she doesn't even know that she has heavy black hairs on the insides of her thighs. Maybe she never saw them (and only I did) and maybe I shouldn't worry her about them. I know she knows about the pits and deep scars on her skin—she couldn't miss them since she is in front of mirrors all day, behind the ladies who are getting haircuts, and in front of the bathroom mirror while she is giving shampoos. I have watched Gilda put salves and hot packs on her face. Once, on Avenue P, an old woman stopped her and said, "My heart goes out to you, darling, or I would never say this, but it might help. Try urine on your face. Your own urine, on a sanitary napkin, tied around your face at night." Gilda ran all the way home after that, with me flying along, holding onto the stroller handle.

My mother doesn't hide body secrets—she acts instead as if they aren't hers, but that someone has attacked her with them, has forced her to have a body when she would prefer never to live in one, eat in one, sleep in one. She lays out her suffering for everyone to see—her headache secrets, her vomiting secrets, her bloody-pants secrets. Now her big-stomach secret. She has a message for us: "Look how I have to suffer. Look what the world does to me."

She has other secrets I'm interested in—how she makes her behind squish from side to side when she plays boogie-woogie while she rocks on the piano bench, how her dimples made the soldiers laugh, how the curve of her hip makes my father cup his hand on it, makes him say something low to her, makes her tilt her head toward him and forget me! They both forget me when he has his big hand on her hip. I feel the thing between them; his powerful interest and her pleasure in capturing it. I know these things without thinking about them—she doesn't *enjoy* his hand on her hip, but she loves how she has his full attention when she lets him do it.

The truth is, I will never get him to love me best, not while she is around. It's too bad, things like this. They are facts of life, like Gilda's skin, Bingo's bad smell.

* * *

While the new baby is growing, my father works in a defense plant. He makes wings for airplanes with machines that stamp them out like cookie-cutters make cookies. I know how sharp a cookie-cutter is, I know how hard you have to press on the dough and how careful you have to be while knocking the cookie out. "Be careful," I warn him. That's what all the women in this house say all the time: "Be careful," as if being careful is some kind of guarantee that nothing bad will happen.

I have to be careful petting Bingo, I have to be careful not to slip in the bathtub, I have to be careful eating fish because of bones. Little needles of "careful" are always sticking in my ears and my eyes—what if I forget for one second to be careful, what will happen then? If I am always thinking "careful," I can hardly enjoy playing with the dog, or splashing in the bath water. (I never enjoy eating fish, whose bones can give you an injection in your throat at any moment.)

"Be careful you don't choke on your food," Gilda tells me, as if swallowing isn't bad enough. What if, while I am swallowing, I choke? How can it be that the food I eat to keep myself alive could also kill me? These are dilemmas that fill my days—dying seems to be at the heart of all my private imaginings. Why did the old baby die and will the new baby die? Will I die? Will my grandmother die? What if everyone dies, my mother and father, my aunt and my grandmother, Bingo and the new baby, and just I am left alone in the house with the furnace? I don't even know how to turn it on and off. I will freeze to death in the winter. Who will find me in my bed, stiff as an ice cube, and when will I be found?

There is no one I can talk to about these matters. Even Gilda, lately, has been harping on food, and on a specific type of food. Crusts. It seems that when my mother goes to the hospital to have the new baby, Gilda wants me to astonish everyone by eating the crusts of my bread. I don't have to do it yet, but only when she goes to the hospital. "Then we can tell her she's crazy—that you do eat your crusts." I don't see why it's so important that this be done: crust is hard, it cuts my gums. But Gilda adds this information: "Issa, no man will marry you if you leave the crusts of your bread all over your plate." This stirs up many questions: why wouldn't a man marry me if I did that? Do I want a man to marry me? If I'm married, does it mean I will have to vomit and have headaches and carry around babies, like coconuts, in my stomach? But because it seems important to Gilda, I practice eating crusts. I hold them in my mouth till they get soft, I suck them, I grind them, I wet them, I strain them against my teeth. Crusts are a challenge. Crusts will help us prove to my mother that she is crazy and that Gilda understands me best and can make me do anything.

The day comes that my mother leaves the house, leaking water from her body. I don't even say goodbye to her, worrying about crusts. For ten days I practice eating them.

On the day the baby is to come home, I hold my triumph like a trophy in my mouth: "I ate my crusts." I am waiting to tell it to my mother, who has been gone all this time without contacting me. They are getting ready for her as if for a queen—my grandmother is shining the windows, Gilda is baking cookies, the bed sheets of the big double bed are tightened and tucked, pulled and pressed to icy smoothness.

They bring in a new baby carriage—my father bumps it up the stairs to the bedroom and my grandmother cleans it with ammonia, shines the very spokes of the wheels. I have heard that the baby who died was a boy; this new one is a girl like me. Why we need two girls in a house is beyond me. I walk down the hall and kick Bingo. He snarls and bites my leg. I love the pain, I could hug him for giving it to me. The wound bleeds, much too serious for iodine. They—Gilda and my father—run with me to see Dr. Trutt down the street, who hurts me even more, with stitches, with an injection. Oh, how the body hurts. How inconvenient it is to have one, how dangerous, how delicious. To live in one is the biggest risk in the world, and the more dangerously you live in it, the more attention you get. I wish Bingo had torn out my eyes! Then I would be the queen, they would shine the spokes of my wheels, they would adore me.

* * *

But as it is, no one cares that I have eaten crusts. I say it over and over—as my mother comes creeping in the front door, leaning on my father. I say it to the nurse who comes in carrying the package of the baby. I shout it while they climb the stairs to the bedroom. I tell it again and again all that afternoon—while the nurse is doing something to my mother's breasts, while the baby is wailing in her new carriage, while my grandmother is stirring chicken soup. I come right up to my mother's ear and shout it at her, right in the opening of her ear: "I ate my crusts!"

And she slaps my face.

"Stop that, Issa! You'll wake the baby!"

I do wish they had died. I wish they had all died in whatever ways were possible—choking to death or drowning in the tub or being killed by bombs, any way at all. Then I would have been left alone to freeze to death in my bed. It would have been better than this, any day.

7

Because the baby is here, everything has to change. For one thing, the house has to be cut in half. My mother argues with Gilda for days before Gilda will agree to the plan to have a carpenter convert the house. My mother wants Gilda and my grandmother to have the top half, and we the bottom half. There will be a staircase with doors that lock, top and bottom, so my grandmother can't get down and I can't get up, at least not without knocking or ringing a bell. There will finally be—right here in Brooklyn—this thing everyone wants so badly: privacy. Doors and locks and keys will be between my mother's scaring me and my reaching Gilda's side. The ladies and the shampoos and haircuts will be upstairs; the stories and busyness will be upstairs; the chicken soup will be upstairs, Bingo will be upstairs—and where will I be? Downstairs, with liver flaring on the grate, with nothing to do, and with . . . Blossom.

For that is the name they have given my sister—Blossom. The lilac tree that I love, with its sweet purple blossoms, now is spoiled because she has a name like its fragrant parts. My sister (I have to call her "my" sister although I don't want her to be mine) has a red, screaming tongue that vibrates day and night with anger. It flails in her little open mouth like a flipper. Why do they all hold her in their arms and look into her face? Hot steam comes up from her mouth—she's a small, wild furnace.

"I can eat crusts!" I shout, going from one person to another, pulling on their arms, punching their thighs, "Watch me chew!"

Nothing looks the same. The upstairs bedroom where my mother and father slept is now becoming the kitchen-living room of the upstairs apartment. The beauty parlor is staying the beauty parlor, but the bathroom where I had all my stomach aches is to be used only by Gilda and her customers and my grandmother. We, downstairs, will have our own, new bathroom—free of hairs in the sink.

I already feel lost: the dining room has become the living room (and the piano is moved in there), the living room is now where my mother and father sleep, and the sun porch is where "my sister" and I have to sleep, close to the street, close to the cars whooshing by on the icy road, close to the wild outdoors. I have lost the room of my own. The Screamer's being here has cut everything in half. My mother and father are only half mine; Gilda and my grandmother are divided in two, also. Although The Screamer is little she gets *more* than half. Our shared bedroom is full of her things—carriage, Bathinette, little swing, little rocking chair, little rocking horse—my father went somewhere and bought out a household of baby furniture. What belongs to me in my bedroom? Just my blackboard, nothing else. I hate this sun porch room, which has nine big windows in it—not even counting the front door with a stained glass peek-a-boo window. Anyone could look in at us.

Hammering and sawing goes on all day. The Screamer screams and the drills drill, and the radiators clank, and not once does my mother get a headache. I am looking forward to the day she gets one—then she and I can rest in her bed together as we used to in the old days and I can bring her a wet washcloth. I wait and wait, but it never happens. Her head never hurts—instead the pain goes to her breasts. She holds her breasts, which drip, making her rock in pain. The Screamer is not drinking out of them—

though Gilda told me that mothers have always fed their babies this way (I can't believe it). I am relieved to hear that my mother refuses to do this, it is a great relief to me. When they drip and tears come to her eyes, my mother covers their drips with my father's handkerchiefs to catch the drops. He watches her cover them with his handkerchiefs. Once he has to help her squeeze the drops out with a rubber pump. When they see me watching, my mother tells me the doctor said they have to do this. She says she has "milk-fever."

I run away to watch the carpenter and his helper make the new pantry and the new bathroom where before there was nothing—I watch them lay the tiles, two pink and one white, over and over again in the same design. And then they put the doors at the top and bottom of the staircase which before was free and open. Big heavy doors with locks. I start to cry at the sight of them. How will I ever get into the upstairs if I don't have a key? How will I ever find Gilda when I need her?

* * *

"Isn't it wonderful?" my mother assures me. They are now building an open back porch where just "our" family will eat in the summertime; Grandma and Gilda are getting a new side entrance for themselves, for "their family," complete with a stoop, a black steel mailbox, and a gold doorknob. Gilda and I will now have different addresses: mine is 405 and hers is 405 and 1/2.

The first night I sleep in the new room I watch the moon coming in all nine windows. Nine moons. And then I see what I was afraid of: the faces of nine little men hanging onto the nine windowsills, watching me.

* * *

In the summertime, my mother puts Blossom out front in her carriage. My job is to sit there and watch her sleep. Bingo sits near me under the bench. Sometimes my grandmother sits next to me. We watch till there is nothing to watch. The Screamer is either asleep, or waking up and getting ready to boil, her tongue curling up like a slice of cooked liver. I think, for the first time, that we are all made of meat. That if we put my sister on the grate over the flame, she would cook and could be eaten.

One afternoon while I am watching my sister, a dog comes over to the carriage and pee-pees on the wheel. He lifts his leg and a stream comes out of a tube on his belly. His tube points up toward his face, while my father's tube hangs down toward his feet. Or so it seems to me. I don't know if my father lifts up his leg—he never lets me watch him make.

Then another dog comes along—he's white and fluffy— and he also makes on the carriage in short squirts. What is this? A parade? I wonder how many more will come. Only two—it seems they are all traveling together in the neighborhood, these four friends. The others arrive and do their pee-pees as if they are playing follow-the-leader. Just then my mother comes out and sees this happening. She screams. She runs in and gets a broom and starts to hit all the dogs. She smashes them on their heads. They run away howling. It's too bad—I liked seeing them pee on the carriage. It was the only entertainment for a long while.

Now my mother snatches up my sister and yells at me as if *I* have peed on her. At dinnertime (we are now eating separately from my grandmother and Gilda) she says to my father, "Bingo is attracting these dangerous animals."

"I don't think so," my father says.

"We can't have this," my mother says. "They could attack the baby. They could kill her."

My father is busy eating. Working in the defense plant makes him hungrier than ever. He still eats in big chews and great swallows. He tears meat from the bones with his powerful teeth. He scoops potatoes up as if his spoon is a shovel and he is digging a hole to China.

"I wonder what they're eating upstairs," I say.

"We're our own little family now," my mother says

sharply. "Don't think about them."

* * *

Gilda has to go to the bank. My mother suggests that I go along for the walk. This is a treat for both of us. Gilda hardly ever has me to herself anymore. We get spruced up ("spruced up" is what Gilda says as she sprays perfume on both of us. I am allowed to be in the old bathroom with her for this—my mother is feeling very generous). Gilda puts a lilac bloom in my hair with a bobby pin. She lets me wear a gold locket of hers that she keeps in a blue leather jewel box. Inside the locket is a picture of her father, my grandfather. "If he had lived," Gilda says, "my whole life would have been different. I wouldn't be beholden to your mother for every bite I eat."

We walk in the sunshine to King's Highway. The vault in the bank where treasures are kept has rows of silver drawers filled with the gold lockets and rings of the whole Kingdom of Brooklyn. Gilda takes me with her into a secret room (a guard in a uniform is there to watch us) and we look at our precious things: a pair of diamond earrings that once were worn by my grandmother and war bonds and birth certificates.

"Someday these earrings will be yours," Gilda whispers to me. I shake with a thrill. Then I think of The Screamer. Maybe they will forget her when it's time to give the earrings away. Otherwise, I will kill her. I will have to.

* * *

When we get home, Gilda goes around to the side door and then upstairs to her house, while I go in the front door and in the downstairs to mine. While I am having my milk and cookies, I hear her running back down (her shoes pound on the stairs), and she bangs on the locked door that enters to our new living room. "Where is Bingo?" she calls through the closed door to my mother. "He's not upstairs."

"I don't know," my mother calls back. She looks at the ceiling.

"You *do* know," Gilda says. She hits the door with her fist. I think my mother knows, too. Where could he be? Bingo is *always* under the table in the upstairs kitchen, waiting for scraps of chicken heart.

"Where is he? Tell me!" Gilda shouts, pounding on the door.

"In the cellar," my mother says.

There is complete silence. Then I hear Gilda turn around to run upstairs, where she has to get the key to the outside cellar door. Then down again, outside, and to the cellar door, where she pokes the key in the lock. I hear all this in my ears. I can get into the cellar by opening a door at the side of our kitchen, but I never do because why would I ever go into a black hole where the furnace is breathing fire?

But once I know Gilda is down there, I slide the bolt on the kitchen door and peek down the steps. I see the shelves above the steps that contain soap powder and bug Flit. I see Gilda's dim form at the bottom of the stairs. She is calling, "Bingo! Bingo!"

"Forget it," my mother calls from over my shoulder. "Bingo is gone."

Gilda and I both turn to look at her. *Then why did she say he was in the cellar?* My mother is smiling, but it's not a good smile. "He's gone, Gilda."

"Where?"

"The pound came and got him."

"What do you mean?"

"I mean I gave him away. He was a danger to the baby."

"You gave Bingo *away*?"

I can't believe it either.

"He was gentle as a *lamb*," Gilda says, but the word *lamb* goes up like a scream. She runs up the few extra steps to where my mother is in the kitchen and butts my mother in the stomach with her head. Gilda is butting my mother as if she has horns in her head. My mother falls down, she has no breath, and the smile has gone off her face.

"Oh God, you bitch," Gilda says. She runs to our phone, which she is not allowed to use anymore. "Oh God." She is trying to use the phone book.

"Don't bother," my mother says when her breath comes back. "They've already put him to sleep."

This takes some time for Gilda to understand—even I understand it first.

"They should put *you* to sleep," Gilda cries out finally, tears jerking out of her eyes. Her shoulders shake. She is choking on her tears. "Oh my precious baby Bingo."

Oh, my mother is bad. She has been very bad lately; I have had to punch her many times. This time a punch isn't enough. I don't know what will be enough. I decide I will go upstairs and live there in the better house. I take Gilda's hand and tug on her. "Let's go back upstairs," I tell her, patting her and kissing her backside. "I'll come and live with you," I tell her. "Don't worry, darling Gilda. I'll take care of you."

Even when the worst things happen, the mind calms down. People still have to go to bed at night and eat cereal in the morning. No matter how hard Gilda butted my mother in her stomach, the two sisters still have my old grandmother to take care of, they still have me walking down there, below the level of their hips, talking up at them, asking things, needing things, demanding what I want. That I can be afraid and then stop being afraid, and that they can hate each other and stop hating each other, is an amazing fact to own. It smooths out the long story ahead, which is bound to be full of terrible times, of fights and yelling and hating.

Best things can go the other way, too—the dropping off of excited, wild feelings down to dull and ordinary. If I get a new ball—which I actually have got: pink, bright, clean, a Spalding—that bounces as high as my head and higher, I am so happy that I think I will always be happy, even if The Screamer screams and even if Bingo is gone forever. I wake up thinking about the new ball; I look for it the instant I wake up and bounce it; I clean it with my toothbrush so it stays pink, I rub it dry on my dress. I kiss it to my lips, feeling that rubbery hard pink curve against my mouth.

Happy! Oh, I am so happy! I will always be happy!

Won't I? Won't I?

And then what happens?

One day I wake up and think about something else, not my ball. Even when I do think of the ball, I don't want to leap up and bounce it. It is still clean. It is still rubbery. It still has that same smell. But I don't feel so much love for it. I am not even close to happy, thinking of the ball. When I finally get up and bounce it, I am thinking about something else already, and I forget I am bouncing it.

This is mysterious to me—how the shape of the thing I love, the thought of it, feel of it, smell of it—what used to be everything I needed to feel happy—now is getting away from me, shrinking, getting smaller and littler and tinier until—even though it's right in my hand—I no longer feel any love for it.

I bring it right up to my eyeballs, I blink my eyelashes against it, I feel them scrape the rubber, and I look, look, look at it. It's right there, sticking into my eye.

But I don't care.

Now I want roller skates.

Ruthie has them. Myra has them. Myrna has them. Linda has them. Everyone on the block has roller skates. The little girls who live on my street roar along the sidewalk, pumping away over the cracks, making a sound like ZZZSHEE, ZZZSHEE. One knee and then the next pumping along.

I want, I want . . . I tell what I want to everyone in my house. All of us happen to be standing outside in the street buying cupcakes from the bakery man. My grandmother. Gilda. My mother. My father. They can't help but hear what I want.

"Too dangerous," they all say, which is the twin sister to "Be careful." They tell me I can't be careful enough if something is too dangerous, though I have no idea why. I can be careful. I tell them so. I'll do it carefully, I assure them, whatever that means to them. The little girls are doing it out there, on the sidewalk, ZZZSHEE! ZZZSHEE! over the cracks. They're not getting killed.

"That's enough," Gilda says. My mother agrees. My

father agrees. "Don't ask again." This time they all—miraculously—agree, they all say the same thing.

"Do you want to break your neck?" Even my grandmother chimes in. The chickens she cooks have all had their necks broken by the kosher butcher—do I want to be like a dead chicken?

I can never be a chicken, dead or alive. They are stupid and wrong. I'm just a child. I just want to roller skate, to fly fast along the sidewalk, to see the hedges go by in a blur. What do they know? They are too old to see any use in it, but I know it must be the secret of happiness. Flying fast, making wild noises. Forgetting whatever it is that goes around and around in my mind, the stuff of stomach aches.

Linda and Myra and Myrna and Ruthie. For years they didn't interest me, being wheeled in their strollers by their mothers, or driving by in their fathers' cars, or sitting on their front stoops eating chocolate pudding or having a glass of milk before bed. They were just other helpless children like me, being guided here and put there and told what to do, but suddenly they are out here on the sidewalk, ZZZSHEE, and they have turned into what I want to be: free. I must meet them, join them, despite my mother's assurances that other children are of no interest, are dumb, bad, stupid, useless.

How odd, that just as I determine I need to be outside, they all determine it's best that I be locked inside. Eating the cupcake the bakery man has given me (free! he does it to be nice, seeing what I have to contend with), I sit on the front stoop listening to their boring arguments. Dangerous traffic. Dangerous germs. Dangerous old men. Dangerous insects. The women circle around me, doing the dance of danger. Best to stay inside, best to color, best to read, best to help Grandma cook, best to . . .

"How can I help Grandma cook if I can't go upstairs?"

They are silent.

"Then can I go up to the beauty parlor?"

Gilda and my mother look at each other. My mother does a calculation, I've seen that look on her face when she's doing the budget envelopes—so many dollar bills in here for the milk, so many for the butcher, so many for . . .

"Well, maybe. Once in a while."

So easily I have forced her to lift the ban. By a clever trick I have changed the iron rule. Look what they will do in order that I not fly down the street on skates!

When we go in the house, the doors between upstairs and downstairs are unlocked. My mother issues the revised orders. Once in a while, at her convenience, when everything I have to do is done, when I have eaten all my food, when The Screamer doesn't need me to rock her, when my mother doesn't have an urge to do rhymes with me, once in a while, I can go upstairs to the beauty parlor.

"Even now?"

She is backed into a corner.

I run, I fly up the stairs, my first time in months, to the new apartment, to see the new sink, the new stove, the new carpet, the new dishes. Gilda has a new dryer, a green monster helmet that fits over the ladies' heads, that dries their hair twice as fast as the old one. It has a clear plastic edge, so the women can see, can move their eyebrows to indicate too hot, not hot enough, just right.

Oh, I have missed this place. I get busy bending hairpins in the crack of the linoleum; I am happy, and I never want to go home, go downstairs, where it's boring, where The Screamer smells of pee and worse things, where no one cares about me! *Where no one cares about me!*

Something thumps in my chest as I think that thought. *NO ONE CARES ABOUT ME!*

"What's wrong?" Gilda asks me. I am clutching my chest, where a hammer has begun to strike. I look down and see my dress shaking with each hammer-blow.

"Issa! What's wrong?" I don't know myself. Something has got into my chest, like a bird or a dog or a baby, and it's flapping and kicking about. I feel it and see it happening.

The thing wants to get out. It doesn't care if it tears through me. I am amazed, but I want it to get out as fast as it can, I want it to stop hurting me. Maybe I need a pill, like the one my grandmother takes when she has heart pains. I need . . . I need . . . *what I need is roller skates!*

But I realize I cannot ask for this now. However, it's perfectly clear to me—roller skates would fix me. Just as The Tree Trunk gave my mother headaches, not having roller skates has given me this monster in my chest, pounding against the walls of my body to get out.

9

The war should stop. Why does it go on this long? How annoying it is that they still say, "Shush, shush," to me when the radio is on. Cooking grease will help to win the war if we save it in a tin can. Tinfoil we find on the street must be packed and smoothed into a ball. (Chewing gum wrappers are good, cigarette wrappers are the best, if, with the tip of my fingernail, I can get the foil to separate from the white paper without a tear.) I have an enormous tinfoil ball—bigger than a tennis ball. How this is going to kill the Japs, whoever they are, is a total mystery. When I examine my silver ball, I think that perhaps the good soldiers dangle these in front of the bad soldiers; then, while distracting them, they pull out bayonets and stab their bellies. Thinking this, I want to throw my silver ball in the bushes, or bury it.

Gilda takes me with her around the neighborhood to sell war bonds. She gets me away these days by not asking permission; if she finds me outside, she just grabs me, telling my grandmother on the bench to tell my mother we went for a walk, *but only if she asks*. Half the time we will be back before my mother notices. Of course I know this is forbidden; I am never supposed to leave the premises without permission. But it's only Gilda—how dangerous could she be?

Lately my mother goes too far with her rules; I *have* to break them, there is no other way to get what I want. Otherwise I think of the trouble I would have to go through: all that asking and begging (all her arguments and finally her refusal) and then—after she tells me that she owns me—the rest: my sulking and crying, and her yelling at me, or hitting me, or giving me that look, with her eyes getting narrow, and her mouth going tight and mean—and finally, that baffling and disgusting change, her turning to "my sister" Blossom, wherever she is, there in her high chair, or there on the Bathinette (my sister is everywhere, everywhere, she never disappears, even for a second), and my mother's face changing like a red light to a green light, turning on for The Screamer, putting on her high, baby-talk voice, getting cute, tickling and cooing to The Screamer.

She has two faces, whereas most of us have only one. When she returns to cooking, the ugly face comes back, a result of my grandmother's now being assigned upstairs to her own house: down here my mother has to be the main cook. And, oh, how my mother hates onions on her fingers. How she gags at the smell of garlic. How she won't ever, ever, ever cook a chicken because she said to my father that chicken feet, with their scales and claws, with their turned-under toenails, are the most disgusting things she ever saw.

Upstairs, a chicken is treated like a peaceful pet. My grandmother pats a dead chicken as if it were her old, sweet friend. With a silver tweezer, she plucks out the sharp, big feathers. And for the little ones, she sears the chicken over the gas flame, *zzst, zzst*—little blue bolts of fire sizzling along its skin. The flames dance. Not ferociously, as when liver flares, but sweet little sparks, dying out over the burners.

Whenever I can get away with it, I sneak upstairs to watch her cook, but I watch with fear in my blood. Any minute, any second, any *half instant from now*, my mother could open the door between our place and theirs and scream for me. "Issa, are you up there?"

If my mother didn't exist at all, I know I could be total-ly relaxed, watching the chicken being sparked into its clean skin. If only I didn't have to be afraid of her!

On this day, my grandmother finds the lucky treasure: inside the chicken's tummy is a cluster of yellow eggs, veined with red. She holds them up like a prize. I hug her thighs to congratulate her; we don't talk much to one another, but we look at one another's faces and smile. She is going to plunge these eggs into the chicken soup. As soon as they boil hard, as soon as they become sweet and soft (nothing like the slimy eggs my mother tries to force down my throat), she will give me one. My grandmother sneaks me the first one that cooks up to the top, rising to boil in the foam like a little sun. Oh, it's wonderful, like meat in its solidness but also like cake in its crumbly soft-ness. If all meat were like this, I could eat till my mother turned blue waiting for me to refuse; I never would.

"Issa, are you up there, goddamn it!"

Now my heart convulses into its wild dance: the pause (it stops beating) and the deep falling thump, and then the animal sleeping in my chest comes to life and starts its struggle.

"Go down, go, go, Issa!" my grandmother says. She is also afraid, we are soldiers in the army against my mother. This is war, this is the real war. Down I go, holding my chest together so it doesn't burst with my fear, going downstairs, slowly, to face that look on my mother's face, as if I have opened the washing machine door while the water is skidding around inside, as if I have opened the furnace door and let the fire roar out to engulf the house. Some awful cellar thing is what her face reminds me of.

"You can't get enough of those two, can you?" she hisses into my ear. She jerks my arm. She drags me into *her* kitchen where some mess is boiling and steaming, where the pressure cooker is popping its hat and could explode and kill us, where The Screamer in her high chair is sticking applesauce into her nose.

* * *

My father walks in the door with his arm in a bloody bandage. He fills the doorway with his pained face. All the women in the house used to run to him, surround him, when he came in, but now there are too few down here to matter. He says he has ruined an airplane wing today. His bosses are very angry in the defense plant, the war could be lost because of this. They want to know: why did he do it? He doesn't know why, he didn't know the machine would do what it did, tear into the metal, break off the wing tip. If he had gone to college and become an engineer, then they could ask him why it broke.

Already my heart, which was pounding from her yelling, is pounding now even more from the blood on his shirt, from the blood seeping through the gauze.

"Why weren't you more careful?" my mother demands, even after he said all that he said.

He looks at her with Bingo's sad eyes. Those must have been his eyes as they put him to sleep in the pound. *How can you do this to me?* (I think—every day, every night—about how Bingo must have felt. I think about what Bingo was thinking when they gave him his shot.)

"The foreman called me a saboteur," my father says. I have never heard either word, *foreman* or *saboteur*, they're not in my mother's rhyming lists (though she hasn't rhymed with me in a long, long time). "He says I could be arrested for sabotage."

He sounds scared. My father, who is never scared, is scared. His being scared scares me. Who around here is strong enough to take care of me?

Oh, I need Gilda! I need the chicken eggs! I need the smell of the soup upstairs, bubbling with celery and onions and carrots. I can't stay here with the pressure cooker about to blow out the roof.

I escape. Up, up, up, I go—she's too busy with the bloody bandage to chase me, too busy with The Screamer, with the cauldron of stew on the flames. How fortunate the doors are not locked between upstairs and downstairs, kept open now so I don't ask for roller skates.

Up I go, here I am, look, I want to live with *you*, stay with you, sleep with you. I grab the silver dishtowel rack on the side of the sink, and I swing on it.

My grandmother warns me, "Don't do that!" But it's too late, the rack breaks off, I fall down, I feel my hand go under me, and I hear the bone crack.

Oh great emergency! Oh joy! But must it hurt so much to get to this place? This is what I would love to have happen every single day if it weren't so painful. My mother never yells at me when my body breaks into pieces. She gets the sweetest I have ever seen her; she actually sometimes cuddles me in her arms, embraces me. And my *father!* He *adores* me—as now, bloodied and bandaged as he is, he lifts me up in his arms and runs with me through the street to Dr. Trutt's. They believe the doctor can perform miracles—he can actually keep me from dying.

You can't feel good or loved around here unless you're starting to die or in pain. This is a strange arrangement, but it's the truth.

10

How does Gilda become a bride? One night she appears downstairs like a ghost, like a dream, like a bride doll. Her white dress is so white a light seems to shine from inside it. Her veil is white gauze held on by a white headband crowning her hair. A red cross burns in its center. Gilda's lips are red and shiny with lipstick.

We all stare. My father puts down his newspaper and tilts his head to take it in. The Screamer, in her chair eating a butter cookie, sticks her wet finger through the cookie's round hole and admires Gilda. Lines grow across my mother's brow, as they do when she begins to get a headache.

Gilda laughs; she spins around once, her skirt blowing up to show her calves and delicate ankles, and then she runs back to the staircase and disappears up to her own house.

We hardly know if she's really been here or not. All that's left is the scent of Lilies of the Valley, her perfume.

A box in the beauty parlor fills up with jewelry. Gilda says it's fake, but I don't know what she means. It's as real as my fingers that jangle and untangle the chains—as real as my cheek that I hold the cold, round stones against. Rubies and diamonds glitter on the table with the nail polish bottles and shampoo tubes and all the clips and curlers and bobby pins. Women arriving to get beautiful drop off these strings and rings and things of gold. I'm told the jewels will build air strips in New Guinea. The natives there will do anything for a shiny necklace. I don't blame them. I would do anything to have one myself.

One night Gilda has a *Kits for Russia* party. The next night she has a *Bandages for Our Boys* party. Her customers come to our house at night and go upstairs to sit at Gilda's kitchen table. We hear their comings and goings. Laughter, footsteps on the stairs, the doorbell ringing and ringing. My heart yearns to fly up there to celebrate whatever they are celebrating. Gilda has told me they roll gauze into neat bandages for the soldiers on the front and make kits for Russia because "they have nothing in Russia." It seems the Russians desperately need sugar for their tea and soap for their baths and thread because their clothes are in tatters.

My mother keeps casting her eyes at the ceiling; all that noise from upstairs, all that chatter and wild laughter. She doesn't like it. At night I'm not allowed to go up and watch because soon it will be my bedtime. My father says to her during one of these parties, "Why don't you go up and roll bandages?" She says to him, "Why don't *you?*"

Something is changing in Gilda. She's braver and noisier; she's busier and bossier. She gets on the phone and tells people how to get busy to win the war. "I can't carry a gun, but I can shoot my mouth off" is what she tells one of her customers.

* * *

A great event takes place in our neighborhood. Gilda marches in a parade carrying a magnificent American flag on a long pole. She leads an army of brides like herself down Avenue P, all of them in white with red crosses, their skirts and hair flying in the wind, their gauze headdresses shivering like butterflies' wings. The Avenue N shul is sponsoring a war bond rally on Avenue P. I am on my father's shoulders, high above the crowd. My grandmother stands down below, spinning her head from side to side, in order to see better. My mother has stayed home with The Screamer, which is always perfect for me.

At every corner are bridge tables where women are selling war bonds. I'd like to be as important as those women. They take money and write down names. My father—counting out five- and one-dollar bills—buys two twenty-five-dollar war bonds although my mother warned him not to do anything that would put us in the poorhouse. I worry that he might be doing something bad. But it doesn't look bad. He's very happy to do it. He's proud. Besides, he pays only eighteen dollars and some change for each war bond. This, he tells me, is a bargain because in a few years they will be worth more than he paid. And, in the meantime, they will be winning the war.

Gilda and the women march to drums and flutes. The women march like beautiful soldiers in a ballet, without heavy boots and guns. They march but really they dance and their dresses blow in the wind. I tangle my fingers in the curls of my father's head and love being this high, this far-seeing.

When the parade is over (it goes for two blocks), Gilda comes up to us, her cheeks flushed, smiling happily. She talks to my father, not once letting the smile slip away, and holds onto my leg, but I have the feeling it's my father she's really touching although I know it's me. They are both laughing—their faces are lit by laughter. I feel my father's shoulders shake under my behind. Something about the red lipstick has transformed Gilda into another woman. That, and the gauze headdress. And the red cross. And the flag. It's as if she turned into another person overnight.

I know I will have to keep this knowledge a secret, at least till I see if the changes stay changed. I also wonder if someday I can change into a laughing, red-lipped woman from the shy small person that I am.

CHAPTER

11

No matter how far away in time a bad thing is, it will happen. The Screamer will walk, my grandmother will die, the furnace will explode—it is just a matter of holding it off and trying to forget about it in the meantime. I have forgotten about school as long as I can. Now the day has come. I know I will doubtless be torn to bits. No one will be able to protect me.

My school is fourteen blocks away. If Avenue P is only one block away, how far is fourteen blocks? My mother and I count streets as we batter our heads into the wind. I can hardly believe we are in this moment, that it has really happened; they didn't forget me or skip over me. They sent the letter that said I must come. The very event I have dreaded all my life, the horror that will trap me with worthless children who will attack me and murder me, has finally moved up, day by day, till it arrived. In the same way that my father had to give up the happy sunshine of Florida and come home to have his arm sliced up at the defense plant, I have had to give up my childhood and surrender to this moment.

Now I am being dragged, jerked and tugged by my mother in order that we not be late, I in my new Stride-Rite oxfords, in my cotton stockings held up by garters, in my plaid skirt and sweater, in my undershirt and woollies, carrying my plaid briefcase in which there is a new pencil case, in which there are new crayons and new pencils sharpened to needle points.

My heart has gone crazy. I could tear away from my mother's hand and run away forever. I could dash in front of a car and let it squash me as Bingo was squashed somewhere, probably right after they killed him with an injection. My mind is knocking about, my heart is thumping, my feet are flopping every which way and my stomach is spinning as my mother hurries along, pulling and pushing me.

Why does it have to happen? *Why* does everyone have to go to school? Who makes these rules and why can't they be ignored or broken? Why would anyone take a good little girl out of her house, where she has her dolls and her books and her special hidden chocolate cupcake, where she has her bed to sleep in, and her tub to bathe in, and her backyard to sit in, why would they pull her out and make her sit all day in a huge stone square building with bars on the windows and sharp pointy fence posts all around it?

The only reason is that she must not be a good girl. She must be bad. Every boy and girl being dragged to school this morning, and I see them now, coming from every direction, must be bad! And that is why they will murder me.

Doesn't my mother know this? Why has she been so careful with me all these years but now is willing to turn me over to *this*? I go over the bad things I have done. Oh! They are so numerous, they are so tremendous in number, that I can't begin to count them, or even think of them in some carefully ordered way. The meals I have not eaten! The milk spilled, the plates broken, the mud tracked in, the dresses torn, the paper wasted, the lights left on, the lies told, the mittens lost, the promises broken. And those are just the things they know about. There are those things no one knows about—the secret thoughts, the mean thoughts, the looking at my body from underneath with a mirror, the trying to break The Screamer's finger off, the wishing Gilda was my mother.

I begin to cry. I won't last a minute in there—I know it!

"Don't do this to me, Issa!" my mother cries, turning her face sideways to look at me as we rush along. *Do it to her?* I don't even recognize her face at that angle; it's as if a stranger is yelling at me, a pinch-faced witch dragging me along. My tears aren't enough, obviously. I bend over and vomit on my Stride-Rite shoes, on my cotton stockings.

"You bad girl!" my mother screams.

Well, of course I am bad, this is all happening because I am bad, incurably, permanently bad. The taste of vomit is what I deserve. I deserve to go to the Peter Pan Nursery School, if they would still take me. There is no end to what I deserve.

But school is what I will get. I will get it today, no matter what. I will get it walking along in my own throw-up, because it's clear my mother will not take me home, not let me creep back into my bed and hide there forever.

She takes me into a little Girl's Room and washes me roughly with a wet paper towel. "You'll calm down, you'll get over this, it can happen." She averts her face as the smell comes up from my shoes. She drags me down the hall as if she can't wait to get away from me and my smell. And she turns me over to some lady. The teacher. Who holds me between two fingers by my collar.

* * *

Such tiny tables and chairs they have in school! Such tiny sinks and such low toilet seats. What little drinking fountains—not like at the playground where you have to lift yourself up on the rim of the concrete bowl and lean over to drink. The idea that at school you don't have to grow up into things, but that the things bend down to you, is very strange.

In the wardrobe closet, we each have our own black hook; it has a number. Beneath the hook we have to put our boots on rainy days. There are rules for exactly when to take off coats and how to hang them; rules for how to ask to go to the bathroom and what to do there; rules for what to do when the bell rings, for when the flag salute takes place, for when attendance is taken. I decide rules are what grownups love to force on children; I think of the rules at home, about how I have to touch The Screamer gently and not punch her on the skull, about how certain bad-tasting foods have to be eaten before good-tasting foods can be eaten, how when you wipe yourself you can only use three sheets of toilet paper, how when you wash your hands, you rub them back and forth as high as your wrists before you dry them.

I wonder, if we were left alone, if we wouldn't all do things very well in spite of rules. If we were left to figure things out, wouldn't we find the best way? I look around at all the children who are crying and vomiting. So many of us are protesting the rules and the prison for the day, this terror is quite a common thing. Some of us are even wetting our pants. But I have no desire to do that. My shoes and stockings are disgusting enough, getting stiff now.

Louis and William Andanopoulos are twin brothers who are wearing white shirts and ties. Joe Martini has a harmonica in his pocket. Ruthie and Linda and Myra and Myrna are also here! They are without their skates, but as I look at them I can hear the sound in my ears: ZZZSHEE. I try to stand near them, but the four of them hold hands and don't look at me.

This is a surprise, that they won't even blink at me. Even when they do look at me, I see they don't know me. I know them. I know their faces. I know the color of their coats and how their knees bend when they skate. I know how their mothers and fathers and their cars and their houses look. How can it be, if I know them, they don't know me?

Oh, I am so lonely here. We are getting our desks, we are each getting our special box of crayons, we are getting our silver scissors without pointy tips. At home I use very sharp, very pointy scissors. I use Gilda's worn out hair-cutting scissors. I am insulted by blunt scissors. How can I follow a clean line for my cut-outs if I don't have the sharpest cutting point? They ought to trust me. But how can they? They don't know me here. They don't love me here.

No matter what happens at home, they love me. That is the first rule behind all their punishments. But to be in a place where I am locked inside, where they push and pull me around, where I'm not free to think my own thoughts, or do my own deeds, where there is the smell of vomit on my shoes, and no other shoes to put on, this is impossible!

The teacher asks, "Who can tell time? Can anyone here tell time? Raise your hand if you know how."

No one raises a hand. Miss Fenley is her name, and she has a yellow bun of hair.

I can tell time, but why should I tell her that? Is being able to tell time good or bad?

I raise my hand. It goes up like a balloon, without my permission.

"What is your name?" she demands. I tell her.

"From now on Issa will be our time monitor," Miss Fenley announces. She walks to where I am standing by my desk and holds up my hand. "Take a look at Issa, boys and girls. If you need to know the time, you will ask her and she will tell you. She will look at the clock there in front of the room. Before long you will all know how to tell time. But for now, remember: this is Issa, she has had the good fortune to have a head start in time, and, therefore, in this classroom she is in charge of time."

12

I am in charge of time.

To be in charge of anything is something. But *time*. What could be more important? Time will make me tall and brave and beautiful. Time will get me everything I want. Maybe even roller skates.

I puff out like a peacock, keeping my nose high—as far from my shoes as possible—and I accept the dull scissors, the baby box of crayons (these have only eight Crayolas; at home in my private box I have rainbow tiers of sixty-four; even in my pencil case I have sixteen).

We are assigned desks, inkwells in the right-hand corner with glass jars inside, our own slot in which to slide and hide books and secrets. We must settle down now to hard business, our first lesson. Hands folded. No wiggling, rustling, jiggling or sobbing. We are to learn . . . colors.

Is it possible? That the twins wearing ties, the four roller-skating girlfriends, the harmonica player, is it possible they don't know pink, green, red, and blue? Have they never heard of orange, yellow, white, and black?

We all know colors. We have to. We have been alive at least five years, maybe six. Is school going to be a waste of time every day? Gilda told me I will have to be in this school for nine years; after that there are schools beyond:

four years in the next one and four years in another and even more perhaps after that.

How can the teachers in these schools know if I already know what they are going to be teaching me? Will they ask me first? If they don't, it will be pointless, unbearable!

But—I now see that there is a boy who doesn't know any of his colors! Miss Fenley holds up color card after color card.

"Alvin," she calls him. "Alvin, what color is this? Don't you know red, Alvin?"

He shakes his head.

"Red?" she prompts him. "The color of Santa Claus's suit?"

He refuses to know.

"The color of your Christmas stocking?"

No.

"The stripes on your Christmas candy cane? That color?"

What is all this talk of Christmas? The word strikes terror to my heart. My father hates Christmas and has forbidden me to talk of it. My mother wants us to start having it, Christmas tree and all. The Jewish problem is at the heart of it, though I can't see why. But I didn't think we would have to discuss Christmas at school. Will we also have to discuss not using butter in mashed potatoes if we eat meat? Will we have to worry about wearing Jewish stars around our necks?

Also, why do we have to fidget in our chairs while only Alvin learns the color red? I could be telling time. I could be standing up at the front of the room, telling it to everyone, minute by minute. *A quarter after nine. Twenty after nine. Twenty-five after nine.* If time is what this class wants, time is what I will give them. They could all look at me and get to know my face, as I know the faces of Linda, Ruthie, Myra and Myrna. If they all knew my face, they might smile at me and maybe get to care about my fate as people do at home.

But this is the real world, and no one wants to look at my face. Neither does anyone want to learn the color red.

The twin brothers are breaking a stick of Black Jack gum between them; another boy has put his head down on his desk and is crying. The Skaters are whispering together, and one girl who looks like a bulldog is actually spilling the ink from her inkwell over her desk.

To think that this will be my home for most of every day, to think that I am glued to this seat with my hands folded for hours each day, to think of it! How did this come to pass? And could I have had any choice in the matter?

* * *

Tomato juice and two Ritz crackers is my first course. Now there is a new element to eating: it must be done as fast as possible in order that I get back to school in time. I have to run home all fourteen blocks, with my mother pulling me along. The meal, made by her earlier in the morning, is served in ten-second intervals; tomato juice, tuna fish sandwich, milk, go to the bathroom, put on your coat, run the fourteen blocks back to school.

Again it dawns on me that this is real, that it has to happen every day. That it's not a joke or an experiment or a temporary trip. That it doesn't end, that it is perpetual and unavoidable.

I tell Gilda privately what I feel. She looks at me with pity. It simply has to be done. We stare at each other in the understanding of something hard and unmovable. I never knew there were going to be things in my life like this, and now I know. Nothing can stop it, and nothing can save me. There is a whirlwind beyond me that spins through its patterns. I can observe it, I can consider all the possibilities, but I cannot change it.

No! I won't have it! This is not what I want! Even as I think this, I am making plans as to how to endure it. Bring Black Jack gum and make friends with the twins. At home, go outside when The Skaters are skating by and offer them chocolate cupcakes that I've saved up in a secret place after the bakery truck's visits. Force some children at school to look at my face. Make them know me! If I mean something to them, they'll offer me advantages. They'll invite me in. No one keeps an eye on me just because I'm there, lost in the army of children. I have to be valuable to someone first.

How complicated!

* * *

"Ride! Ride! Ride!"

We are reading a book. The whole book has only this one word in it. Ride. On every page there is a picture of a different kind of ride: a car ride, a pony ride, a train ride, a wagon ride, a bus ride, a trolley ride, a sleigh ride, a bicycle ride.

Miss Fenley is going around the room, having us each read a page of the book. "Ride! Ride! Ride!" When she comes to me, I will know what to say. In the meantime, all I can do for entertainment is to look out the window. The classroom has tall windows that can be opened from the top by a long pole with a hook on the end. Outside, the day is dark and snowy, the sky black, heavy with cold. Soon it will be lunchtime and I will have to start pulling on my boots, which exhausts me. My mother will be there at the gate at a quarter to twelve; then we will race home, our breath coming out in puffs of smoke, so I can eat my balanced meal. Snow will get down my neck. Snow will get in the top of my boots. My mother always whimpers a little as we run, almost as if she is crying. Together we will slosh in the slush and slide on the icy curbs.

Why don't the other children go home for lunch? My classmates bring a paper bag lunch, or they eat in the hot lunch room. Why am I the only one required to have a balanced lunch at home? Because of this rule, my mother has to come and get me since the crossing at Ocean Parkway is too dangerous for me by myself. One rule leads to another. She must leave The Screamer with my grandmother every day at noontime because Gilda is busy with her customers; my grandmother, who might have a heart attack and drop my sister, is almost as dangerous as my crossing Ocean Parkway. My mother's constant fear is that something terrible can happen anywhere at any moment.

Here in my classroom, lit by yellow lights, with the black sky outside, I can almost forget The Screamer, forget home with the nine windows in my bedroom, forget liver broiling, forget my whole life. It's rather nice, sometimes, to beam my eyes like a flashlight across the room and light up new faces, not the old ones from home. I wonder if a person can get tired of faces at home and one day decide never to see them again.

Joe Martini closes his reader with a slapping sound. Doesn't he want to take his turn reading "Ride! Ride! Ride!"? He gets up from his desk and wanders to the window. Ruby, the girl with the bulldog face, pulls up her plaid skirt to let her garter belt show. Miss Fenley doesn't see any of this, she's so busy trying to get Louis Andanopoulos to read the words in the reading book. Even after she explains to him how to read the first "ride," he can't read the second "ride."

The sky gets darker and darker. A wind roars through the schoolyard. Tree branches rattle and shake across the playground.

"Oh, goodness, this is a real blizzard," Miss Fenley says. Just then the lights flicker and go out. We can't read anymore. We can hardly see the teacher. Because it isn't really night, there's enough dim light in the room to see the outline of everyone's heads, but not their faces.

"Boys and girls," Miss Fenley says. "Boys and girls . . . ," but she can't think of what to say next. We sit in the semi-dark and look around for comfort. Joe Martini comes back up the aisle, not to his seat, but to mine. He bends down right next to me and says, "I hate to read ride ride ride, don't you?" I'm astonished. I stare at his face, and he stares at mine.

"I hope the whole school blows down," he whispers to me. Then he is gone. But my heart is bursting with joy. He looked at my face. Now someone at school knows me.

* * *

A messenger comes to the door of the room with a note. By now Miss Fenley has found a flashlight and is shining it on the alphabet letters above the blackboard. The same children who didn't know their colors also don't know their letters. It's not so bad when it's my turn, but with so many children it's almost never my turn. Also, my turn goes by very fast. I read ride ride ride, or I read one letter of the alphabet, and then I have to wait forever for my turn to come again. I begin to make rhymes in my head. *Ride, slide, bride, glide, hide, tide.* My mother would be proud of me.

"Issa," says Miss Fenley. "Your mother has called the school. All the lights in Brooklyn are out. Even the traffic lights. She cannot come to take you home for lunch. You will eat in the hot lunch room today."

"But where is it?" I ask.

"Who will volunteer to take Issa to the hot lunch room at lunchtime?"

Joe Martini will. This is the luckiest day of my life.

* * *

Never mind that the smell in the hot lunch room is of vomit and tomato soup. Or that the sandwich is peanut butter on whole wheat bread and we have to eat in the semi-dark. I can get this food down. I can swallow anything as long as I don't have to run fourteen blocks each way and be watched as I eat and drink and even as I go to the bathroom. I could manage crusts here, liver here, soft-boiled egg if I had to. Joe Martini and I sit at a long wooden table and each get our bowl of soup and our half-sandwich. We get our milk. Some children look sad, but I can't imagine why. Would they rather be racing home in a blizzard? Home is fine for some things, like having a cold, or getting an enema, you wouldn't want to be in school for those things, but for eating anywhere else is better than home.

School may not be as bad as I thought. It's terrible for learning things, but it has its advantage for eating food and for sitting with Joe Martini. At school you can forget home if you want to. At school you have a kind of privacy in your mind that no one can enter. Miss Fenley might think I am reading "Ride ride ride" every time someone reads it, but she can't really know what I'm thinking. No one knows what is going through my mind as I stare out the window at the trees blowing in the wind, or even as my eyes follow Miss Fenley's pointer going along the row of alphabet letters. I am learning things, but not the things Miss Fenley is teaching me. I give myself special lessons that light up my mind like flashes of lightning. I walk through a blizzard of my own thoughts and cross my own dangerous streets.

CHAPTER

13

On the radio, Christmas is as big as the war, even bigger. Songs come on—"Silent Night," "The First Noel,"—that my father switches off and my mother switches back on. A little green plastic Christmas tree appears in the kitchen and then disappears. At school, decorations go all around our classroom. Tinsel (which I never saw before) and stars and elves and Santas and candy canes and camels and donkeys and reindeer and Jesus The Baby and Jesus The Lord and Jesus The Savior and Jesus The Father. Joe Martini knows all about Jesus and can't believe I never heard of him.

"I'm Jewish," I tell him, hoping that will explain everything, but wondering why even Jews don't know news this big about Jesus.

"Jesus was a Jew," Joe Martini tells me. "So you should know." This is definitely something I will have to ask my father about since he is the expert on Jews in our family. But I know he won't want to talk about Jesus. He won't talk about Christmas either, except in fights with my mother. The word *Christmas* is between the two of them like the word *liver* is between my mother and me.

"Issa is in school now," she informs him, which seems to make it plain why she should have the Christmas tree she wants in our house. Not just the little plastic one, but a big one, a real one, a forest tree with green piney leaves, with mirrored balls on it, with tinsel. *With presents for me under it!* She doesn't want to deprive me, she says. Or Blossom, my sister. "This is a Christmas world," she tells my father.

"Not in this house," he says.

* * *

Gilda is on his side. I hear them talking out by the garbage cans after lunch on Sunday, where they have met by accident, each depositing his bag of garbage.

"My sister was born a *goy*," Gilda says to him. "There's nothing you can do about her. The same as she was born having tantrums. It's in her nature."

"But she can't force *Christmas* on me," my father says. "I can put up with everything else. But this, this is bile in my throat." His eyes seek Gilda's. Their faces, in profile, have the same expression, as if they are two parts of the same person.

Bundled up in my winter coat and leggings and kerchief and gloves, I am playing Russian Seven against the brick wall in the alley. *One*, you just throw the ball and catch it. *Two*, you let it bounce once. *Three*, you clap your hands twice and spin around before you catch it. *Four*, you throw it under your leg and catch it on the fly. I can't get past Four, I'm not even sure I know what Five is.

"Tell her she can only have *Chanukah*," Gilda whispers to him. She pats his arm, and lets her hand rest there.

* * *

Now we get a houseful of menorahs. My grandmother digs one out from a closet that she bought for five cents in a grocery store when she first came to America at the age of fifteen. It is tin and has eight sharp rings that hold the candles. It's so light that it tips over as soon as she stands it up, even though there is a lion embossed on the front of it. My father brings home a big brass antique menorah, shaped like an archway, heavy, on a pedestal, on a round base. Gilda has her old one but also buys a new one at the Avenue N synagogue, gold plated with two fierce lions with great manes on it. She also buys me a book, *The Adventures of K'Ton Ton*, about a little Jewish boy. Suddenly everyone is handing me books about Jewish children and Jewish holidays with juicy names like *sukkoth* and *tu bish vat* and Rosh Hashonah; saliva bubbles in my mouth when I say those words. My mother spits when she repeats them, angrily, "I will not have her mind filled with Rosh Hashonahs!" she cries, ". . . with yiskors or whiskers or whatever that nonsense is, I will not have my child repenting for her sins. What kind of sins does a child have to repent for?"

I both agree with her and I don't. I have many sins, but I don't want to repent for them.

The Chanukah candles come in many colors. I prefer blue and yellow, I like white. The green looks grim. The red reminds me of Christmas colors, and I'm not allowed to like red in this season. But presents! I would love presents, a pile of them under a tree, all for me! Maybe even the sacred roller skates, which appear in my dreams every night. Silver, with sliding adjustable panels, with clamps that tighten with a skate key, with leather straps. Oh, what beautiful complications are woven into a pair of ordinary skates.

I would love to have a puppy, too. Maybe a Captain Midnight decoder. If they asked me, I have many ideas. But how likely is it I'll get a pile of Christmas presents? And not even on my birthday, but on *Jesus's* birthday?

* * *

In school, we are rehearsing a Christmas play to be put on in the auditorium for the seventh and eighth grade. Miss Fenley says that because I have a good memory, I have to be Mary, Mother of Jesus. Mary has to give a long speech. I repeat it to myself many times, at home in bed, in the bathtub, during endless dinnertimes. I discover that keeping my mind on something far away and fascinating lessens my fear of the man looking in the window, lessens the degree of my shivering with cold after my bath, lessens my disgust at having to eat lima beans, whose grainy thick insides make me gag. This way I keep my mind on some far-off place and become someone else:

> *Oh Goodness, we have nowhere to stay on this cold winter's night. There is no room at the inn. Whatever shall we do? I fear our long-awaited child may be born soon. Joseph, my good husband, do you think they would let us stay in the manger, on a bed of straw?*

Joe Martini is Joseph my husband, which embarrasses and thrills me. They put a beard on his face with a rubber band to hold it on in back. I hope I really can marry Joe someday and have our long-awaited baby with him. They have no donkey for me to ride, but someone brings a wooden hobby horse to school, and I have to rock on it. I think it's a mistake. No pregnant woman would ride a bouncing horse.

* * *

Joe Martini has a plan. Instead of eating in the hot lunch room every day (which I am now allowed to do), we will one day go instead to his house for lunch. He lives only a half-block from school. He will bring a note from his mother inviting me, in case Miss Fenley tries to stop us, but his plan is not to give it to her. We will just walk down the hall, as if to the hot lunch room, but instead we will walk out the door and run down the street to his house. He says his mother will be glad to have me.

"What about my boots and my hat and my coat?"

"Who wants to bother with them?" he says, giving me a new idea that never crossed my mind. Putting on my coat on a cold day has always struck me as a law of nature. I admire this boy; he is my teacher more than Miss Fenley is.

His house smells different from mine. Food is cooking, but it smells rich and spicy, not fatty and slimy. His mother is different, too—her breasts are soft and big where my mother's are hard and skinny. She hugs me, too, though I am a stranger. I can't help but love her.

"That's Jesus," Joe says. And sure enough, there he is, floating over us in a pink gown, in a painting that goes from the floor to the ceiling of the hallway. His eyes are astonishing; they see right into your deepest mind. He has a girl's face, but he has a beard, too—it reminds me of the beard Miss Fenley attaches to Joe with a rubber band. Joe has a sweet face like Jesus. How come we don't have a god I could appreciate? Our god is mixed up with white shawls and not eating and unshaven men and sour smells.

Joe has told me that when they die in his family they are all going to hold hands and fly up together to heaven, where they will all live together on soft white clouds. I don't know much about death, but I know it isn't soft wherever Bingo is, and wherever the dead soldiers are, and especially in the place my grandmother fears when she clutches her chest.

This is good here. Mrs. Martini feeds us spaghetti and meatballs and, oh, they are delicious! They slide right down my throat, even if Joe says, "Watch me suck down this worm!" We get milk *and* wine, if we want it, although we don't. We each have an empty wine glass, ruby colored, which the light shines through, casting pink lines on our plates.

This house reminds me of Mrs. Esposito's because of lace doilies on the backs of all the chairs and the dark flowery smell of the carpet.

I wonder, if I had been allowed to know other children, would I also have been able to come into their houses? This is very nice, looking around in someone else's kitchen, seeing their dishes and glasses, eating their food. There is no grandmother here, or aunt, or beauty parlor upstairs, and there may be no cellar, either, for all I know. But people live here and have fun, even so.

Mrs. Martini wears an enormous gold cross on a chain;

as she moves about energetically, it swerves across her chest, back and forth like a pendulum. She doesn't even glance at our plates; doesn't she care if we chew and swallow? Doesn't she worry that we may be late? There's an easy carelessness here that astonishes me.

Joe takes me upstairs to his room, and that's where he tells me he has ten grownup brothers and sisters! They're all married; he says he was his mother's little angel, who flew into her life just when she was lonely.

You flew into mine just when I was lonely, I want to tell Joe, but you can't say something like that. Then it is over—we each get a hug from Mrs. Martini, and we pass under the kindly eyes of Jesus, and without coats we run back to school in the freezing wind. The icy blasts take my breath away.

In the afternoon, we practice Christmas carols, but I don't know what to do when we come to the words, "Christ the Lord." My father, who is kind in nearly every other way, has become vicious about this problem. "You will not sing those words," he told me, "and you know which ones I mean."

I don't see why I can't. Will I be cursed? I sing them. I sing them all, Christ the King, Christ the Lord, Holy Infant, he'll never know.

But that night I get chills, and then I get a 104° fever. Dr. Trutt comes in the morning and says I'm very sick. Two days later he says I have pneumonia. Now I can't be in the Christmas play. Now I can't be the mother of Jesus. I can't ride my donkey/rocking horse. And I can't be Joe's wife. All because I'm Jewish.

CHAPTER

14

Sundays always start out well enough. For breakfast, my father buys rolls and bagels and lox and cream cheese at Irving's delicatessen on Avenue P. He buys *The Brooklyn Eagle*, which is fat and soon covers the floor all around my father's easy chair. He buys me Greek black olives which, though I can't say why, I love although my mother makes an awful face when she tastes one. They're quite disgusting for many reasons; they have slippery, oily skins, they're soft and wrinkled. They are not only salty and black, but they have a hard pit in each one. There's the usual problem of pits; you can choke on one if you swallow it; you can break a tooth if you chew hard on it, or it can just take you by surprise if you forget it's in there, and shock you by being a rock in your mouth when you expect ordinary chewable feelings.

But, disgusting as they are, I love Greek olives; my father calls them something like *misslinnas*. They make my tongue curl. I have to drink three glasses of water afterward. But that's how I am. I love them.

My mother can't understand me. When I love something she hates, she looks at me as if I'm not hers. I look right back at her because although I may be hers, I am not *her*. My father does not expect me to be him, Gilda does not expect me to be her, but my mother wants an exact copy of herself. My mother has decided The Screamer is exactly that—a copy of her. The Screamer likes what my mother likes and hates what my mother hates. I have seen my mother chew meat for her and put it with her fingers from her mouth into The Screamer's. Liver she chews especially long and hard for her, whereas I always had to chew and gag on my own. The Screamer is the one who naps with my mother now, when her headaches are bad (and they are very bad. They are worse than they ever were). No one thinks to invite me to nap anymore; does she think I don't get tired? Does she forget what wonderful times we used to have, napping together, each one of us with a wet washcloth on her forehead?

Today is Sunday, a day when Gilda has no noisy customers running up and down the stairs, a day when the papers are spread in a colorful circle at my father's feet, a day I have a greasy container of olives all to myself. Sundays always start out this way—peaceful and full of promise.

My mother says she can't read the papers because of her headaches, but I notice she can read music without any trouble. She plays the piano on Sunday. Sometimes she plays too loud, and she plays too long; I have learned ways to close my ears to her music. When she's finished, my father always says something nice, like "Very nice," and then he looks at me, and I say it also. "That's nice, Mommy." She plays her Chopin, and she plays Stephen Foster songs, her boogie-woogie, and she always plays "Oh, Danny Boy," to which my father howls along like a dog. She likes to tell the story of how, when she was seven years old, her father bought her a piano because he knew she had musical talent. "But Gilda had none," she says. "She wanted a violin, but he wouldn't buy her one. He knew she had no talent."

My father never lets this pass: "But if he never bought her a violin, how could he know?" My mother throws him a look that says he is not only not like her, but also stupid. I know that look—we all know that look. I suddenly understand that my mother has always hated Gilda just as I hate The Screamer; I feel a sudden rush of *likeness* to my mother. We *are* the same, I *am* her, but in ways she just doesn't recognize; we are both good haters—maybe the best.

On this Sunday, in springtime, we have the windows open, and warm, lilac-laden air is coming in on a hot breeze. We begin to discuss what we will do today. Even though we appear so content, reading the papers and hearing music, even though no one has to go to work or to school, we all know a moment will come when we get unhappy. The day, full of endless hours, lies ahead. How many more times can my mother play "Oh, Danny Boy" and how much longer can my father read the paper? Soon we will have to move on.

Somewhere out there in the world we have relatives, and I am told that on Sunday people visit relatives, but we don't. My mother won't have it. She said relatives are the most stupid people of all, and most of them belong to my father, and his are the worst. I remember a few of them, Aunt Clara and Uncle Charlie, Aunt Tillie and Uncle Harry, but that was from a time I was very small. I don't remember much, and what I do remember is not interesting to me. Uncle Harry had sharp whiskers and Aunt Tillie could not talk without sniffling and snorting. Uncle Charlie smelled of whiskey and Aunt Clara snapped the box of chocolate truffles out of my hands when I wanted a second one.

So what shall we do? We are at that moment. My mother asks it from the piano bench, her back toward us.

"The zoo? Issa would love the zoo," my father says.

"Too smelly. The monkey house makes me want to throw up."

"Prospect Park? We could rent a paddle boat?"

"Too many hoodlums there on Sundays."

"What about the museum?"

"Blossom will get restless."

"We could eat out at the automat."

"Who knows how long those sandwiches sit in those windows?"

"Issa likes it there."

"Well, she would. She's a child."

"I like it there," my father says.

There is silence. I know this whole play so well. Now my mother will turn back to the keys and play something fast and loud: a military march or the "Minute Waltz." My father will pick up another section of *The Brooklyn Eagle*. That's the end of that. We won't go anywhere today.

Then, what happens is what always happens. The day turns dark. There is the feeling of the end of freedom coming. Tomorrow is school, tomorrow my father goes back to work at the defense plant, where (because they couldn't prove he was a *saboteur*) they have given him a much simpler job. Tomorrow Gilda's customers run up the steps like cackling hens (says my mother) and tomorrow the long week starts without a hint of respite.

I want, I want . . . There ought to be fun for me. There ought to be roller skates. If I sit on my bed and look out any of the nine windows, I will see The Skaters going by, Linda and Myra and Myrna and Ruthie. Now they know I am in their class, they know my face by now, I tell them the time every day, but still I have no skates. If I had them, I could fly with them like the wind, I could play their noisy games, their rolling games, their racing games, their falling-down games. Whose fault is it that I have no skates?

My mother won't let me, that's all. If she would, the others would stop saying be careful be careful. My father does what my mother makes him do. Gilda, also, is led by her. She is terrible. I hope something terrible happens to her. Because of her we can't go to the zoo or rowing on the lake or walking in the museum. Because of her everything in my life is the way it is.

* * *

Good, we are getting a thunderstorm. Good, because it will shake the house with thunder. Good, because the rain will pour on the roof and streak the windows with mess and dirt. Good, because it will drown all the ants and soak all the birds and batter all the flowers, and make all the plants and trees bend down and shiver. Good, because my mother is down in the basement washing The Screamer's diapers and now she won't be able to hang them on the line and they won't get dry and they'll smell bad and The Screamer will have to wear her wet ones and get diaper rash and all that is good, because no one will take me to the zoo or get me skates.

Sundays are poison. I would go upstairs and bake with my grandmother, but she is clutching her chest today and moaning. I would go upstairs and roll bandages with Gilda, but she is checking her record book of war bonds and has to concentrate.

No one wants me, so I turn into thunder. With the thunder I roar and bang and clap and shake the very walls of the house. It is so dark outside that nighttime would seem bright with its moon and stars.

If only I could get sick they would pay attention to me, but I am healthy, I am strong as an ox, I am gaining weight from eating peanut butter sandwiches and tomato soup with Joe Martini. I could try to break my arm again, but even that didn't keep me sick enough for long.

What could happen that would change the dark furious feeling inside me? If I wait, something will have to happen. There is no way this feeling can go on without something to stop it. It is too ugly and terrible.

* * *

The clothes are washing in the basement in the Bendix. My mother is making bacon sandwiches for lunch; the smell of bacon grease gives my father a headache. He won't touch it, he won't even sit at the table when she serves bacon, but she makes it because she has to do things to stir him up. I know she likes to get him angry; it makes things happen, it makes the deadly dull Sunday come to life. I am just like her, so I know how she does things.

What I do is reach under The Screamer's knitted blanket and pinch her thigh. She can't talk, so she can't tell. I love to make her cry. I know it's bad and I love to do it. That's the way I am. Why I am bad I don't know, but I am.

The lightning is exploding through the windows. I used to be scared, like Bingo, of lightning and thunder, but I believe Gilda's telling me that it won't hurt me, so I let it happen now without screaming or hiding.

This is what I see; I am opening the refrigerator to check if my chewing gum is still stuck in the inside bottom corner. My mother is at the sink, in front of the open window, rinsing the bacon fat out of the frying pan. The bacon strips are lined up like curly snakes on a brown paper bag. The Screamer, still screaming from my pinch, is in her carriage near the stove. My father is not here: he has gone down to the basement to bring the wet clothes upstairs where we will lay them all over the backs of chairs.

And then my hair stands on end. I can feel it lift up at the back of my neck and rise up toward the sky. There is a tremendous crackling noise, and the room lights up. I turn around, and a ball of flame, big as the sun, has flown in the window and is hanging in the air, just behind my mother's back. It dances with fire, it's blinding me with fire, it hangs there in the space behind my mother till she turns around and almost takes it in her open mouth when she screams.

No one can move, we are paralyzed as it crackles and sparks. My father in the basement hears it and howls, "What? I'm coming!" and dashes up the stairs; he sees it just as it vanishes from the air. With a pop, it disappears, leaving a black hole in the air, an inside-out space.

We look at one another. We are all alive, but no one can move. We have been visited by a ball of fire. We have been electrified. We have lived through another Sunday.

CHAPTER

15

My mother is convinced she will die by fire. Terrified since the ball of lightning came in the window, she won't open the windows. She won't let anyone take a bath or shower if the sky is cloudy. We can't even get a glass of water from the sink if there is one dark thunderhead in the sky. Could it be that she is being punished by God for making bacon? Could that *possibly* be the case? I don't think about God. How can I think about an invisible person who never shows up, never speaks, never shows the slightest indication that he exists. But maybe, as my father suggested, I should take this event as a warning and not eat bacon any more. Maybe my father is right, that God is everywhere, that he sees everything I do and knows everything I think. I have a sense that, if God does exist, his presence is especially dense in the area where the Jewish shawl and the Jewish prayer book are in sight. My father may know something: a ball of fire has never crackled at *his* back.

I watch my mother when she isn't aware of me; I follow her into the bathroom where there are only the two of us. The Screamer can't walk, so she has to stay wherever they plop her. She's like a lump of dough. One of these days her mouth will talk and her legs will walk, but not yet, not yet.

I walk, I talk, I see my mother leaning forward, looking at her face in the mirror, examining it as if it is spoiling, like a piece of molding cheese. She has a sad, disgusted look around her mouth, which she never opens to smile. Her pretty round behind comes toward me as she leans over the sink—even when she's sad her behind is always pretty, the way her skirt clings to it and then swings free down at her knees. When my mother walks, she dances, despite herself.

Very suddenly, I throw my arms around her legs and kiss her behind. She jumps, as if I have bitten her.

"Issa! Don't do that!"

"Why not? Gilda likes it when I do that to her."

"You must never kiss people in those places," she says. "And you must not kiss Gilda all the time. You're not a baby."

"I wish I were."

"Don't be silly."

"Well, I do."

My mother wants me out of there. I think she probably has blood on a napkin and wants to take it off and put on a clean one. I have seen her wrap the old one in toilet paper and put it in a paper bag. But that was when I was little and she would do those things in front of me. Now, I suppose, she only does them in front of The Screamer.

I don't think there is a reason for me to be in this house any more. I would like to live in some other house. With some other mother.

* * *

When Gilda wants to take me around the neighborhood to sell more war bonds, I ask her if we can go to a Skater's house. "Please, can we visit one of the girls from my class?" I beg. "Linda, Ruthie, Myra, or Myrna?"

"I don't see why not. I know all their mothers, every one of them is patriotic," she said, hitching over her shoulder the canvas bag that has her record book and her money box in it. "Everyone is patriotic these days." As we pass Mrs. Exter's house, Gilda points out to me the four gold stars pasted in her window. "A four-star mother," she says, "poor thing. Four boys lost in the war. I'm glad I have no sons. I'm glad you aren't a boy, Issa." Just then Mrs. Exter comes to her window and waves to us. She doesn't look too bad. When your children die, you can still smile and wave. What does that mean?

"I love the summer," Gilda says to me as we walk on. Even after she has told me about four boys dying in the war, she can think of something ordinary like the summer. What does that mean? When grownups have feelings, do the feelings only last a minute or last forever?

"I love the summer, too," I say, switching from dead boys to summer thoughts. I do the same thing grownups do—go to another subject. But what happens to the bad thought; if I bring it back later, will I get the bad feeling? Can I switch on and off like a lamp?

We walk along the summer streets, under the leafy shade of maple trees that drop little wing-shaped seed holders. I gather them up, snap them open in the middle and glue the wings to my nose. There aren't many cars on the street in the daytime; the fathers who have cars are all at work, including my father. Summertime is calmer than wintertime. I wear less clothes. I don't have to run to school. At night fireflies wink and glow against the hedges, and we sit out on the stoop to get cool, licking ice-cream pops we buy from Willy, the ice cream man.

But now that it is summer, I never see Joe Martini. I thought he would find me no matter what; I wonder if he has already forgotten me. He promised me he would walk over to my house as soon as he could, but he must have counted the fourteen blocks and decided I wasn't worth it. Or maybe his mother didn't like me and forbids it. Or . . . could it be . . . Jesus may have told him with his powerful eyes to stay away from me.

I wish Joe loved me. I wish everyone loved me. I wish anyone loved me.

Suddenly we are at the door of Linda's house. To my amazement, once the door is opened, there is the real-life

Linda, just a little girl playing Monopoly with her father on the rug. There is Linda's mother, cooking in the kitchen. There is Linda's little sister, Evvy, pale and thin, because her heart is weak. (I thought only my grandmother, who is old, could have a weak heart, but look at this: a child younger than I am has a weak heart. This too could happen to me!)

"Hi," Linda says. "Want to play?" Just like that, the invitation I have wanted for so long is laid at my feet. She pats the rug beside her and I rush to the place, folding my legs under me, grateful and weak with gratitude. Gilda goes into the kitchen to talk to Mrs. Levitz, and, because the game is beginning, I am just in time to get my money from the banker, who is Mr. Levitz. He has two missing teeth, and a stubble of beard, but he has a sweet face.

"I hate Miss Fenley, don't you?" Linda asks. "I can't wait to see who we have for our teacher in first grade."

"Me too," I say.

"We should walk to school together," Linda says. "You and I only live across the street from each other."

"Will you be allowed to cross Ocean Parkway?"

"Of course! I'll be in first grade. Won't you be allowed?"

"Sure," I say. I decide I will push my mother in front of a car if she doesn't let me walk to school without her.

"Your turn," Linda says, giving me the dice. She has short brown straight hair and bangs that fall into her face. She's pretty. I try to see into her bedroom. I try to see her whole house from where I'm sitting. I wonder where she keeps her skates.

Mr. Levitz is reading an Archie comic book while Linda and I take our turns. He laughs out loud to himself. I know he drives a truck—he delivers furniture but he doesn't work every day.

"This is fun," I say. But Gilda, I notice, has finished her business and is ready to leave. My heart turns over.

"You want to stay?" she asks me.

"Oh please!"

"Your mother will kill me," she says.

"Well, if she does, I'll kill *her*," I say; the words just fly out of my mouth. Mr. Levitz laughs. But no one seems to think I am bad. Gilda blows me a kiss and leaves without me; she says she will be back to get me in an hour.

So I get to stay and play with a friend. I could explode with amazement as I think about it, *Issa playing with a friend!*—and I do think about it, all the time I am playing Monopoly, buying houses and getting put in jail and collecting "Go" money. So much money—if only I had my own money I could buy skates.

When I have to go to the bathroom, Linda directs me to her bedroom next to the kitchen; the bathroom is through there. As I pass her dresser, I see six quarters sitting on a mirrored tray, gleaming like silver moons. I take a quarter. I just take it without hesitation and quickly bend to put it in my sock. When I go back to the living room, that wild bird, my heart, is flapping its wings inside me. The quarter is red-hot in my sock. Do they know? Can they know? Why did I do it? Maybe Linda will discover the quarter missing later and tell her mother. They will come to my house. They will shine flashlights in my eyes.

I am so bad. Why does it feel so exciting to be bad? The thudding inside me is spinning my breath out in long strands. Linda's mother is making potato pancakes, I can smell the onion and the oil, flowing in a delicious cloud from room to room. My heartbeat shakes me! I have discovered that if I pretend to bend down to pick something up, if I let my head hang low, the wild bird in my chest will eventually slow down, beat and pop, then stop flapping. I try it, shaken hard by this excitement; so much has happened in one day it is almost too much to bear.

When Gilda comes for me an hour later, I am better. My confidence in myself expands; I can survive this kind of shattering expedition away from home. The inside of my mind is glowing with new matters to think about. I walk home with Gilda, feeling the quarter in my sock like a chocolate cupcake, hidden and delicious.

* * *

Easy as pie, they now call for me. Four friends call for me, at my door, Linda and Myra and Myrna and Ruthie. I hardly believe it, looking out one of my nine windows and seeing the troupe of them coming up to the front door. The doorbell rings like a fanfare of trumpets. I can't believe that eight legs that can skate, eight eyes that have seen the sidewalk flying by beneath, are now walking to my house, looking for me.

* * *

My mother has to have all her teeth pulled. She never smiles, anyway, so I think it won't be so bad, but it is. She comes home from the dentist on my father's arm looking like a witch, her lips drawn in on a string of pain. Blood comes out of her mouth all night. When I come into her bedroom, she throws the sheet over her face, and talks from under it, in the dark, like a lamp without a bulb. Her words sound to me like, "Wis is to wis my yay-yay."

"This is to fix my headaches," is what my father translates. A certain doctor thinks that it's my mother's teeth that are causing all her headaches, causing all her nausea. The doctor should have asked me and I could have told him it isn't her teeth. It's me. It's Gilda. It's not being able to rhyme her rhymes to applause in a big parade on Avenue P, carrying a flag and wearing a crown. I can feel where my mother's unhappiness comes from: it's from my father's not being rich or fancy, it's from living in the same house with the beauty parlor and Gilda and my grandmother, it's from the endless war and the accident at the defense plant, it's from having to cook and get onion-stink on her fingers and tears in her eyes. It's from her being beautiful and having no one looking at her. The doctor ought to have asked me. I know.

She comes out from under the sheet, holding ice to her mouth in a washcloth.

"Wo wahwy wah-ing" she says, but I unpeel the words

to find that she said, "Don't worry, darling." For that *darling* I would give her all my teeth this minute. I would give her my life.

"Poor Mommy," I say. Saying it gives me an amazing power, as if I am the mommy and she is the child. I never knew she could be a child; right now she is crumpled on the bed like a little child, she is weak like a little child. I never knew my mother could be this weak. I never knew I could be this strong.

This is another new idea to think about. Look how every day is a surprise.

CHAPTER

16

Teeth take over. The Screamer gets her first one, so what is the commotion about? One tooth. I have a whole mouthful. My mother has none, my sister has one, they are the strangest things; with teeth, if you think about it, a person is like a wild animal, having those white, sharp, pointy prongs that clamp down into meat, that grind it and tear it. So what about smiles? The same prongs that are so sharp, that can hurt, that mince matter, are displayed to show friendliness.

"Smile more," Gilda reminds me. "If you smiled more in school, you'd have more friends. You'd be elected class president." How little she knows. I already lost two elections, each time nominated by Joe Martini, in first grade, for president and for vice president; each time I had to go out into the hall and stand there with the other nominees for three minutes by the clock while the class raised their hands for or against me, and then go back inside, head bowed, heart agog, to find out they didn't want me. Not me: someone else. The hands that didn't come up for me were like fists that punched my stomach as I came back into the room.

Gilda doesn't know everything—I was wrong to think she did. I used to think she thought I was perfect. Why then did she discuss my smiling with my mother? Why did my mother write a jingle for me and prop it up in front of my orange juice:

> *If smiles she won't hoard,*
> *I'm pretty sure she'll get a reward!*

Why should I smile? How much I smile should be my own business. A smile isn't something you *do*; it comes because you feel a certain way, and it isn't often I feel that way. Besides, I have too much gum showing over my teeth. My teeth are too small. Whose fault is that? I am beginning to see and envy parts on others that are prettier than mine.

The Screamer clicks a spoon against her one ragged tooth and everyone laughs and laughs. One afternoon The Screamer sneezes and my grandmother says, "*Gesundheit.*" The Screamer laughs at this funny word. Then everyone says "*Gesundheit*" every time The Screamer sneezes. One day when she isn't even sneezing at all, someone says "*Gesundheit*" to her and she makes a sound like a sneeze, a little baby snort through her stuffy nose. How brilliant they think she is. How they carry on, day after day, saying "Gesundheit" and going wild when she makes the snuffly sneezing noise.

When *I* catch a cold and sneeze for a week, no one says *Gesundheit* to me. They are all worn out from saying it to her.

* * *

Teeth aren't the only odd things. Look at ears, those cups glued onto the sides of our heads. And eyes, like marbles, that come in different colors and roll around, roll around. Luckily, in children especially, they are at the very top of the head. If they were lower, we couldn't see far at all. Children are too short to do almost anything important.

At first my mother goes around with her lips sucked in, to hide her toothless mouth. When she gets her new teeth,

big, square, white, even teeth, with their pink plastic tops
and bottoms, she gags putting them in, she gags taking
them out. Even if she tries to do it quietly, we know when
she is putting them in and taking them out.

Though I am just now getting my second set of teeth,
my grownup teeth, I have to worry about losing them
someday and getting plastic teeth. I also have an unstable
heart to think about, like my grandmother's. I have all
these body parts, all over me, and all of them breakable,
dangerous.

Suddenly cavities spring up in all my teeth as if my bub-
blegum had infiltrated every crack and sprouted seeds of
rot. Dr. Ellen's office is opposite the playground, and I sit
at the waiting room window, not reading *Jack and Jill*,
but watching free children roller skating on the blacktop;
they are doubly lucky, to have roller skates and not have
cavities. My stomach churns at the threats from within:
the low burr of the drill, the smell of antiseptic, the cries
of a child.

They have to hold me down, my mother and father
both. They have tricked me, lied to me, bribed me,
dragged me into the chair. I have made them promise not
to let Dr. Ellen pull my loose tooth. My mother promises.
My father promises. Dr. Ellen promises. He says, in a
kindly way, "I just want to wiggle it slightly." Then he
thrusts his hairy fist into my small mouth and pulls the
tooth out of its socket with a violent wrench that I feel in
the core of my brain. Blood pours out of my mouth.

I scream so loud the mirrors crack. I don't want to have
teeth to rot, and a heart to flop inside my ribs, don't want
to vomit, have babies, make poopies, pee, gag, break my
bones, have sore throats. Die! Next to my cry: *I want! I
want!* is my other cry: *I don't want! I don't want!*

It doesn't matter. I get what there is, and so does everyone else.

* * *

There is a party in the street when the war ends. Dancing on the sidewalk, balloons, whistles, hats in the air. My father brings out a tambourine and dances around like a wild monkey, his knees going cockeyed. My mother is wearing a brown silk dress and beautiful, delicately heeled alligator shoes as she lounges against one of the tables. Gilda and my grandmother are setting out honey cakes and sponge cakes and mandelbrot and candied orange peel. There is a special bottle of Manischewitz grape wine.

It suits me. War news on the radio has always been the cause of people shushing me. There's nothing good about war, except for the war bond parades and Gilda's collecting jewelry for the natives in New Guinea.

My father drinks two paper cups of wine and begins to sing one of his war songs:

> *Praise the lord, and bless the ammunition.*
> *Praise the lord, my Blossom's goin' pishin,*
> *Praise the lord and hurry with the diapers*
> *Or we'll . . . all . . . get . . . wet!"*

He seems to think it's all right to say "lord" in that silly song, no one gets excited about it at all. I think it's nasty to talk about The Screamer's wet diapers, no matter how much she disgusts me. But everyone, even my mother, even Gilda, seems to think the song is cute.

There is another song my father bursts into:

> *Off we go, into the wild blue yonder,*
> *Flying high, into the sun,*
> *Down we dive . . .*

(he stops here to drink another cup of wine and adds:)
> *Atta boy, give 'em the gun!*

Why does he have tears in his eyes? Is he happy or is he sad? Does he wish he had flown off into the wild blue yonder? Does he wish he were a gold star on someone's window?

We know one thing: his job at the defense plant is over. My mother wants him to get rich. She says so often, now.

She wants us to buy a house of our own. She wants to move away from Gilda and Grandma. She wants an alligator purse. She wants gold jewelry. She wants a vase of gardenias on every table. She wants a maid to cook and another maid to wash clothes and another one to clean the house.

My father says why can't she learn that the best things in life are free. She turns her back on him. The war in Europe is over, but a new war is starting, right in our house on Avenue O.

CHAPTER 17

No more blackouts, enough sugar for a thousand chocolate cakes, plenty of soap powder for the Bendix and The
Screamer's diapers, new leather shoes for everyone, nylon
stockings for Gilda and my mother; just when our spirits
are lightening, just when my father goes back into the
antique business (at an auction my father buys three
locked trunks—contents guaranteed unknown—and finds
some rare china bowls and a bronze elephant with which
to start out in his new business, a store he rents on
Hansen Place); just when I get my first ballet slippers and
start to take lessons in a basement studio on Avenue P, my
grandmother's heart stops.

I come home from school one day and see Dr.
Schwartz's black car in front of the wishbone tree. (We
don't use Dr. Trutt for my grandmother; she thinks his
wife is a floozy and if he can't take care of her, how can
he take care of sick people?)

I run into my house and upstairs, where my grandmother is on the couch in the front room, her face twisted
like a corkscrew. Gilda is bending over her, Dr. Schwartz
is bending over her, even my mother, knotting a handker-
chief in her hands, stands far back, but watching. This
isn't the usual emergency that a few white pills under her
tongue can fix up. This is the real thing. My own heart in

my chest does a loop-the-loop, skids, flutters, begins to pound. It could also just . . . stop. Who is to say mine won't stop even as I watch my grandmother, whose pasty face is the color of pale chicken fat?

But no, Gilda turns to assure me it's not her heart, her heart is strong. Dr. Schwartz thinks there has been an explosion in a blood vessel in her brain. See how her mouth turns down on one side? See how one hand and one leg seem unable to move? He shouts at my grandmother, his voice seems to be thunder flung out of a storm cloud: *"DO YOU UNDERSTAND ME? BLINK YOUR EYES IF YOU DO."*

She stares like my doll with painted china eyes. I feel a sudden and hideous gurgle of diarrhea in my lower parts; my insides are trying to come out to escape what is inside me that is treacherous and can kill me.

I hate this, hate it, it's the worst invention in the whole world: *fear.*

* * *

Now there is the bell. My grandmother's voice has turned into a bell that rings and rings. I hear it in my sun-room bedroom in the deep of night, that distant, imperious clank of the brass bell she can clutch and shake in her good hand, and I imagine I hear Gilda's footsteps running in desperate, fearful reply to it. This drama all takes place overhead, on another level, in another world. We downstairs don't have to worry—my mother has told me so. Gilda is good at this. Gilda will handle it. Gilda was born to be a nurse and a soothing presence. Gilda loves my grandmother and wants to take care of her.

When I ask if my grandmother is not terrified that she can't walk or talk, when I ask if she isn't scared every minute of the night and day, my mother shrugs. She seems to think my grandmother never felt very much to begin with; I see with amazement my mother doesn't love her.

Don't you love your own mother? It is a question I frame, but it's too incredible to say aloud. I realize that the truth I've heard all my life is a lie. *Sticks and stones can break my bones but words can never hurt me!* Wrong! Words have the *most* power. Words can do damage far beyond a slap or a punch or a rock in the side of the forehead. And likewise, but in an opposite way, wonderful words, like Joe Martini's saying I'm his wife and I can always come and live with him, do the most good, bring more happiness than any present, last forever, and creep out in the warm sweetness from the depths of my mind as I lie in bed and say them to myself, over and over. They are better to burrow into than my feather pillow, sweeter to wrap myself in than my layers of wool blankets.

I try to imagine my own mother frozen in one position in her bed, without a mouth to talk with, without legs to walk with, not like The Screamer who will soon, is now, getting a mouth and legs that work, but frozen forever, helpless and silent. My heart pauses at the thought—it only starts when I jump, literally jump in bed like a jerked puppet, to start it again. This is how I can also die, by thinking of my mother's total weakness, her loss of power over me. What would keep me going if she were not behind me, holding me up, pushing me, disapproving of me, liking me only when I am like her, hating me when I am not?

Nothing would keep me up. I'd fizz out like a popped balloon, I'd whoosh away and fall to shreds like a tattered, ruined balloon.

This is too hard to think about. I would rather be in my ballet slippers, in Madame Genet's basement studio next to the Claridge Theater on Avenue P. I would rather be doing my eight hand positions to "The Merry Widow Waltz."

* * *

Gilda is run ragged. After I get home from school, I hear her overhead racing up and down the hall, from the beauty parlor to the persistent jangle of my grandmother's bell. Sometimes I go upstairs and try to help: "See what she wants," and I approach the sickroom in terror to look into my grandmother's frozen eyes, her crooked face, and I say "What do you want?" but all she can do is shake the bell at me, jab the bell at me, stab at me with the bell, her mouth vicious with the misery of not being able to tell me anything at all.

"Oh, Grandma," I say. Her fingers are furled into a curled claw; her white hair is electric with static and the chaos of being loose and wild. I always have to get Gilda: "You go, I can't understand her," and Gilda drops her scissors and comb and runs, leaving me there to look at the lady in the chair, who is half done, half cut, half curled.

"It must be hard for you to see your grandma that way," the ladies say to me. If I agree, they will say something else about how hard old age is.

I don't think it's hard, I think it's disgusting and that suffering like my grandmother's shouldn't be allowed. Laws should stop this, wars should be fought to stop this. No one, no one I love, and never, never, never *me*, should ever have to experience this.

* * *

Gilda wants her moved downstairs. Gilda is crying and my father is patting her back after my grandmother has fallen out of bed upstairs, and two neighbor-men have been called to help my father lift her back into her tangled sheets. She is like a load of old laundry nobody wants around. Does she know it? Inside those steel blue eyes, is my grandmother in agony? I used to wash her back in the bathtub, I used to watch her cook chicken soup, she used to give me those golden jewels, the boiled baby egg yolks from the hen's belly. She came from Poland in the hold of a ship when she was fifteen. She married a tailor, my grandfather, who died before I was born, but he knew my mother had talent for the piano, but was certain Gilda had none for the violin. If he had known me, what would he have seen in me?

"Let my sister take her!" Gilda is sobbing. "I can't handle it anymore. She's downstairs all day, she does nothing but play with Blossom, Issa is at school, why should she be the prima donna? Why can't she take Mama for a while? This is going to kill me!"

My father smooths Gilda's hair back with such tenderness that I begin to shiver. I think he is going to kiss her and I am afraid of what I will see when he does.

"Shh, shh," he says to her, stroking her hair. "Yes, yes, this is too much for you, isn't it?"

"Let her have it!" Gilda sobs.

"It would kill her," my father says.

"But it's all right for it to kill me?" she asks him. "I don't know how to bear it anymore," she says. And it occurs to me that she's stuck the way Mary was stuck when she had no place to spend the night and the baby Jesus was about to be born. People get stuck somehow, at sometime; grownups get stuck, and don't know what to do. So they cry. Or they beg. Or they give up and let someone else figure it out.

"We'll figure it out," my father says. "I'll find a solution."

"Please!" Gilda begs him and she throws herself into his arms. He hugs her there in front of my grandmother, whose eyes stare out from the puffy queer twists of her skin as if they are desperate to close and shut out what they see.

* * *

And then there's no more Grandma in the house. Just like that, we're one less. She isn't dead, but she's worse than dead. She's in Sherman's Rest Home on Ocean Parkway. They take her there in an ambulance, three black men stagger down the stairs with her, her sheets dragging like animal tails, and they stuff her into the back, and Gilda, sobbing and screaming, climbs in with her, and neighbors are in the street watching, and my mother stands leaning against the doorjamb, leaning with her hip out and her hand resting delicately upon her hip bone, her face without expression, looking like a sculpture. Looking cold as marble.

18

This is a new feeling: feeling for someone else. I think of Gilda alone upstairs. I feel how alone she is, eating alone, sleeping alone, just sitting alone on her couch, while we—downstairs—are four in the living room, four sitting around the radio, four having dinner, four going to bed and knowing the other three are breathing in the nearby shadows of darkness. I ache for Gilda's aloneness, I want to draw her down to sit with us, to give her noise and light and chatter and the plain comfort of company.

The others don't seem to worry about her; if they do, they don't tell me. I know just when it happens, when her last customer comes down the stairs and hurries past my sunporch windows along Avenue O, hurries home to make supper for whoever lives in *her* house. It's close to five o'clock and dark out already. My mother is making something on the stove, I have already set the table with plates and silverware, with napkins and glasses. Soon my father will be home.

And upstairs, I see in my hidden eye, Gilda alone, Gilda taking out a piece of fried fish and some bread, Gilda sitting down at the dining table and looking out her front window at the houses across the street, *their* windows warm and bright, and behind their glowing panes, families sitting down together to eat.

The silence upstairs is like a vacuum, sucking me up. I want to rush up there, fling on all the lights, dance and sing for her.

I don't have this feeling for my grandmother—I don't think of her, wherever she is, alone, without us, paralyzed, unable to move or talk, because I can't imagine it. I haven't been to visit her yet, nor has my mother. Only Gilda goes three times a day, and my father has gone once, to carry for Gilda heavy jars of homemade gefilte fish, chicken soup, flanken and potatoes.

My mother won't go. "I don't have the heart for it," she says. What does that mean? What *does* she have the heart for? She reads magazines all day and talks about getting a decorator for the house if we're not going to move away yet. My father has protested that we can't move yet (if we ever can): not now, not when he's starting up a new business, not with my grandmother paralyzed, not while Gilda is alone.

Why does she need a decorator for the house? I could decorate it for her if she asked me—I would make crepe paper streamers and tie balloons on a string across the ceiling. I would hang a Halloween skeleton from the front door. I would glue devils and angels around the moldings, I would put an enormous Christmas tree permanently in the middle of the living room.

"She wants new furniture," I tell Gilda. Gilda has had bad luck today. She has burned a customer's scalp, she has cut her own finger on the manicure nippers. At the rest home, she found my grandmother lying on soiled sheets. I am trying to keep Gilda company. I have run upstairs after supper, run so fast I pretend I don't hear my mother calling me back. I know she won't stand and come to yell up the stairs after me; she has The Screamer on her lap and is doing "This Little Piggy" with her.

Safely upstairs, I sit beside Gilda on the couch and hold her injured finger. I kiss it with my lips. I tell her I am giving her a "raisin," and it will make her better. Usually she loves this, she adores it when I do this. But tonight she is staring out the black front windows; she has not even lowered the shades. Ice patches have formed along the window frames, blurring the view from the edges. I try to think of things to tell her.

"Mommy says she has to have a new couch. She says she hates to sit on furniture where strangers' behinds have been."

Gilda looks at me and I know she doesn't see me. She's somewhere else, and she says something I find very strange: she says, "My sister thinks she was born without a body, that she has no behind. Then what is it she shakes in everyone's face? Your poor father, he doesn't even know what she's doing to him." She says it in a trance and she has no idea she has said it aloud, or that I have heard it. I know that, because when her eyes come back to seeing, she sees me, and she hugs me, and she's gentle, and she offers me a cookie, not homemade, but from the store.

I don't talk to Gilda anymore about furniture, though I am thinking about what will happen when we get new furniture; we won't be able to put our feet up, we won't be able to play on it.

Our old furniture is "new"—we get new furniture whenever my father comes upon a second-hand piece he thinks we might like better than the old piece, or he thinks he can sell the old one and can't so easily sell the new.

I don't mind it. There are often treasures under the cushions of used furniture: I have found a pipe, a pen, a penny, a penlight. I have found licorice His Nibs candies, and sticks of Black Jack gum, and safety pins. I know my father hunts treasures, also. Sometimes at night he closes the shades and spreads out newspaper on the kitchen table and cuts open pin cushions he has bought at an "estate" sale—he thinks he will find hidden diamonds. He has heard of this happening, and he hopes it will happen to him.

I love it, love it, when the sawdust spills out onto the paper and carefully, with his big thick fingers, he spreads the crumbs out before our eyes. Who will see it first, that sparkling gem, that glowing fiery stone that will mean we will be rich? We will have new *everything*—and I will get

skates, dolls, tea sets, toeshoes!
But it's always only sawdust.

* * *

The Screamer can't be ignored. She's here and she
belongs here as much as I do. She's annoying in every
way; she screams. She is cranky after her naps and kicks
till her breaths stops and her face turns blue. Her crib
smells of throw-up and pee; they think she's wonderful.
They play with every part of her, tickle her ears, count her
toes, blow on her belly-button, bite her tummy.

Why is it that my hair looks wild in the morning, a tangle of golden curls that won't lay down, while her hair
wakes up combed and neat, straight lines of fine, dark,
neat hair. We both grew inside our mother, but we're not
the same. We're both my mother's daughters, but my
mother loves her more. She is of no interest. She is in the
way. We'd be better off without her.

* * *

I need something strong in my mind. I am so tired of
another Sunday. Gilda is going to the rest home. I will go
with her. I have to find out someday where we all go
when we're old, don't I?

I don't beg, or ask, or plead, or argue. What I do is
make my grandmother a miniature honey cake while
Gilda is baking special foods for her. They can't refuse me
now—I know how they think in this house. They will
have to let me bring my grandmother a present. How
sweet an idea, they will say. What a good child!

But we don't even have to ask because my mother is
out looking at furniture. They have taken The Screamer
away and left me home with Gilda and there's no discussion because Gilda can't leave me home alone, and she
can't not go to visit my grandmother this middle time of
the three times a day she goes to visit her.

I hold the honey cake like a little dead child as we walk

along Avenue O, as we turn on Ocean Parkway and pass
the old people sitting on benches, pass the bicycle riders
on the bicycle path, pass the little gold, pointy rails that
separate the benches from the bicycles. I walk in my good
Stride-Rite shoes, the ones that are wide on me even in
their narrowest size, the ones the salesman wants me to
grow into by eating my potatoes standing up.

"I don't want you to be scared," Gilda says. "I'm used
to it by now."

"I'm not scared."

"But you will be," she tells me. "There's no way I can
prepare you for this."

"Is she going to die?" I ask Gilda.

"Not soon enough," she says.

* * *

My grandmother is strapped into a wheelchair. Her
head flops forward, her white hair has never been
combed, I think, since the day they stuffed her into the
ambulance. Her face has fallen away and all I see at first
is the grin of her huge false teeth. They smile even as tears
come out of her eyes when she sees me.

Her hand shakes at me although she has no brass bell
in it. The smell in this room is so bad that I can't breathe.
I hide behind Gilda as she tells my grandmother what she
has brought, shows off the little treats for everyone to
share, including the other old women who are strapped in
their wheelchairs.

I bury my face in the little honey cake, breathing in the
scent of sweetness and warmth.

"Where are your earrings, Mama?" Gilda asks. My
grandmother's ears have become stretched out, long flaps
of hanging skin. She is all teeth and ears. Gilda looks
around at the other women. "Did any of you see what
happened to her earrings?" As if any of them can talk,
explain, solve problems.

Gilda finds someone in the hall; she grills the nurse, a
colored woman with a big white smile and a hearty laugh.

"Oh them, they got flushed down the toilet by accident," she tells Gilda.

"But they were my mother's diamond earrings!" Gilda cries.

Are they *my* diamond earrings? The ones I once saw in the vault? Who flushed them away? How dare they take what was to be mine?

I start to eat the honey cake. I eat it with my fingers, in big handfuls, crumbs of dark honey-colored cake smash into my nose and glue themselves to my lips.

"Issa, what are you doing? Aren't you going to give that to Grandma?"

But this isn't my grandmother, this grinning witch, this smelly pile of rags, this empty pitcher with enormous ears, this silent, foreign, absent, blank-eyed soul.

I kick Gilda. I kick the wheelchair. I will kick down the walls of this ghost-house, I will pull down the roof and throw the bricks into the ocean. I will bring my real grandmother home with me, where we can sit outside on the bench and smell the lilacs. Where we can cook chicken soup together and smell the onions, layer by layer. Where things can be the way they used to be.

CHAPTER

19

I will be a great ballerina. I will do backbends and *pliés* and grand *jetés*; I will hold onto the *barre* (and, when practicing at home, to the sunroom doorknob) and will execute perfect *pirouettes, arabesques* and splits.

Madame Genet's senior class performs for us in the studio: how I love the calf muscles of the sixteen-year-old girls. How strong and smooth their thighs are, how they leap with perfect ease across the shiny wooden floor. Their gauze tutus shimmer and vibrate, flying up in delicate pulsations to reveal the secret white space of the cave between their legs. I will be this powerful one day, this strong, this graceful, this womanly.

It is better, of course, to have long, straight hair that shimmers across your shoulders when you do a backbend, straight hair to twist high into a tight, dark little bun. But, if I have to, I will wear a wig when I am older. I will pull out my wild golden curls, hair by hair.

My mother leaves me alone here; I am dropped off while she takes The Screamer to the playground to push her on the swings. I have one complete hour to dream about becoming a beautiful sixteen-year-old with thighs like iron, with calves hidden by veils of lace.

When the older girls dance ballet, we're not supposed to think they are gasping for air and sweating, but they are. I know it because when I dance, I am. Illusion—the discovery that it is possible thrills me. Why should the audience suspect perspiration and sense the wild beating of each heart? No, all they want to see is the dance, all they want to hear is the music. I find it a grand conceit that we can conceal so much, pretend to be colorful butterflies when we are really sweating horses with thudding blood, that we can pretend to be dreamy floating angels when we are actually counting beats and remembering the sequence of steps.

How much of what I see in the world is illusion? Is *everything* not what it seems?

I begin to examine everything with this standard in mind. The ladies who come to Gilda have been through hours of sitting and cutting and curling and baking in order to look nice (not beautiful like ballerinas, but simply nice, simply neat). And, my mother, even to play "Danny Boy" has had to learn her scales, her chords and her notes. She always tells me how hard she used to practice when she was a girl, but why is it that the learning part of her life seems to be over. She never practices new songs now. Nor does she read books now. The headaches, she says, prevent it.

Couldn't she take an extra aspirin and keep reading, keep playing, and not be angry so much of the time? If I were practicing ballet every day, for hours, I would be too tired and satisfied to be unhappy. If she were busier, maybe *smiles she would not hoard.* (That rhyme she wrote to me sticks like a burr in my throat. *If smiles she won't hoard, I'm pretty sure she'll get a reward!* Where is my reward? I'm smiling, I'm smiling. I smile into her face whenever I can, and she doesn't seem to remember. *Where is my reward?*)

On the way home from ballet lessons I stop at intervals to do the eight hand positions to myself, then the five foot positions, humming "The Merry Widow Waltz."

As we walk up East 4th Street my mother stops the stroller and looks at me. She says, "Issa, you have such powers of concentration."

Is that good or bad? I can never tell what she's thinking when she analyzes me.

"Doesn't Blossom?" (This is my test. Blossom has no faults at all.)

"Oh no. She's just a baby. But she hasn't got what you have. She's a free spirit."

"And what am I?" My blood is thudding louder than it does when I do ten *pirouettes*.

"You're a determined little thing."

I'm a thing. "Is that good?"

"You might be famous someday. Rich and famous."

"Would you like me if I were rich and famous?"

"I'd adore you, darling."

Adore. Darling. Rich and famous.

I dance home on winged feet. That night I practice *pliés* till my heart bursts in my chest. I spin till my eyes fly out of my head. I backbend till my spine splinters.

She will adore me, darling!

* * *

It is a Saturday afternoon in spring. I am now in third grade. I am sitting on the back porch reading a book called *Katrinka, The Story of a Russian Child* and wondering how I might feel if I woke up some morning to discover my parents and Gilda gone, leaving me in charge of my sister. Outside snow would be rising to the windowsills. There would be hardly any food in the house. A freezing blizzard would be swirling about the windows.

My fantasies are thicker than the snowflakes. I would leave my sister in her crib and start out to get help. I would leave enough wood burning in the stove to keep her warm for two days. (Then, when it was gone, if I weren't back—no fault of mine—she would freeze to death.) Before I left I would pack Zwieback biscuits around her body to keep her fed. (I would take with me all the rest of the food in the house: particularly challah and halvah and black olives.) Wolves would be howling from the edge of the forest, and Indians (do they have

Indians in Russia? Do they have them in Brooklyn?) would close in upon the house with tomahawks raised. They would either scalp her, abduct her and raise her as an Indian princess, or eat her. (Are Indians cannibals? There is so much I don't know yet.)

Suddenly, I hear the slam of my father's car door out front. I know his car sounds, just as I know his two-tone whistle, his laugh, his voice. Why is he home? He is supposed to be at his store. He is never home this early on a Saturday. What is he doing here?

The street is quiet, the house is quiet. Gilda is at the rest home visiting my grandmother. My mother and The Screamer are taking their afternoon naps.

My father is home! I sit in perfect silence, the book balanced on my knees, and I hear him come up the alley. He knows where to find me—it is he who takes me to the library each Friday night to get an armful of books to read over the weekend. He knows where I am on a Saturday afternoon.

He has a carton under his arm! Aha! A surprise! I smile at him. He has his pipe in his mouth and a sweet expression in his eyes. Oh, how I love my father! How nice it is to see him. And a carton brought home means a surprise. He loves to surprise me, bringing me treasures from his business like costumes for Halloween (one year a clown costume, one year a hairy gorilla), or games that children used to play long ago, or a gum machine from the subway, or a ukulele whose strings have come unstrung.

But my mind is reluctant to swing away from that delicious vision I was embroidering a minute ago: The Screamer alone in the cold, dark, abandoned house, the blizzard roaring outside, bears at the windows (or were they wolves?) and myself, the heroine, setting out into the storm, heroically, chewing chocolate-covered halvah.

My father carefully sets the carton down on the floorboards at my feet. There is a scuffling sound from within. What could it be? The slide of some object that is loose in the carton? A new doll whose glass eye has just slithered across the cardboard bottom?

My father's eye is merry. My heart starts to pound. Skates? Am I finally getting skates? The Skaters are already riding bikes, they are now The Bike-Riders. But I still dream of skates, that sawing, buzzing freedom of skates on cement. Can it be? This visit has to be special, my father is home at midday, curls of caramel-flavored tobacco smoke swirling around our heads, his merry smile—he can't contain his pleasure.

The top of the box pops open and a puppy sticks his head through.

Oh ecstasy! Oh heaven on earth! Oh joy forever! Oh no! My mother's face at the screen door. Go away! Let me have this first union with my Beloved with no looming axe above me. Let only my father witness my passion. Let me have something I want, at last! At last!

* * *

Beloved to me. Spotty to all others. A pink tongue and little pink nipples, brown and white fur, so soft, so smooth: heaven on earth. I have never known such happiness. The weight of him curled in my lap as I read. The heft of him in my arms as I carry him here and there.

"He can walk, don't make a cripple out of him," Gilda says. But she picks him up too, a look of deep pleasure crossing her face as she feels what he has to give: warmth, adoration, peace, physical surrender. My Baby. My Beloved. My Reason For Living.

I get melodramatic in a way I have never been. I would give my life for him. I would save him first in a fire. I would sacrifice *my whole family* in order to save his life.

There are rules, of course. Not to touch him while I am eating. Never to allow him on the furniture. Never to let him lick my face. (I will break these rules at every opportunity.) My mother will tolerate him, but barely, and only because it's too late to give him back. (My father accepted him from a man who disappeared into thin air afterward. In trade for a couple of English teacups. My father never even learned his name.)

I sit out front with him and The Skaters/Bike-Riders stop to admire his delicious little snout, his sweet brown eyes, his thrilling pointy tail. How did this luck land on me? I have something that others want. Issa is enviable! Issa is lucky! Is it possible? That the arrow of luck has finally landed on *me*?

Myra and Myrna and Ruthie and Linda want to start a girls' club. They invite me to be in it. Before I can agree, I have to gather all the information and give a full report to my mother: why they're forming the club, what their long-term goals are, who will be in it, what the weekly activities will be, where they will meet, how much the dues will cost—this is worse than doing a book report for school on the causes of the Civil War. I don't think my friends know what their long-term goals are. I think they just want to have fun.

I can tell they are inviting me as a kind of afterthought: they are quite complete as they are, forged in friendship from the early days of their skating together, and now they ride on the Ocean Parkway bicycle path every Saturday, two abreast, their shiny Schwinns moving in tandem, a red and a blue in front, two dark blues just behind.

They don't know I see them every Saturday as I sit on a bench in front of Sherman's Rest Home, waiting for Gilda to come out, and holding Beloved close to me on his leash. (I think they might want me in their club *because* of Beloved, because none of them have a dog, and they love him because he's so lovable, because they can't resist him, and because they want something to hug and kiss, like everyone in the world wants.)

At least he's mine. I bend way over to kiss the top of his brown and white head. A beagle, a hunting dog whose ears get stiff when he hears the squeak of brakes and thinks he has just heard a mouse make a noise.

I think about my friends (and enemies) all the time. I think about Joe Martini, who was left back in second grade because he wouldn't stay in his seat and do drawings of little houses with smoke coming out of their chimneys. I think about Ruby, the girl with a face like a bulldog, who stole my pencil case and threatened to push me in front of a car. She did push me down on the sidewalk, and now I have two scars on my knees. I will never be a Rockette. Gilda told me they have to have perfect legs. I probably can't be a ballerina, either, though I practice every day. The reason is that I can't touch my heel to the top of my head in a backbend. I didn't get the right muscles from my family. Only little miserable teeth. (Do other girls look at their new teeth as they come in, those ragged-toothed teeth, and beg them: "Grow! grow!"?)

But Myra and Myrna and Ruthie and Linda are the true mysteries. How does one get to be part of them? Can there be a group called Myra and Myrna and Ruthie and Linda and Issa? It sounds wrong, it's got the wrong poetry. It's proof that I got not only the wrong muscles, but the wrong name, too. Issa: my name sounds like a secret that others whisper to keep me away; my name is like a hiss, like steam escaping, like the pressure cooker when it's about to pop, like the furnace before it explodes. I *feel* like steam, as invisible as a secret, as violent as an explosion. To look at me, I am just a little girl on a bench, but I am all those things. I rattle inside myself with the beings that I am—the lover of Beloved, the daughter of my father, the hater of my sister, and the grandchild who will not go in those doors behind me, into that house where dying is what they have to do. Dying is bad enough, but should it smell like the monkey house?

Gilda is inside that hall of horrors. She brings the special food she makes for my grandmother, the salted chicken fat on rye bread, the chopped chicken liver, the kreplach soup, the kasha varnishkas. I don't know why she makes this food; my grandmother can barely chew or swallow—she eats only farina and the cornmeal mush called *mamalega*. But they don't allow me to go in. I haven't seen her since that one time, after which I came home and had nightmares for two months. To think that every day that I am jumping rope, eating ice cream, letting Beloved lick my tears away, dancing *pirouettes*, my grandmother has been in one place, strapped into a wheelchair! In a room with old witches who don't know her or love her. To think of it!

I don't think of it. Neither does my mother, who won't visit her. My father has gone there with Gilda, but he doesn't speak of it, and no one asks him how it was. I imagine he just goes in and smiles reassuringly at my grandmother. That's all he has to do; that's why my father was born. For his sweetness.

How come I didn't get his sweetness? They are always talking about what I "got" from them. I have curly hair from him and have my good rhyming from my mother. I get the shape of my big toes from my grandfather, who died before I could meet him. As for teeth: I get my small teeth from someone with horrible small teeth, I will never know who. I can't check my grandmother's, because of her false teeth, nor my mother now, because of hers. I will probably get *my* false teeth from both of them. I try not to think about this either. As soon as the thought pops up like a nasty worm, I kick it back in its hole. Why add a reason for another stomach ache on top of all the other reasons?

Gilda is in that terrible place now, in that prison, that enormous toilet, that torture chamber, with her beef and barley soup, offering it to my grandmother and to all the old abandoned ghosts without teeth. (She will leave it, finally, for the colored helpers.)

Her cooking isn't a bad idea; I know she's upstairs at night peeling and frying, grinding and chopping. After the customers leave and she's all alone, she's not so sad, being busy in the kitchen that way. When she's busy, I don't feel so bad. And when I go upstairs to say goodnight, it isn't just the two of us, it's now three, with Beloved who comes everywhere with me. Three above, like the three below, is more fair. For those few minutes it's more like a family.

* * *

This is how we make better friends. Everything is as usual: I am on the bench waiting for Gilda who is in the rest home. Beloved is at my feet eating Milk Bone biscuits, which I drop down to him, one by one, to keep him happy. I am only supposed to wait ten minutes today; Gilda is going to give herself a permanent because she has no customers coming in this afternoon. Tomorrow she is supposed to meet a widower who is the business partner of Mrs. Exter's husband, who is in the chicken business. This chicken-man is rich and owns a chicken farm in Little River. His wife died of something terrible, and he is very sad. He is having dinner at Mrs. Exter's and Gilda is invited. She is going to take me along! And why? Because Mrs. Exter, even though she is a four-star mother, is rich enough to have a television set! And there will be a circus shown on the screen!

All of this is wonderful—to have so full a calendar when usually on the weekends all I do is read books I get from the library on Friday nights.

Timing is very important in life. You can't arrange these things. You might call something like this a miracle: The Skaters/Bike-Riders are coming along just as a black cat jumps out of the window of a parked car and just as I let go of Beloved's leash to reach into my pocket for another Milk Bone biscuit. The cat races across Ocean Parkway and Beloved dashes after it. Cars all across six lanes screech and bang on their brakes. When I can breathe again, I see that the cat is squashed and flattened into a bloody, furry pile. Myrna throws her bike down and runs after Beloved without even looking both ways. She, too, is almost squashed, but she scoops him up and kisses him freely all over his snout, while I cry out his public name,

"Spotty, Spotty, come back here!"

Myrna runs back to the sidewalk with her rescued armful and claims her place in his life by letting him lick her lips. I have to thank her. I have to hug her. She has to give him to me. The Skaters have to hug her and hug each other. Then Linda hugs me. We are better friends than I am with the others. One reason I feel so warm toward her is that I once stole money from her. She has enriched my life by excitement and guilt.

"Oh, the cat is dead," she says, and we all burst into tears. We cry and jump up and down and hug one another. Gilda, coming out of the rest home, finds us sobbing and laughing and hugging. The poor cat is so easily dead; we should bring my grandmother's wheelchair out here and push it across six lanes of traffic. Then Gilda could laugh and cry with us.

But she has that white look on her face; the air in the home powders her skin with grief. She is very grateful to The Bike-Riders for what they have done for me. We all are extremely happy, standing there, and Gilda invites them to use her living room for club meetings whenever they want to. She lives alone, she says—she would love to hear the sound of young happy voices in her living room. (But she won't stay around—she'll make herself scarce, she promises.) It's settled then, that fast. I am absolutely in the club and my house is where the first meeting will be.

Who would ever think that a fatal accident for a black cat could end up like a party?

CHAPTER
21

Food at other people's houses looks amazing to me. Mrs. Exter has laid out a feast that makes me hungry in a deeper way than just wanting to eat everything. I want to put my head down on the table and wrap my arms around all the dishes and bowls and platters. It's the excess of wonderful things that is thrilling—it's there for me and anyone who wants it, it's free, and nowhere is there anything slimy or gristly or grainy or gluey.

I mostly eat chocolate-covered halvah. It comes in little squares covered in dark chocolate with two wavy lines on the top; no one watches me, I eat ten. Mrs. Exter is watching Sam Marcus and Sam Marcus is watching Gilda and Gilda is staring at her plate.

"Gilda has a wonderful business that she runs all by herself," Mrs. Exter says loudly.

"I have news for you," Sam Marcus says. "It isn't often these days that a woman can run her own business. Especially a business in the home. But a license must be expensive. These days you have to work half a year just to pay off the license."

"I don't have a license," Gilda says.

"So you like to take chances, eh?" says Sam Marcus. "What if someone reports you?"

"Only my friends are my customers," says Gilda. "I

don't worry. I couldn't be in business if I had to pay for a license."

"Friends can turn into enemies," Sam says. "You should trust no one."

"The truth is Gilda trusts everyone and everyone trusts her," says Mrs. Exter and claps her hands together. "A beautician with fingers like an angel. And you don't find a better cook, either."

"I'm not as good a cook as you," Gilda murmurs. Her face is down so that no one can see it, although at home, as I watched her get ready, she hid her skin under layers of Acnomel. She's wearing a starched pink blouse with a white collar and a black skirt; she has on her jade ring. Sam Marcus is bald and short. He is wearing two rings on two next-door fingers, both heavy gold, one ring is a lion with glittering ruby eyes, and one is a single diamond stone.

"Sam is lonely since his wife died," says Mrs. Exter. "The poor thing, how she suffered."

"It's true, she suffered," he says. He digs into his pot roast and kasha. He puts his mouth down low to the plate and shovels the kasha kernels in with a spoon.

Something is very odd here; the conversation drops like blobs out of a meat grinder.

"Why can't we turn on the television?" I say.

"A good idea," says Mrs. Exter. She jumps up and goes to the machine. The circus comes on, far away and very small. Behind glass it's not the same as when my father took me to the circus in person. I have a pungent memory of sawdust and elephants with wild intelligent eyes and the smell of their leathery skin.

I tell everyone at the table—a confession brought on by the food and the endless supply of halvah—that I wish I could have had a souvenir turtle when I went to the circus, but that my father wouldn't buy me one. I don't know why I betray him in this way—the need to make him seem less good than he is comes over me like a chill. It's a trick I'm doing, but I don't know my purpose. I say it especially for the benefit of Sam Marcus. "My father wouldn't buy me a turtle because he said they cost too much." (The truth is that the turtles come in little boxes with gold safety pins; people who bought them pinned the turtles by their tails to their lapels. My father assured me I wouldn't want to buy a painted turtle whose shell would soon go soft and rotten. Nor would I want to pin a living creature to my collar—that it was too cruel.) But I tell Sam again. "My father said they cost too much."

"Well," he said. "If I had a little girl as pretty as you, I would never tell her *that*."

There grownups go again—lying. *A little girl as pretty as you*. He knows I have small teeth and wild curly hair. If he has eyes, he knows that. Just as I know he is bald and not kind and untruthful. At least I don't say to him, "You're more handsome than my father. I wish you *were* my father." I have *some* limits. No one is more handsome than my father—Gilda and I both know that. But there is something I'm telling him, I feel as if I'm doing a circus trick. I just don't understand what it is.

* * *

I get a turtle. That's what it was. That's what I wanted. I realize this a few days later when Sam Marcus rings Gilda's bell with flowers and candy for Gilda and a turtle for me. The turtle has a palm tree painted on its tiny back, and it comes in a glass bowl with a rock in it. I have to add water and sprinkle in some flakes of food.

I am extremely excited by my successful technique of achieving this gift—as much as by the gift itself.

* * *

Every Friday night Sam Marcus comes up the steps with a present for Gilda and a present for me. I make it my business to be upstairs even if it means skipping my trip to the library with my father. Gilda wants me there. She doesn't want to be alone with him. We have signals to indicate when she wants me to sit between them on the couch, or when she wants me to serve the cookies. If she tilts her foot back on its heel, it means rush up to him with a tray of honey cake or sponge cake slices. If she crosses her ankles, it means come and sit very close to her, if possible between the two of them. The rule is that I must never, never leave her upstairs with him unless my mother actually gets hysterical.

My mother has become very interested in the proceedings; she asks me a hundred questions. What does Sam talk about with her, what present did he bring her, how many children does he have, does he own a house in Little River, how new is his car. I tell her what I can because that's the price of my being allowed to stay upstairs so long and so late. But I can't stay past nine—I have to go to sleep and there's no arguing about my bedtime. Usually Gilda makes Sam leave by nine, so it works out perfectly. My mother is beginning to imagine that Gilda will marry Sam Marcus and move to Little River. Then she and my father will have the whole house to themselves.

My father's jaw trembles when Sam Marcus walks up the steps to Gilda's house; my father reads the paper and grinds his jaws together every Friday night. I don't think he would want to take me to the library even if I begged him to. What is he so worried about?

Gilda and he used to meet every night at the garbage cans in the alley; it was almost as if they had an agreement, both of them, to carry out the garbage at exactly six-thirty. And if I were outside, in summer playing ball, or in winter walking Beloved up and down just in front of the house, I would listen to them talk to each other, in low soft voices, as if they were carrying on a conversation left in mid-sentence the night before. They talked of household things: the storm windows, the price of heating oil, my grandmother's misery. But their voices sounded like singing to me, so very much in tune, blending in a comforting harmony.

Now my father has me take out the garbage when I go out to walk Beloved. He won't go out. He won't talk to Gilda. My mother doesn't notice; she never notices things like that, the things people do because they feel a certain way.

* * *

I am upstairs when the kiss happens. I am *between* them when it happens. Gilda is holding a bouquet of roses Sam has carried up the stairs. He wants her to wear one of them in her hair; he sends me into the beauty parlor to get a silver clip. I throw Gilda a glance of apology—I have to leave the room, but I do it as fast as possible. He takes it from me and tries to fasten it in her hair but he doesn't know how to work the clip. I do it.

Gilda is wearing bright red lipstick that matches the rose. Her dress is navy blue with lace at the edge of the hem. We three are sitting on the couch; it feels as if it is moving. We're perfectly still, but we're careening into space.

Them Sam Marcus leans over and pulls Gilda's shoulder forward and kisses her fast on the cheek; then he kisses *me*! We all three are caught in a hug, I am being crushed between them. I push Sam off me and look at Gilda. She looks very worried behind her smile.

"Well," she says.

"Well," he says. "You have some Manischewitz wine?"

I know just where it is. I hand the bottle to him. He hands it back. "Pour us, sweetheart. We'll have a toast to an understanding."

* * *

"They have an understanding," I announce the minute I come downstairs to go to bed. For punctuation, we hear Sam Marcus's car start on the street.

"When is the wedding?" my mother asks. She is sitting across the room from my father; he has been reading the paper, I don't know what she has been doing.

"Not for a year," I say, proud to have this information. "They will be keeping company."

"You'll have your own room, Issa. Blossom will have *her* own room. Your father and I will redo the whole house! The sunporch can be a sunporch again! We'll get rattan furniture—I know a decorator who specializes in rattan."

"Gilda's not moving out," I tell my mother. "When they get married, Sam will move in upstairs. Then he'll be near Mr. Exter and they can drive to Little River together."

"What about his house in Little River?" my mother asks me, furiously, as if something has happened that's all my fault.

"He doesn't have a house there. He lives in a little building on the chicken farm."

"I thought he was rich!"

"He wants Gilda to invest money in building modern chicken coops," I tell her.

"He wants her money!" she shouts at my father. "They're going to live *here!*" she shouts at my father.

My father's teeth are pressing down on his pipe. He is nearly biting his pipe in two.

"Answer me!" my mother screams at him.

"They're only keeping company. Nothing may come of it."

"I won't have it," my mother hisses. "He will not move into my house!"

"It's not your house!" my father says. "We all live here. It belongs to Gilda as much as to anyone."

"She has never paid her way!" my mother says to him. "I was the one who worked to pay the mortgage after my father died. I was the one who didn't go to Hunter but had to go to secretarial school! I couldn't even *think* of college where I would have met educated men!" She stares at my father and I see again how false her teeth are, how they hang there in a kind of skeleton smile when she is as far from smiling as she has ever been.

My father bows his head.

She doesn't know what she's just done to him, but I know what she said. I could kill her. She's doing one of her lists: "I rode into the city every day to be a secretary and she stayed home and baked cookies. She stayed home and gave little haircuts. Now she thinks she owns half the house! With her pathetic little income! From polishing nails and curling hair! How dare she offer my house to some stranger! I *need* this house! The *whole* house. I deserve it! I've been waiting years for it. Finally Mama is out of here, and now Gilda thinks she can just invite strangers to live here. I won't have it! I'll stop her—any way I can."

There is nothing to say when she starts her lists. Usually they're about what I won't eat, or how I aggravate her, or why she needs a decorator, or how she can't live another day without a maid. This is much worse. I thought she would greet my good news with a celebration. I thought she would rush upstairs and invite Gilda down and play some music on the piano. I thought we would all have hot chocolate and marshmallows.

Just when I am sure of something, I find how wrong I can be.

22

"I don't want him in the house anymore," my mother announces.

My father and I both think she means Sam Marcus. "It's her place," my father says in a dull voice. "She can have who she wants up there."

"Not him. The dog," she says. "I want him living outside."

"No!" I rush away from the table and from what we are eating—boiled corned beef and cabbage—and I wrap my arms around Beloved's neck.

My mother and I glare at each other. Beloved has become the new reason for my mother's unhappiness. She suspects I am spitting out food I don't like and feeding it to him under the table (I am). She suspects, from a bad smell in the living room, that he peed under the piano (he did). She believes I love him more than I love her (yes!) and better than I love my sister (definitely! definitely!).

I bend down and kiss him all over his furry face.

"You know you are *never* to touch him while you're eating!"

"I'm through eating!"

"You are not through. Sit down and finish your meat."

It always comes down to meat: meat red and stitched through with fat. The cabbage is limp and sour. Boiled carrots also taste wrong. They're much better raw. How come my mother can't cook good things after all these years of cooking?

I try to understand my mother. I do try; I thought we had reached a kind of peace, now that I am allowed to go upstairs and listen in to developments in Gilda's newly forming life, now that I am allowed to walk Beloved around the block without my mother's permission each time, now that she lets me read in the backyard for hours without demanding I rock The Screamer or play with her. (The Screamer is now walking by herself, she plays with toys, she doesn't scream as much as she used to.)

"My dog *has* to live in the house. He sleeps with me," I tell her. How can I say more than that? That I *live* to sleep with Beloved, that I can't *wait* for nighttime so he can jump on top of my blanket and curl deep into the curl of my body. That the fear that has lived in me since I was a baby lessens only when he is breathing beside me in the dark. That his wet black nose is my guide through the startling dreams that erupt from the cave of my sleep.

"It's not healthy," she says. "I read that you can get asthma from dog hairs. He might have ticks that will suck your blood."

"I brush and comb his fur all the time." I look to my father for help, but he's frowning; he's been so silent lately. Where is his laugh? Where is his sweetness?

"It's too cold outside in the winter," I say, finally. "He'd freeze to death."

"We can get a doghouse," she says. "Your father can build one for him."

"No, I can't," my father says. That's *all* he says. He gets up from the dinner table and whistles to Beloved, who is lying at my feet. His tail starts beating against the floor.

"Come on, boy," he says. He snaps his fingers and Beloved leaps to follow him.

"Take the leash!" I cry. My father has been trying to train my dog to walk around the block without a leash. He thinks Beloved needs freedom; everyone needs freedom.

"But he might run away! He might get hit by a car! He might get lost! He might run after a cat! He might . . ." I am not my mother's child for nothing; I can make lists as fast as she can.

But my father's coat is on, the door slams, he's gone. I am left to wait among the cooking pots. This kitchen is the scene of my entire life—will I always live here in this kitchen, cowed by broiling meat and the requirement to eat it? I want to fly away from home; I dream of flying: in dreams I point my hands into a spire above my head and I take off. My praying hands steer me between skyscrapers and over the tops of tall trees. I sweep like a bird but I'm sly as a snake, dipping, curving, the wind like laughter in my mouth.

"God damn it, you will chew and swallow every bit of your dinner."

Mommy, Mommy, what is devouring you? I can never be a good enough eater, dancer, rhymer, daughter. I can never fill you with joy and happiness. You are getting a maid, you are getting a decorator, you are getting rattan furniture. But your hair is going white. Your eyes are burning. You are sinking down and you can't catch hold of anything.

* * *

Suddenly I hear it through the walls and windows: snarling, shouting, the vicious wilderness sounds of an animal fight.

"Beloved!" I throw open the front door and there in front of my house is pandemonium. My father is kicking at a clump of quivering animal haunches. I see the yellow flash of bared fangs. Panic is in my father's shout: "Get away! Get out of here!" His eyes swing to find me. "Issa, get a broom, hurry!" I hurry, I smash into my mother who is coming toward the door and I take her breath away. Good, she can't yell—I run outside with the broom so my father can beat at the attacking dog (it is Bully, the boxer who lives on East 4th Street: he snaps his razor teeth and hangs on while Beloved yips and yelps with pain). My father howls and smashes down with the broom; the boxer runs away, his cut-off tail beating like a stump in the air.

Blood. My father's shin streaming blood. Beloved's ear torn off, streaming blood. My own tongue, bitten by my own teeth, bleeding. My screams. My mother's screams. We limp and drag our shredded selves into the safety of the house.

* * *

So this is the price of freedom. So this is what happens when the leash is left hanging on the door. So this is what's out there in the world.

* * *

The maid is called Margot; she's from Holland. She wears a pillbox hat with a veil and speaks English oddly so that everything she says sounds interesting. She is here to scrub the tub and dust the furniture and beats the rugs; she is here to wash clothes and hang them on the line; she will also care for The Screamer while my mother is out with the decorator, looking at rattan.

I don't know what to do with myself when only she and I and The Screamer are in the house. I don't know what to say. I don't know why someone who hasn't made the dirt here should have to clean it up for any reason. Because I am embarrassed to watch her on her knees, scrubbing, I would like to go upstairs and stay with Gilda, but my mother wants me to be sure Margot doesn't steal anything. I have to follow her around, watching her, wondering what anyone would want to steal from our house. We have old lamps, old chairs, old radios, old plates, old pots. No wonder my mother wants new furniture; now that I am looking for things someone might steal, I see we have nothing at all.

My father doesn't even leave quarters around on his night table; he takes all his loose change to the store and keeps it in a cup there. He plays a game in his store: a sign leaning against the cup says "What will you pay me for this change?" Sometimes someone will offer him five dollars, or ten dollars, or even twenty. Sometimes only one dollar. And he always sells the contents of the cup. He never knows if he wins or loses.

When I'm in the store with him, I hate that game because he doesn't let me have even a nickel for a candy bar from the candy store next door. He knows I have terrible teeth, pitted with cavities, and he is against my having candy. Yet, he will easily give away twenty quarters free if it turns out that someone offers less money for the cup than it contains in change.

He's not perfect, my father. Not quite perfect. Still, he's having a good time in his antique shop. He sometimes buys a clock for ten dollars and sells it for a hundred. That's why my mother is looking at rattan with a decorator.

* * *

It could happen any time. His arrival with a carton. It's the great hope of my life. Nothing could rival the arrival of Beloved; this is certain, and I have accepted it. No life can contain two days like that one day. It's just as well.

But there are close approximations. Book deliveries are almost as exciting. This is how it happens: with his key he opens the front door of the house (this is in my sunporch bedroom) and disappears outside for another minute, returning to his car. Then he arrives with a heavy carton in his arms, pushes open the unlocked door with his foot and makes a great show of exhaustion as he sets the box down on the floor beside my bed.

He wipes his brow as I grin at him.

"Whose were they?" I always ask him. Sometimes he knows but mostly he makes it up: "These books belonged to a pirate who was shipwrecked for twenty years on an island; then he was rescued and the first thing he wanted to do was give them away because he was sick of reading them over and over!" (This was the carton that contained *Little Women, Mother Goose Nursery Rhymes, Grimms' Fairy Tales*, and a tattered copy of *Heidi*.) Once my father said, "A famous brain surgeon read these in his spare time." (Then he unveiled a huge comic book collection: Archie and Jughead and Superman and Dagwood and Nancy and Sluggo.)

I always piled them beside my bed; the best ones would go on the bottom: Nancy Drew mysteries and books about collies. The others I would arrange judiciously—textbooks on chemistry and histories of ancient wars would go on top; these I would dispatch very quickly although my rule was I had to consider them, I had to get a distinct sense of what they were about. But I didn't have to read every word.

* * *

Today, my mother is still out with the decorator, Margot is on Avenue P with The Screamer buying bread at the bakery, and Gilda is upstairs cooking paprika-chicken for my grandmother, who is now barely able to hold her head up. (They don't strap her in a wheelchair anymore; she has to be tied to the rails of her bed.)

There is the fanfare of his key in the lock, the return to his car, the carton of books preceding my father in the door, but he doesn't want to hang around long today, he has to get back to business. I unpack the books and see two identical Nancy Drew mysteries, two Albert Payson Terhune novels, two Bobbsey Twins books.

"Two of each!" I cry in delight.

"You can give the extra copies to a friend," he says.

"What friend?" I say to him. "I have no friends."

"You will make a friend if you give away a book."

"Two books is twice as good as one," I argue.

"You will end up like your mother," he says.

What does that mean? But he disappears up the stairs

to Gilda's house, informing me that I am to stay down-stairs and examine my books.

"What if I want to come up?"

"You stay here," he says. It is the kind of comment that invites no question. I don't argue. I get busy reading the top book, on diseases of the intestinal tract. The next one on collecting foreign coins. I have a long way to go to get to Nancy Drew. But even as I read, I recall a fairy tale in which a starving beggar asks an old woman (dressed in a red cap and white apron) who lives in the woods if he can have some food; she agrees to bake him a muffin, but each batch of muffins comes out of the oven too big, too fragrant, too delicious looking. She keeps trying to make him a tiny muffin, but the dough rises and the muffins grow big and beautiful. She can't bring herself to give away anything so good; finally, impatient with waiting, the beggar casts a spell on her and turns her into a wood-pecker, with a red cap and a white apron, who will have to peck away at the bark of trees into eternity, to get her small bit of sustenance to live.

Still, I won't give away a book, not one.

23

I am getting older and older and still I have no skates.
Now I want a bike. I often dream about a bike shaped
like a horse with wings. The horse is called "Schwinn"; he
has a beeper horn on his flank. I ride him over the
rooftops of the Kingdom of Brooklyn, dipping and dart-
ing between chimneys and under elevated tracks. In every
dream in which I fly, there is a moment during which
something happens to my tongue; it inflates, like a bike
tire, it swells in my mouth and emits something like a
taste. I don't know what I taste, but I can almost taste it.
When I wake, the feeling is still there, the appetite for
something I cannot name, the fullness of my tongue, pal-
pable in its nearly tasting something extraordinary.

The Skaters/Bike-Riders and I have our first club meeting in Gilda's living room. Sam Marcus is taking Gilda to
the movies, so we have no constraints. The Skaters/Bike-
Riders get right to the point: I have to be initiated. This is
a ceremony without which no one can ever belong to the
club. It's simple: I have to be blindfolded; I have to taste
something they serve me on a teaspoon; and I have to let
them do something to me that's "scary but not dangerous."

I will allow anything done to me to belong to their
club. I reason that it must follow from belonging to The

Bike-Riders that I will somehow then be given a bike. I feel sure they can't kill me—murder is against the law—and, after all, I am in my own house, all I have to do if they try to harm me is run down the stairs and burst into my house, calling for help.

I turn myself over to them. The giving-up of myself as I let them cover my eyes is a form of gaining power itself. In surrender, I become brave and strong. In being blinded, I have new vistas opened to me.

Wild with excitement, I open my mouth. They are preparing something, laughing and giggling, and I await my fate, eyes closed, mouth open. The swollen tongue of my dreams is becoming ready to accept a gift—I am ready to faint and fly, live and die, all at once.

"Swallow it!" they command me, the order I have taken from my mother every day at every meal every day of my life. And always I have resisted: fought her, rejected her, gagged and spit and vomited and cried and begged. Now, not protesting, I let them feed me the spoonful of my joining them, of breaking out of my mother's house. The thing they put in my mouth is so vile, I can't give it a name. It's sharper than a knife, thicker than honey, more tangy than raw onion, more bitter than bitter herbs. But delicious.

"Don't spit it out!" they command me.

"I won't." I am totally obedient, swallowing the brew. Stars are sparking on my tongue, rivers of fire run down my throat.

Still locked in darkness, I am led to the couch, pressed down, wrapped in a tunnel of cloth, lifted up, tossed downward, flung upward, hurtled and bounced and thudded and dumped. Out on the floor.

They remove the blindfold. I see them folding Gilda's bedspread, in which I have been slung about like a sack of grain.

"What did I swallow?" I need to know if I will die shortly. I want to know how long I will have to enjoy my last happy moments.

"We'll never tell." But on Gilda's sink I see mustard

and horseradish and vinegar and Manischewitz wine.

I stare at the new world of my friends. I toast myself silently. "To freedom. To survival. To friendship."

* * *

I am sometimes Issa and sometimes I. I sometimes don't remember how old I really am or what my duties for the day are: I am just Issa in all of time, deep in the heart of all I know. This is a deeply comfortable place to be, the heart of home, where nothing changes, where I will always understand myself. More and more I like to go there, to float in the sensation of Issa Nowhere, Issa Knowing.

But there is so much to do in the other place, they are always calling me, do this, do that. *Keep out of my way*, I want to tell them. *Let go*. I want to curl up and be in the great moments of my mind, when Beloved first popped his head out of the carton, when I was Mary, Mother of Jesus, when I stood on the beach in my butterfly pinafore and all the soldiers in the world applauded me. I don't only choose happy times: I also want to remember the ball of lightning sizzling behind my mother, the moment Dr. Ellen pulled my tooth out, how my grandmother looked in the bathtub and then later was folded to a flat soul in her wheelchair. I am so busy in there, where my mind swirls and ticks and circulates new scenes and old scenes, sometimes in the straight line of how they happened, and sometimes in new positions that make all the old arrangements seem different.

This moment, blindfolded in the dark with my friends around me, trying to trust them and knowing they could kill me, wanting to take that chance and doing it—this moment will go into the deep other place and be there forever. You know at once when moments like this are happening, but you can't create them. You wish you could make them happen, but they take you by surprise. If you wait long enough, *something* happens. I have to remember that when I am so bored, so tired. Just wait. The earth is turning slowly, but soon it will take you off balance and topple you. Just wait.

* * *

The antique store is on Hansen Place, across the street from the Railway Express truck station. My father has his wooden Indian outside on the street—he often stands outside next to it, smoking his pipe; when a customer comes in, he sticks the pipe in a hole in the Indian's mouth and goes into the store with the customer.

I am here for the day with Beloved. Wall-to-wall carpeting is being laid down at home, and I am in the way. So I get to help out in the store.

Everything in the window is dusty—a bronze elephant, a punch bowl with cupids painted on the inside, old pocket watches, chiming clocks, perfume bottles, a fat Buddha, guns from the Civil War, Japanese swords.

Nothing here is interesting to me. Next door, at the candy store, everything is alive, illuminated. Red wax lips, chocolate licorice whips, candy dots on a white strip of paper, orange-and-white chicken-feed corn, Popsicles, candy bars, comic books. Couldn't life have been good to me and given my father the candy store instead?

The cup of coins sits on the counter—it's a big cup and sometimes it's full, sometimes it's half full. If you look inside, you see mostly pennies on top, quarters below: there's no way to tell if it's all filled with pennies or quarters. My father doesn't know. He gambles at every opportunity. He offers the cup: "How much will you give me for it?" Some of his customers, mostly men, love the game—they think they will win money. I think they always do. Now and then someone will actually come back and say, "Remember when I paid you ten for the change? There was twenty-two in there."

Luckily, my mother has never heard a remark like that. She would be angry for days. I am always angry about it. He won't give me money for comic books. ("I can get you dozens of them free; don't I get you dozens at estate sales?" "But they're never the ones I want." What does he care? He thinks comic books are comic books.)

Beloved behaves perfectly outside the store. He sits at the Indian's feet in the sun, his leash tied to the Indian's tree-trunk base. He has only one ear now; his scar is made of little star-like stitches. My father has a matching scar of stitches on his shin. And I have a scar on my tongue that no one can see. I can feel it with the bottom of my top teeth. I am less perfect all the time: first my knees were ruined for being a Rockette and now a damaged tongue. By the time I am grown up, I will no doubt be in shreds.

A nun comes into the store. She has a tight white band above her eyes, round glasses, a dark long dress, black shoes, a black cape.

My father is very respectful. I see his honor in his eyes. He definitely won't offer her the cup of coins. She browses at the back of the store while he takes care of another customer. It's Jack, a dealer—a dealer is another man in the same business—and they talk what my father calls "shop talk." They talk about Otto and how he fences stolen jewelry. They talk about how old gold coins are hard to find. They talk about Persian rugs being too big to handle—you'd need a huge store. Jack points to a painting on the wall of a girl with a basket of flowers and asks to see it. He examines the back more than the front and he offers my father ten dollars. It's a deal, although the price marked on it is twenty-five. Why did my father just give away an extra fifteen dollars? I could have had a Sparkle Plenty doll. I could have had a bike. I could have had . . .

Just then I see the nun at the back of the store sweep an object off a shelf and hide it under her cape. I think it was a vase.

I tug at my father's sleeve. "Daddy, Daddy!" I whisper the news to him. He stares down the aisle at the nun, who is strolling toward us, holding her cape tight against her chest. Jack, who heard my whisper, is looking, too. My father stands motionless and says nothing. The nun comes past us, smiling sweetly. She leaves, passes the wooden

Indian, bends and taps Beloved on the head. She is gone.

"Jesus!" says Jack.

"It's okay," my father says.

"What's missing?" Jack says. "What did she get?"

"It doesn't matter. Don't worry about it. Who knows? She might donate it to charity."

"Yeah," Jack says. "Like I'm Jesus Christ. Well, buddy. Easy come, easy go." Then he lays the painting he just bought on the counter and rips off the frame. Just like that, he rips the wood apart and tears off the backing and then he shouts: "Holy cow! I had a hunch! Look at that!" Hidden behind the backing of the painting are twenty-dollar bills in rows. Jack is counting them. When he gets to number twenty, I feel myself start to cry. I go outside and lay my cheek on Beloved's warm little triangular head.

My father never once found diamonds in a pin cushion, not once. Why aren't we ever the lucky ones?

* * *

Late in the afternoon, my father buys me an ice-cream pop next door. He buys pipe tobacco. We stand outside and watch the traffic on Hansen Place; we watch the big green Railway Express trucks pull in and take off from the lot across the street.

My father is tamping new tobacco down into his pipe when a blue car careens around the corner, jumps the curb and crashes into the plate glass of the candy store window.

The big car hangs there, half on the curb, half into the shattered store window, with its motor racing. The man in it is slumped over the steering wheel, but the motor is roaring.

My father hesitates only half a second. Then he rushes to the car, tries the door on the driver's side, runs to the other side and tries that door, runs back and gets the wooden Indian, and carries it with him, Beloved dragging along on his leash, toward the crashed car. I run after him, grabbing and freeing Beloved. My father hurls the Indian into the back car window, smashes the glass, reaches in to unlock the door, pulls the man out of the car, lays him gently on the ground, jumps back in and shuts off the motor.

The man's face is blue. My father lifts him in his arms and opens his shirt button. The candy store man has run out and run in. Police come. The man may be dead or he may not be dead. I don't know him. But I feel as if I don't know my father, either. All these years of watching him read *The Brooklyn Eagle* and seeing him pick peaches off the tree in the backyard, and hearing him sing "Danny Boy" and I don't begin to know the depth of the things inside him. I have enormous respect now, I am in awe of him. He is stronger than I ever realized. And I am his. I may be like him in some amazing way. Why, oh why, didn't I ever think of that?

24

Gilda is having an engagement shower. The customers crowd up the stairs with white gift boxes while my mother sits motionless in our living room, on our new rattan couch, which rests on our new wall-to-wall flowered carpet.

"Gilda says you're invited," I tell my mother. "She says to come up. I'm going up soon."

"No thank you," my mother says. I know that look on her face, I know trouble when I see it. I don't stay to hear her opinion, but run upstairs to observe the party.

So much giggling and laughter from the women; they sound like young girls, like The Bike-Riders and me at our club meetings, but they are all older than Gilda and she is nearly forty. There is the delicious moment of suspense as Gilda peels back the tissue paper, then her exclamation of delight: a red lace nightgown, satin slippers with roses at their toes, perfume, bath powder with a big feathery powder puff, a box of chocolate-covered cherries.

Gilda is radiant, her teeth are white, her lips red. She has never laughed so much, or blushed so rose-red as she is blushing. I help her serve tea and homemade honey cake, special mandelbrot with chocolate marbling, delicate pastries from the bakery. She laughs with the women and they make her blush. I've never seen her this relaxed and happy when she is with Sam Marcus. When he's here, her back is straight, her lips are pursed with nervousness, she keeps her hands folded in her lap. Why is she going to marry this man?

It's only after the ladies go home, after Gilda and I are examining the presents, that my mother comes charging up the stairs.

"You can't go through with this!" she says in a tone of voice so severe and icy that Gilda's head is flung back against the couch.

"I am getting married," Gilda says. "You can't stop me. This is my last chance."

"Yes, I can stop you! I won't allow you to ruin yourself and I won't allow him to move in here and live in this house that we've killed ourselves to pay for. He's a crook, Gilda. He's after your money! Your little bit of savings. Mama's jewelry. He wants a free place to live and you as a cook and laundress. He wants to bring his daughter here to live!"

"What? You're crazy! His daughter lives with his dead wife's sister."

"But not for long! They want to get rid of her. She's a filthy pig. This is a girl who eats sardines with her fingers!"

Gilda is shivering. She sits on her couch and I sit next to her. I'm afraid to take her hand under my mother's gaze.

"Who told you that?"

"I went to visit Mrs. Exter yesterday. I caught her off guard. She admitted these things: Sam isn't rich; in fact, he's nearly bankrupt. The chicken farm is on its last legs. They need new equipment, new coops, they need to tear down the little house Sam's been living in and build a place for egg-candling. His wife's illness used up all his money, so he's got nothing, Gilda! He sees you as an easy mark! Free room and board, someone to iron his shirts, make his meals, someone who lives around the corner from Exter, so they can drive to the farm together. Look— can't you see how convenient it is for him to have his business partner around the corner? They all cooked this up, Gilda, the Exters and Sam, behind your back. You're such an innocent fool! I forced the truth out of Mrs. Exter. She couldn't deny it. She says she thought it would be good for you, to get a husband at this late date!"

"It will be," Gilda says softly, all the color gone from her face. Her lips move like red worms, separate from her other features. "What else have I got to hope for? You're not the only woman in the world who deserves to have a husband."

"You'd like to have mine, I know!" my mother says.

This is not to be spoken aloud. I look toward the window for another lightning ball. This thought should never have been turned into words.

"*I* should have had him," Gilda says softly. "Harry Cohen brought him to the party to be my date, but you got to him first."

"That's ridiculous! He wasn't interested in you! He was sitting in the sunporch all alone, smoking his pipe when I came home that night."

"Yes, you came home from a date, all worked up and smelling of perfume. In that fur cape Papa made for you. Looking like a movie star."

"He wasn't interested in you, Gilda! You were a shy, timid little nothing!"

"I didn't have a chance!" Gilda cries. "You were so busy shimmying around him, you took his eyes out."

"Stop!" I cry. I take Gilda's hand and kiss each finger. Her fingers are freezing cold. "Mommy, *stop!*"

"Just look at the facts, Gilda," my mother carries on. She's like a truck that can't stop. She's barreling along as if she weighs a thousand pounds. "This Sam doesn't want you—he wants what you have. Don't make the mistake of thinking he's in love with you."

"If we were moving away to his place, you wouldn't be saying this, Ruth," Gilda says to her. "You just want me out of your life."

Will my mother admit it? I know it's true, we all know it's true. That's all she ever talks about—privacy; she wants every room of this house for herself.

"If you go through with this," my mother says, "just don't come running to me when Sam ruins your life."

* * *

How can I stop Gilda's tears after my mother leaves? How can I soothe her quivering sobs, comfort her after such forbidden revelations?

"She'll kill me someday," Gilda whispers. "God forgive her, she wants to kill me."

"No, she doesn't," I say helplessly. "You're her sister." (But as I say it, I think of my sister, and know how easily I could do without her.)

"But what if she's right about Sam? Could she be right?" She shudders. "I don't know, I just don't know! She might be right. Your mother looks for the worst in people and finds it. Oh God, what if she's right?"

"She can't be," I say, and we sit there, both of us looking at the red lace nightgown; there in the white tissue paper it looks like a puddle of blood.

* * *

On Friday night when Sam is to arrive (this is the night they will set the wedding date), my mother and I have our ears tilted upward to the ceiling. My father knows nothing of my mother's violent visit upstairs after the engagement shower. We hear Beloved howling softly from the back porch, where he now lives in a little dog house. He can't come in ever now, where there is a new rug and new rattan furniture. Blossom is playing on the floor with a toy elephant. There is the sound of the doorbell upstairs, Sam's step on the staircase. Gilda's voice. My mother's eyes glow. She has so little color in her face these days that it's strange, very strange to see her lit up this way.

We hear an argument start at once, from right upon the staircase. My mother looks at my face and glances away. We hear Sam's loud voice and Gilda's gentle voice. Then

Gilda cries out with some terrible cry. My father's chin shoots up from the low angle where it rests as he reads the paper.

"What's wrong upstairs?" he says and looks at my mother.

"She and Sam have to work something out," she answers with satisfaction.

"Did you interfere?" he asks. "What did you do, Ruth?"

"All I did was warn her. Now Nature is just taking its course," she says.

From upstairs we hear Sam's coarse voice saying "It's a lie! You don't believe that, do you?"

"Should I believe it?" Gilda's voice is so hopeful, so sad, so desperate.

Sam talks; we hear the buzz of his sawing voice.

Then Gilda cries out, "But there is no room for another person here! You know there's no room for her. Not if I keep the beauty parlor. I was thinking maybe I would give it up once we get married."

"Give it up?" he says. "A good business like you have built up here?"

It goes on a while longer, with Gilda begging and Sam denying, with Gilda weeping, and Sam getting louder and meaner. And finally we hear one clear, unmistakable word: "The bitch." I know who he means. It isn't, it cannot be, Gilda.

* * *

In the morning after my father has gone to work, Gilda runs down the stairs and knocks at the door between her upstairs and our downstairs. She comes in without waiting for an invitation. She says to my mother: "You won. I thought you'd like to know. Sam is gone for good." Then she turns around and runs up the stairs, shaking with sobs.

* * *

When one story happens on top of the next one, there isn't enough space or time to arrange all the details before they rearrange themselves. While I am thinking that Gilda will not get married, while I am glad to be rid of Sam, while I am sorry we will no longer get to eat halvah at Mrs. Exter's, while I pray for a bicycle, I am given a bicycle. It arrives like the Star of Bethlehem appeared in the sky: just like that. One day I come home from school and there it is in the sunporch, its kickstand down, a blue Schwinn with a button horn on its side, with my name in gold letters, ISSA, on the front fender.

Why does it come when I have almost made myself stop longing for it? Who wants to please me so much that they put my name on it in gold? And now that it's here, will I be allowed to ride all over the world, or will they forbid me to use it, just as they got me Beloved and now forbid him to be in the house with me.

By now I know everything has conditions, everything has limits, the best-seeming things can turn out to be the worst things.

I don't know what to say about this bike. As I examine it, the bird in my chest begins to thump and skip—I'd forgotten he was there. Where is everyone? No one is in the sunporch—they don't even know I've discovered the bike. It has big tires, it has silver handlebars, it has a little glassy headlight. Will they let me ride *at night*?

Could it be here by accident? Could it be for someone else? No, it has my name on it! Is it my birthday? No. Is it because some terrible thing is going to happen—and this is to pay me back for it? The things I think! Instead of simple happiness! Instead of simple singing and hand-clapping. My club friends would sing and hand-clap; they don't go into all these questions, not one of them, Linda, Myra, Myrna, or Ruthie. They take what happens and they go on. I would love to be like them, but I can't. They know I'm not, but they come over anyway. They like the things my father brings home—a gum machine from the subway, a stereopticon with old pictures to slip into a slot,

bouquets of comic books (my father has given some out
to them without my permission, without letting me look
through them first! He has found my friends on the front
stoop playing jacks with me, and he has given them *my*
comic books!). I have to smile generously when he does
that, but I hate them and I hate him.

I have a bike. I have a bike. I test my feelings. Is a bike
now as good as skates would have been before?

No, no, no. Not as good. But so what. It's here, this is
now. Who shall I ask about why the bike is here? No one,
absolutely no one is in the house. I hear no one moving or
talking anywhere, either upstairs or down. Where are
they? Now I begin to feel alarmed.

Did the Russians take them away, as they did Katrinka's parents in *Katrinka, The Story of a Russian Girl*?
And in trade did they leave me this bike?

I rush upstairs but Gilda is not there. Maybe no one in
my family is left but my grandmother, whom I have not
seen in three years. I know where she is. I could go to
Sherman's Rest Home and visit her. I might have to. She
might be the only one left in my entire family. But could
she help me to grow up? Could she give me advice? She
can't even talk! She doesn't think! She has no teeth in her
mouth. She is a living ghost.

I come back and lean my head against the cold flank of
my bicycle. Blue, it's the color of my dream bicycle.
Where are they?

*   *   *

I go next door where our neighbor, Mrs. Berk, lives and
I ask her if she knows what happened to my family. She
says the police came and Gilda had to go somewhere with
them. Gilda was crying. My mother called my father, who
came home, and they both went with her.

The police? My stomach heaves. Who has The Screamer?

"I have her," our neighbor says. "Come in and wait
with me."

"How long do we have to wait?"

"I don't know. If you have to sleep over, you can."

I go into Mrs. Berk's house and there—playing on the floor—is my sister with her familiar flat face, her brown eyes, her smooth dark hair. An amazing feeling comes over me. I am happy to see her. I even want to hug my sister. I may even *love* my sister. She may be all I have left in life.

25

Actually, now that it's a crime for the beauty parlor to be operated, now that it has to be closed down and emptied out, there *would* be room for Sam Marcus's filthy-pig daughter. But without Gilda having her business, Sam doesn't want to marry her. The whole thing is over. But who told? *Why* did someone tell, someone tattle, someone report that Gilda had no license? Why would anyone want the police to come and close her down?

The police station—not Russia—was where they all were the day I got my bike; they had gone with Gilda to the police station while an officer took Gilda's finger-prints. Gilda thought she was going to jail, forever. But she only had to pay a big fine. Jail! I can't even imagine it.

Today I am out in the alley—leaning on my new bike—as the movers carry away Gilda's green metal hair dryer, the red plastic hair-cutting chair, the shampoo attachment that fits over the sink with a deep cut-out for a customer's neck. They take away her manicure table, her trays of nail polishes and cuticle pushers and nippers and files. The big mirror goes, the metal cabinet where all the chemicals for permanents are stored, the curlers and thinning shears and waving clips—they take Gilda's life away, bobbie pin by bobbie pin.

Who these moving men are I do not know. They keep

their heads down as they go up and down the stairs, and don't look at Gilda, who stands in the street sobbing. Mrs. Berk from next door comes over and gives Gilda a hug. My mother stays deep inside the house with my sister; my father is at work.

Who told? My mother says Sam. Gilda says my mother told. But she told me not to tell my mother she told me that.

I can't imagine what Gilda will do now. I just don't know how she will use her days. As for my bike, I never found out why it came at that moment, on that day. I am afraid to ask, afraid they'll realize I now have wheels and will be rolling down strange streets and crossing busy roads on it.

Maybe my father got it in trade for some antique. Maybe they just felt I deserved it after all those years without skates. Who knows? Some questions can never be answered.

* * *

I get on my bike (oh, what simple words to say, but what heavenly feelings pour over me as I settle onto the hard black seat); I ride over to Ruthie's where she gets on her bike and we ride over to Linda's, and then we pick up Myrna and Myra at their houses. Five Schwinns, five free, happy girls on a Saturday morning going to ride on the Ocean Parkway bicycle path.

I see the five of us in my mind's eye, two and two and one behind (Issa is behind) as we pedal along in unison. Five sets of legs pumping round and round, and five wind-whipped faces looking ahead at what's to come in our path.

I know what's in *my* head: poor Gilda and the end of manicures and haircuts, poor Gilda and nothing to do now, poor Gilda with only my grandmother to visit. Even now—as we pass Sherman's Rest Home there on the left—I think that inside those blank, closed doors is the human being that gave birth to Gilda and my mother, who used to sit in springtime on the wooden bench under the lilac tree. I know what's in my head as we ride along the bicycle path, looking at the scenery (cars and mothers and babies on the benches, and across the lanes of traffic to the bridle path where occasionally horses come pounding along with their riders, their hooves kicking up clods of dirt).

But I don't know what's in Ruthie's bobbing head, or in Myra's or Myrna's or Linda's, I don't know what thoughts are riding along with them on the bicycle path, what images flash on the inside of their eyes as the horses and cars and other cyclers flash by on the outside. I wish I knew, but I don't. Will I ever know anyone's but my own?

* * *

We each have two dollars for spending money and we stop at Schector's Luncheonette for lunch. We line up our matching Schwinns and align the kickstands so it looks like our bikes are dancing in step.

"Let's leave our horses here to drink," Linda says, and we all laugh as though no one ever said a funnier joke. We shuffle in the door together, a little happy army: we are friends out for adventure, we are young girls—eleven years old—we tolerate school but we try not to think of it when we are not there. School is where we mark time till we all have boyfriends, which will be soon, soon. We promise each other—we will soon have boyfriends, every one of us.

"A ham and cheese sandwich," Myrna tells the man behind the counter.

"Make it two," says Linda.

"Three," says Myra.

"Four," says Ruthie. They look at me. I have never had a ham sandwich in my life. I have never even *seen* ham. My mother cooks bacon, but that's the closest we have come to eating filthy pig.

"Do you have tuna sandwiches?"

"All out of tuna."

"Okay, then. Ham and cheese." I tried, and I have witnesses, that I made an attempt to save my soul. As the man turns his back on us and does something hidden on the cutting board, making magic motions with his elbows, his shoulders, seizing tools from a rack (an enormous cleaver, a saw-toothed knife, gobbets of white cream that he smears on bread), I remember the words of the bearded rabbi of last year's Religious Instruction class: "Eat pork and you will go blind. Touch your eyes in the morning without washing your hands and you will die young."

I only went to instruction for two weeks, and only because the school let us out early on Wednesday afternoons if we signed up for the program. When I told my mother the essence of his lesson, she called the school and said I was not to be dismissed early on Wednesdays. "Let your father get on his knees for that hocus-pocus," she said to me. "I won't have your mind poisoned."

Now I sit on a soda-fountain stool waiting to poison my eternal soul. Ham sandwiches are served to us along with bags of potato chips and chocolate malteds. My friends dig in, every one of them a Jewish girl without a Jewish worry; without a pause in their chatter, they eat ham. They eat hungrily, automatically, their pink tongues licking crumbs from their pretty lips. Lightning does not flash. The ceiling does not crumble into their plates and spill their malteds into their laps.

I bite. I taste rubber. Pink, elastic, gummy rubber meat. Oh, meat will be the death of me! It rebounds against my teeth, refusing to be chewed, subdued, conquered. *God help me*, I think, this is the closest I come to prayer, and then the irrevocable happens. I grind the ham into submission with my little pointy teeth—and I swallow.

Jesus, The Forbidden Savior, Father, Lord, King of Kings, flows speedily into my bloodstream; I feel his essence bubbling up like seltzer. I am a new person. I am no longer a true member of my family. I am separated forever. I am free.

I get giddy. I throw potato chips in the air and catch them in my open mouth. I toss my pickle spear into

Linda's mouth and she tosses hers into mine. Ruthie and Myra buy red wax fangs and try to terrorize each other, thrusting their faces forward and growling. We push off our spinning stools and stand at the comic book rack, reading Captain Marvel comic books for free.

My mind is blissfully blank. I laugh and giggle and feel like a regular girl all the rest of the afternoon, as we ride our bikes and buy Popsicles from the Good Humor man and pedal back home.

Only when we pass Sherman's Rest Home on Ocean Parkway, now on the right-hand side, do I feel the clicks of adjustment as the puzzle of my life regains its shape. I am Issa, Issa has this Jewish face, this fate, this fortune, this future. Issa is going home to take on the form fortune has made her wear, to re-enter the life she is destined to enact.

* * *

A new boy has moved on the block, into the house on the corner where the Espositos lived. After Tommy and Joe Esposito both died, Mrs. Esposito moved back to Italy. I think for a second or two about how sad it must have been for Mrs. Esposito to leave her vegetable garden and her grape vines and her goats, but I stop myself. I hardly know anything about Mrs. Esposito except that she gave me a Jewish star when I was little; I don't *have* to think about how sad her life is. I am trying *never* to think of how sad my grandmother's life is. I definitely can't even *begin* to think of how sad Gilda's life is now that she has no beauty parlor, no boyfriend, no dog, no mother with her, and not even me. Because I am growing up. I have a bike, I have friends, I have hope. How can I think about everyone's sadness every minute of the day?

The boy is tall and blond. He has a crew cut. He is strolling up the street, looking my way. I get busy playing stoop ball, a ferocious game between me and myself, my goal being to hit only fly balls, to have every pink arrow of my ball hit the point of the step and arc back to me as high and graceful as a rainbow. No low, sloppy, rolling bounces, no chugging clunks in the dead space of the step.

Wham! Wham! I am hitting the point of the brick, catching those fly balls. I have something to prove, and I'm proving it.

Just at that moment my mother comes to the front door and calls me in for a hot dog.

"I'm busy," I tell her.

"You can play later," she says.

"This is not *playing*!"

"Your hot dog will get cold."

Whap! Another fly.

"Good throw," the boy says behind me. My mother's head snaps up as she stares at him, though I don't look behind me. I just throw another fly ball and catch it.

"You could be on the Dodgers," he says.

This is no ordinary compliment. In Brooklyn this remark, to a girl, is a declaration of love!

"Want to play?" I ask him. I still haven't looked at his face.

"Sure."

I toss him the ball and stand to the side as he gracefully throws an overhand toss, hits the point, catches the rebound.

"Nice ball," he says.

"It's a little dead."

"Not really."

"I might get a new one." All the will inside me wants my mother to go inside and disappear! I am consumed by shame that she has appeared at this one instant of my life to which I want no witnesses, particularly not *her*. I can't put off this moment, do it later, do it when I am alone with *him*. It's here, it arrived at this instant whether or not she's watching. I can't simply go inside and be nailed to the hot dog chair, can't face that long ground sausage of chewing and despair, not while outside in the bright air is this blond boy, this hope of freedom, better than skates, better than a Schwinn.

But he sees the difficulty. "I gotta go; they're eating

over there, too." He motions toward his house. "So I'll see you later, okay?"

But when, when, *when*? I want to have him sign an agreement, in *blood*.

"Later?" I say. I could die at the sound of begging in my voice.

"Sure." He tosses the ball to me. I toss it back, like a reflex. He has to toss it back. We are caught up briefly in a duet of harmony. "I'll come back after supper."

* * *

The hot dog has a certain transcendent quality—sweating beads of boiled water and fat, making soggy the soft bun, sending up fumes of spice and ground innards of cow. Strings of gray sauerkraut, pungent and sour, can't take away the sweet taste of my inner smile; the yellow smear of mustard is like the sun laid out in a line that I will follow to the ends of the earth.

I bite and I burst the skin and taste the hot juices. I tear into this hot dog like a madwoman, and I chew. I relish! I swallow!

Not only does the blond crew-cut boy come back, his name is Izzy, short for Isadore, and together we are Issa and Izzy, we are a pair, we are in love, we sit on Gilda's stairs and play Old Maid, we become co-conspirators in all things. We talk about our teachers, about adults, about parents: how false, how bossy, how wrong they are. Not his parents; he has only one, her name is Iggy (short for Etta) and she's nothing like a parent. She's his pal. And not my parents, because I can't talk about mine while I'm sitting in limbo in my own house, between the upstairs mother I desire and the downstairs mother I belong to.

Forget parents. Be here, in the semi-dark of late afternoon on the enclosed staircase. Playing the game of Old Maid. *She* is what I don't want to be, what Gilda is, whose fate is the worst imaginable, whose demeanor is prissy and sour, who wears a black bonnet tied under the chin, whose forbidding spectacles sit on her beak-like nose, who carries a sharp black umbrella. Everyone else in the deck is paired; Mother Hubbard, and Mary Quite Contrary, the Pied Piper, Aladdin, Jack the Giant Killer, two of each of them makes them jaunty and cheerful, confident and triumphant. Strength in numbers. Safety in numbers. But alone, unpaired, a woman is lost and weak and destined to be sharp as a porcupine. She emanates needles of *keep away, keep away.*

On Izzy's golden head lie needles of another kind, tingling and tantalizing.

"Do you mind if I touch your crew cut?" I ask Izzy, because the needles of his hair call to my hand, call to be tested. He bends toward me over the cards upon the stair and I reach for quills and find a silken sheaf of wheat. The tips of his hairs prickle my palm; they are feather-soft and luscious.

"Issa," he says to me, and his voice is deep, his eyes are watching mine. "What can I touch of yours?"

We are just a boy and a girl playing cards on the stairs, but instantly I know that no moment in my future will ever equal this one, nothing any man will ever say to me in all the years to come can hold the power of what this first boy's words offer me. I shiver in his implication, dizzy with imagination. Even Joe Martini, stopping at my desk in kindergarten, even Joe, the Joseph to my Mary, inviting me to live in his house, doesn't come near to Izzy's low-voiced, unequivocal desire.

What of mine can he touch?

My mouth is an "O" of openness; I am open, waiting for the word to come to describe what he can touch, have, of me, of mine.

And at that moment my mother throws open the door to the stairway.

She knows, from the dark, from the heat, from our silence, where we have been wandering. If Gilda had found us so, she would have retreated, let us be, gloried in my discovery, but my mother's reaction is to turn on the stairway lamp, to plant her feet on the landing and ask how we could possibly see our cards in such dimness.

We blink, Izzy and I, in the sudden brightness, and he's instantly on his feet, up and going, late for supper, pleading his mother's rage (though she never rages, she's his pal) to get himself past my mother and out Gilda's side/front door.

And then I am lost: unpaired like the Old Maid, undefended like the Old Maid, sullen and beak-nosed and bitter like the Old Maid. If at this moment I held the Old Maid's sharp umbrella, I would pierce my mother in the heart with it—for stopping me, for preventing me, for interfering with my moving into the realm of desire. And then—later—I would gladly mourn her, with my black bonnet tied under my chin. Gladly I would mourn my mother.

* * *

A Disney film of bees and butterflies is shown at our Girl Scout meeting. At our leader's house, we sit in our green uniforms and little yellow ties, our knees bent under us on the rug, our innocent chins tipped up toward the screen, where we see diaphanous butterfly wings instead of red blood, and hear the words "Now that you're growing up . . ." instead of "Watch for blood." We have all been watching for blood for months—Ruthie, Myra, Myrna, Linda, and I. Some girls, we know, "get it" as early as nine or ten. We are almost twelve, and so far, nothing. I have a hunch that when I "get it" I will receive womanly power in my thighs. Only then will I be able to become the ballerina that I was too weak to become before. I recall the older girls performing for my ballet class—those girls in the diaphanous butterfly netting of their tutus, flitting and sailing as though on wings, but deep in the core of their bodies: the machinery of blood. Inside their white-stockinged legs were deeply pulsing vessels filled with blood. And not a stain on netting or panties or pink toeshoes. The energy kept inside, where it burned and pulsed and fed those muscles with leaping power.

When our leader says that some day we girls will marry and want to have babies, that some day we'll be glad we have all this baby-making machinery right inside us in an efficient little package, I think of Izzy's eyes on the staircase, his voice saying "What can I touch of yours?" If I say those words to myself, in a little stair-step picture, starting at the bottom step:

yours?"

of

touch

I

can

"What

. . . I am *en pointe* at the top, I am at the height of my beauty and strength, I am strained to exploding.

We Girl Scouts are advised to revel in the fact that we are magically constructed, that in each of us there is a miraculous chemical and biological factory which, at the *right time*, when each of us has married the man of our dreams, will build for us a *perfect baby*, itself a container of life (within life, within life) and like rows upon rows of mirrors, each baby will string out babies unto eternity, and each of us is an essential segment of the string.

I imagine myself as a spider, hanging in air between two web-like threads, hanging far above a chasm, unable to go backward, afraid to go forward. Unless . . . unless . . . Izzy is there to take my hand.

The man of my dreams. This image seems capable of supplanting my desire for bikes, puppies, Captain Midnight decoders. This is a *big* idea, this has a richness I never before imagined possible. I can feel it pushing away even roller skates (the dream of which offered mainly speed and freedom and self-control) and substituting *the man of my dreams*. This idea offers endless fantasies—not only on staircases with decks of cards, but on the decks of ships with moonlight above, on merry-go-rounds, on roller coasters, on subway trains, on rides not unlike the rides in my primer book, sleigh rides and donkey rides and train rides and—(something else happens as I think this—a contraction of my baby-making mechanism occurs, a kind of inner convulsion, shudder, tremor, shock, quiver). I am amazed and totally grateful that I have located this treasure within me; this is the force that drives the world.

* * *

Margot, the maid, doesn't come to work one day and my mother says to me, "She feels sick today. She thinks she may be having a baby."

She thinks? Doesn't a woman *know?* Doesn't she *do that thing* with a man for that special purpose? I ask this of my mother, the time seems right, nothing appears premeditated, though certain questions have been burning in me for months, for *years*, but now there is an opening, a chance to find out some critical things. I hold my breath in hope; if my mother begins to talk about this, I can ask her what "the missionary position" is—described in our Family Medical Encyclopedia, I can ask her what "the woman lies with knees bent and legs splayed" could mean in real time, real life. The dictionary says to splay is "to dislocate, as a shoulder bone." Or, "to slope or slant, as the side of a door or window." Splay also means to spread out, it means awkward, ungainly.

None of this completes the blank space in my mind, fills in the details. Whatever my mother and my father did to make me, I hope against hope that nothing was dislocated, as a shoulder bone.

But my mother can't do this. She says, of Margot, of her possibly having a baby, "Sometimes you know and sometimes you don't."

I have one more urgent question: I have seen a word written on the wall of the playground in school, a word not in any dictionary, a word that causes girls to shriek and boys to laugh knowingly—FUCK is the word, it's always written in capitals, it has such power, such shame attached to it. What could it mean? Who can I ask? Who would tell me a secret so critical and weighted with meaning? Not my mother surely. Not my father. Surely not Gilda. And to ask Izzy is too dangerous; he is one of the boys who laughs, leers, when the word is in sight. I may never know. That's just the way it is.

* * *

But at the next club meeting, at Ruthie's house, I do

ask. We are talking about subjects that make our hearts pound anyway, about bras and sanitary napkins and nipples that get hard when we are very cold, and how long it will be before we "do it," and find out what it's like. And Ruthie says, "Come with me, I'll show you a secret." And in her empty house we follow her single file to her parents' bedroom where she opens the drawer of the night table—and there, inside, is a little nest of knotted white balloons. They are soggy, weighted slightly, we are invited to poke at them with our index fingers, they are slug-like and elastic, they are terrifying.

"That's the *stuff*," Ruthie says. "It's scum. If it gets inside us, that's the end. In there is the seed that makes the baby."

We all shriek and stand on our toes. To be this close to it! To almost have touched it with our bare fingertips!

"Why do they save it?" Linda asks, with my very question.

"Maybe my father thinks he will run out someday," Ruthie says. She pulls the drawer out further, and—with the authority of one who knows—she shows us the box that contains unused balloons—Trojans, they are called— and she confesses that she counts them whenever her parents are out, to see how often they "do it."

Such knowledge. It is almost too much for me. I can't see straight for the beating of my heart. The bird has come loose and wild again, it's breaking my ribs. Whenever I get close to some dangerous essence, the bird of fear comes to life.

"Does FUCK mean when they do it?" I blurt out. My club mates nod. See? I have known all along. Some things are known to the heart. No one has to be told the meanings of certain words. They flare their meaning at you, they shock and stun and burn you.

And to think of it! That ordinary parents play with fire. Mothers and fathers obsessed with tuna fish sandwiches and earning money, who talk about buttoning up your coat and being sure to close the front door do these things, together in the dark night of secrecy where no children can come, these parents of ours contain magical flu-ids and miracle-making machines. My own mother and father are wizards. And I am attached to them by the spi-der's filament, spinning out toward the sun, knowing by heart the natural magic of existence.

27

Iggy, Izzy's mother, wears extremely tight pink angora sweaters, tosses hardballs in the street to whichever of her seven brothers is visiting her, drives an old red Ford convertible she calls "Lizzie," and has never had a headache in her life. Izzy swears to me about this: his mother has never been sick, she never yells at him, she never, once, made him finish anything on his plate. And, just last week, she bought him a pinup of Betty Grable to hang inside his closet door.

Izzy and I are on the front stoop, discussing a subject that sets the hairs on my arms to standing straight up: how a key and lock are like a boy and a girl. He is showing me, in full daylight, how my key is "male" and the front door lock is "female"; he is just now demonstrating the principle by inserting my key into the opening of the front door lock—("See? In it goes like they were made for each other")—when his mother comes driving up to the curb in her red car and yells out in her Betty Hutton-hoarse voice, "Hey, kids, wanna hop in and go for a ride?"

Izzy pulls the key out of the lock and places it, steaming, in my hot palm. "Let's go," he says.

"I don't know," I say. "I should ask my mother."

"Why bother?" He winks, something his mother has

taught him: he does it without grimacing at all, "She'll never know. We'll be back in a flash."

And here it is again, the things men do without conscience or worry. How Joe Martini—and then only in kindergarten—escaped from school in the winter wind without jacket or boots or hat, without permission, and was able to convince me, easily, so easily, to do the same. I have always been ripe for convincing; there's no telling what I could be convinced to do, in half a second. All I need is someone's expectation that a kernel of raw courage is within me. All I need is an interested person, waiting to witness my calling it forth. When someone thinks I can do it, when someone is watching, magic happens. I can't even *remember* fear.

A convertible! I hop in the front with Izzy. We zoom away from the curb and I laugh. I laugh, catching wind in my teeth, past the three playgrounds between 3rd, 4th and 5th Streets, past the windows of Dr. Ellen's dental office (behind whose door poor trembling children wait to have drills bore to the core of their beings) and then—but where are we going? Not *just* around the block! Iggy is driving much further, much faster than was agreed upon. She shakes her wild blonde hair and she laughs and Izzy laughs and they jar me, between them in the front seat, with their shaking shoulders.

Oh no, I am a lost soul, swooning under wind and sun, going further and further from home, going so far I almost can't remember how it will be when it's discovered that I didn't ask permission, didn't tell anyone, didn't ask, didn't think, didn't care!

Coney Island! That's where we're going. We're taking a wild ride to the place of wild rides. Izzy grabs my hand and I feel his index finger move through the circle of my closed hand like a key riding through the opening of a lock.

"Isn't this fun?" he asks. He leans close and says, "Isn't this fun, Issa my kisser?" His hand comes down on the seat between us and nudges my flesh. Whereupon I enter a new extremity of knowledge.

* * *

Kissing, it seems, is the essence of every ride. Bumper cars, merry-go-round, tunnel of love, fun house; with them come speed and thrill and laughter and kissing. We check from time to time and see Iggy waiting for us on a bench at the edge of the boardwalk, smoking cigarettes and staring at the ocean while Izzy and I forget time, forget the world, as we spin, as we bump, as we scream to the springing forth of ghosts and devil-faces in the dark.

"Did you know people could have this much fun?" Izzy asks me as we look at our images—two fat people with enormous feet—in a pair of fun-house mirrors.

I shake my head.

"I didn't think so," he says. "What you needed was me."

Oh yes. It is a certainty. All the years of crying *I want, I want!* and what I needed was him. Do I have him? How can a person know when she has someone? And for how long can he be mine if I do?

Izzy apologizes that he has no father; but what he has is seven uncles, some of them rich. "We can go on any ride we want. Even twice! Even three times! My mother doesn't care. She gets all the money she needs. And she likes it at Coney Island—sometimes she meets men."

One time, as we pass by a doorway in the fun house, we glance across the wild slants of the boardwalk and see that Iggy has company on her bench: a sailor, in fact. A sailor in a sailor suit and a jaunty sailor hat.

"She likes to kid around with guys," Izzy says. "They think she's a hot tomato."

"How does a girl get to be a hot tomato?" I ask Izzy. We are in a new part of the fun house, standing up to our ankles in cold, slimy worms. "Ugh," I add.

"It's only spaghetti," Izzy assures me. "Let me think about hot tomatoes," he says. He leads me to the next room, where we have to sit down on a softly padded bench that collapses under our weight and sends us careening down a slide, at the bottom of which we land

on a bed of balloons. "Only some girls can be hot tomatoes. Most can't. But you—" Izzy says. He pulls me close
to him. "You'd be a star hot tomato."

"Me?"

"Issa the kisser," he says. And we kiss again, popping
balloons as we roll out of the way of the next couple who
are screaming and plummeting down the slide together.

* * *

"Your mother is going to kill you," Iggy says, as we
drive home. She thinks it's a joke, but it isn't: my mother
can kill, and this time she may.

The truth of what I will face at home is beginning to
close in on me; the sky grows darker and darker. It is, in
fact, night. How did I—so easily—forget my whole family? My duty to them? My certain punishments? For a girl
who tries to be good I am definitely bad, seriously bad. I
may even be bad enough to be classed as a hot tomato.
How I hope so!

"Look," Iggy says, reaching over and giving my thigh a
friendly pinch. "What can they do to you? Nothing! They
can't do anything! So you're late. So what? I'm responsible—I'll come in and tell them I took you for a ride
around the block and we ended up in Canarsie. Or Coney
Island, wherever the hell we were."

"Leave out 'wherever the hell,'" Izzy advises her.
"You'll see what I mean when you meet Issa's mother."

"Aah. She can't scare me," Iggy says. "I eat spinach out
of a can."

Both Gilda and my mother throw open the front door
when we ring the bell. Both look as if their faces have
been dipped in white face powder.

"Which dame is this kid's mother?" Iggy asks, putting
her hand on the top of my head.

"Issa!" my mother says directly to me, "we thought
you were kidnapped."

"No such luck," Iggy says, and she laughs like Betty
Hutton, bending over and slapping her knees.

Gilda's mouth is open. Iggy says, "Close your mouth, kiddo, or flies'll get in."

Izzy pokes his mother. "Come on, Ma, tell them how we just took Issa around the block, and then you had a flat tire, and they had to tow us to Bensonhurst, where . . . "

"Yeah, well, that's what happened," Iggy says. "But it's water under the bridge, here we are, safe and sound. And Issa is fine, we took good care of her, just look at her." She pinches my cheek to prove to everyone that I'm healthy and alive.

My mother casts a withering glance upon Iggy's pink, fuzzy sweater. Then she turns her stare upon Izzy. He has a smirk on his face that thrills my entire body. My mother reaches out and pulls me into the house. She is about to slam the door when Iggy says to Gilda, "Hey, neighbor, I'm new on the block, we ought to have tea sometime."

"We ought to?" Gilda says. "You and I? My sister and I were just about to call the police."

"Good thing you didn't," she says. "Police aren't that cute. Sailors are cuter."

Again, my mother begins to close the door when my father's car pulls up at the curb. We all watch him park. He gets out with one of his usual cartons under his arm; when he sees a crowd at our front door, he grins. His pipe is angled at the corner of his mouth, he is wearing baggy pants and a big tweed jacket.

"Hey, this man is better looking than Clark Gable," Iggy says. "Which of you lucky ladies owns him?"

My father grins and when no one answers, Iggy says, "If you're not spoken for, I'll take you."

He can't help but laugh. My mother reaches out and drags him inside: "Come in, dinner is ready."

When they disappear Iggy says to Gilda: "You live in the same house with that dreamboat and he isn't yours? How do you stand it?"

Gilda stares at Iggy as if her heart has been torn open.

"Look, I think you could use a little advice. Why don't we have lunch at the Chink's on Avenue P tomorrow?" Iggy says.

"I don't know . . ."

"Issa and Izzy will be there," she says. "Right, kids?"
We nod.

"Who knows what our fortune cookies will tell us?"
Iggy says to Gilda. "See you then."

28

The Bike-Riders and I have chosen a club song; we sing it at the end of every club meeting and we sing it as we ride our bikes along the bicycle path:

> *Did you ever think when the hearse went by*
> *That you would be-e-e the next to die?*
> *They lock you up in a coffin dark*
> *And cover you over with dirt and rock . . .*
> *The worms crawl in, the worms crawl out,*
> *They crawl in your stomach and out of your*
>   *mouth . . .*

After we sing the last line, we dissolve into laughter. No sir, not us, no worms worming their way through our graceful inner parts. We're young and healthy and soon we will be called upon to exercise our baby-making machinery and the world will be made anew. Worms threaten only the old and emptied out, the ones who have no life ahead of them, like my grandmother. (But Gilda, is she useless? Is she too old to make the world anew?)

Though my plan is never to think about my grandmother, I can be hit with a thought of her, like a bullet through my temple, when I am most unguarded. The simplest act, like racing inside the house from a game of stoop ball to get to the bathroom before I lose it, can throw up a picture before my eyes of her lying twisted in her wet and bunched-up sheets in the steel bed at the nursing home. Food will do it, too; anything that won't go down my throat sends up a silent cry from my lips to her ears on Ocean Parkway, where a colored helper shoves cold oatmeal into my grandmother's slack, unprotesting mouth. But no! I have vowed not to think about her. I make myself stop. These thoughts start up a motor of violence in my body: the wheels of stomach pain begin to churn. *Don't think about it.* I don't want to, but why then does my mind turn back to my grandmother, like a hairpin seeking a magnet? Why does it secretly worm its way back in, bring up technicolor images of horror, though I haven't seen my grandmother since that first time, never go to visit her. (My mother won't let me go, and secretly, in this instance, I thank her. But why do I harbor this dangerous tendency, the hidden intention to make myself feel worse when I already feel bad?)

Gilda says almost nothing about what happens at the nursing home. She only brings up the subject when she has to discuss a medical decision or some financial matter. But today she is begging my mother to visit in her stead, to bring food to my grandmother, to feed it to her.

"Please," she says, a word not easy for her to say to my mother. "I need some time off. I have an appointment. Please will *you* go there today?" Gilda asks her favor standing on the bottom landing of the steps, not quite in our house, but not quite on her property either. She swings on the doorknob, leaning into our house and then out, like a sail blowing in the wind.

"Mama doesn't know the difference," my mother says. "It's all the same to her if you skip a day. You could skip a *month* and she wouldn't know. She's in a black hole. Besides, the smell in that place makes me puke."

"Everything makes you puke," Gilda says.

Oh! Such an ugly word. Something clutches in my bowels when I hear that word. There are words that can make me come alert like a hunting dog (*fuck* is such a word) and others that can make me shiver. *Puke* sends a shudder down my back and every hair on my body stands on end.

My mother knows about words and their power. Not just rhymes, but curses. I am grateful she has never said the word *puke* about me, not even when I have had fever and been racked with vomiting. Even the times I've been heaving and spewing out acid liquid, she has only stepped away from me and screamed for someone to bring a towel, "Hurry, Issa is throwing up!" (Of course it is always Gilda who comes, who holds my forehead, who whispers soothing assurances that soon the racking waves will be over.)

My mother hoards her ugliest words as I hoard my smiles. She waits to let them out, waits for fights, for the best moment to attack. When she's in some uncontrollable whirlpool of fury and contempt, when the world seems full of so many "nobodies" that she can't bear to live in it another minute, she lets certain words out of her mouth like snakes: *bitch* and *punk* and *lousy bastard* and *no goddamn good* and *puke*.

Today Gilda has said *puke*, but only because she is quoting my mother. My mother knows that Gilda's appointment is taking off time to have lunch at the Chink's with Iggy and Izzy. With me. She hasn't refused me, but she refuses Gilda. She will not feed my grandmother. If Gilda goes out to lunch, my grandmother won't be fed. Take it or leave it.

* * *

Gilda is sensitive about the word Chink's. She can't help it if everyone calls the Chinese restaurant "the Chink's," but we don't have to do it. Jews don't like to be called Kikes, she says, and the Chinese don't like to be called Chinks. I never heard a Jew called a Kike; this is news to me. What could it mean?

As we walk together down East 4th Street toward Avenue P (Gilda looks away as we pass Mrs. Exter's house and hurries her stride), she confides she is worried about encountering pork in the Chinese restaurant. She has not been out in the world much; she has never eaten Chinese food, though all her ladies love it, and they especially recommend egg roll.

The Chink's (see? I can't help it) is right down the street from my old ballet studio and near the movie theater. The restaurant has a brown bamboo curtain across the front window and a dusty statue of a red wooden dragon nailed over the doorway. Gilda hesitates at the entrance; she squeezes my hand. I think we both feel as if we are about to enter a forbidden world; we can sense the beyond: strange smells, a dark interior, an atmosphere of danger and excitement.

"Maybe they're not here yet," I say, and we look out into the bright sunny world of Avenue P: the passing cars, the delicatessen across the street, the dry goods store.

"They must be inside," Gilda says. "There's the red car." And, indeed, there it is, Iggy's "Lizzie," parked at the curb like a red fire truck, its top down, brazen and open to the sun. I move with Gilda toward the darkness inside, where the air turns cool, dark and foreign, but still: Izzy is inside. My sense of excitement suggests to me that we could be moving slowly toward the sun's whirling center.

*   *   *

Ivory chopsticks, hard, twig-like noodles in a white bowl, thick-lipped tea cups with thin-legged storks painted on them. Gilda sits primly beside me, against the wall, while Iggy and Izzy play a switching game with their tea cups:

"Gimme that one, mine is chipped."

"Give it back, you goose. Why should I cut my lip!"

"Why should I?"

"We could ask the waiter for another one," I venture. But mother and son are having too much fun, swinging their arms back and forth, making a racket, till Iggy cuffs Izzy on the head and says, "Shaddup or I'll take away your Betty Grable pinup and put a picture of me there instead."

Izzy pretends to throw up. Then the waiter comes to take our order.

We all agree on chicken chow mein and boiled rice; tea comes with our lunch. Izzy asks for a side order of spare ribs. I don't know if I will be able to eat whatever comes; I have trouble with food, especially if I can't tell what it is, or what's in it.

"They don't serve liver here, do they?" I ask, and Izzy thinks this is hilarious, he laughs till he slides off his seat and disappears under the table. Then he makes a grab for my legs and pretends to sob into my lap.

"Oh please, please, waiter, make us liver chow mein, it's a delicacy, we can't live without it."

Gilda sips her tea and makes a face. It has leaves, black as little flies, floating around in it.

"Up here, young man," Iggy says, and she pats his seat until he surfaces, just as the egg flower soup is served. I try mine with its little shovel-shaped spoon. It is very much like chicken soup. I am deeply relieved.

*   *   *

The restaurant is nearly empty, and while Gilda and Iggy talk, Izzy suggests we take a table of our own.

"Go ahead," Iggy says. "But don't make a mess. Have a heart; don't pour soy sauce all over the tablecloth."

Soy sauce. Izzy is at home with everything here. I have never heard of the things he extracts from the tangle of steaming food on his plate: *bok choy, bean sprouts, water chestnuts.*

Izzy holds up a small umbrella-shaped object between his chopstick.

"What's that?"

"What's *that*? You never saw a *mushroom*?"

"No."

"God, you are a peasant."

"It looks slimy."

"Taste it." He holds out his chopsticks. I don't recoil, but I hesitate. And here I am at a threshold again (will it never stop happening?)—the challenge to move into new territory, to risk my life! And indeed the thing looks dangerous: flesh-colored and slippery and oddly like . . . but no, I have never seen one, why do I have this thought.

"So if you throw up, you throw up." (He doesn't say *puke*; I am deeply relieved by that.)

I lean forward, close my eyes and open my mouth. Izzy draws his chopsticks with the thing on it in a heart-shaped line along my lips, and then lays it gently down on my tongue like an offering. I close my lips. Before I can taste it, it slides down my throat and disappears.

Izzy laughs. "Now you're poisoned. You've eaten the forbidden fruit," he says. "Now you have to leave the Garden of Eden."

"You're a lunatic," I dare to say to him. He loves that he has shocked me. But, yes, I feel the mushroom inside me, throwing sparks.

"Tell me more. What else am I?"

"I never met anyone like you."

"Good." He sits back, satisfied. "I'm one of a kind." The waiter arrives with the spare ribs.

"Have one." Izzy holds the plate out to me.

"Is this pork?"

"No, it's liver in disguise." I lift with my fingers a rib, wine-red and hot, almost sizzling, the edges are dark and look succulent.

"Bite it, Issa. Do it. You'll love it."

I take a strip of meat gingerly between my front teeth, which are small; they sink in deep.

"How is it?"

I am making my evaluation. It's sweet, it's crisp. "It's good," I say.

"It *is* pork, you know."

"So I'm ruined."

"Not really," he promises. "There's much further to go to be ruined."

* * *

Iggy makes us come back to their table for fortune cookies and tea. I know the two women have been talking the whole time. I have never seen Gilda's cheeks so red, or her eyes so brilliant.

"Issa, baby," Iggy says to me. "We're going to make a new woman out of your aunt here. We've got to get her out in the world more, take her to Coney Island, make her try pizza, drag her to a Dodgers game."

Gilda laughs, looking down at her plate.

On the wall above our table is a small painted lamp, unlit, covered by a milky glass tube. The picture is of a delicate Chinese girl in pink silk robes, holding a parasol. I notice a black ridged switch at the bottom of the lamp; I reach to turn on the light.

A bolt shoots through me, so sudden, so hot, so shocking, that I gasp, leap up, and begin to dance wildly. My fingertips are quivering.

"What is it? Did you get a shock?" Gilda cries out.

"Bad wiring," Iggy says. "This place is a dump."

Gilda puts her arms around me. She is trembling.

"She's okay," Iggy says. "Relax."

"I would kill myself if anything happened to her," Gilda says. She covers my face with kisses.

Izzy says "Maybe it's just a message from God telling her not to eat pork."

Gilda throws a look at her plate, which has remnants of meat on it. Izzy is still laughing; he doesn't know about the ball of lightning that was aimed at my mother as she cooked bacon. He has no humility in him, but now that I, too, have been electrified, I feel I have been given a warning.

29

Polio lives, a wide green bug with blinking red eyes. It hides beneath the iron grates of the drinking fountains at the park, in the silver sprinklers of wading pools, on the rims of cups in restaurants, on the headrests at the movie theater. If you inhale deeply, it can ride into your lungs on a single breath, splash up from the toilet at school, enter your nose if you lean down to smell a rose. No form of "be careful" has ever been like this, no warning to watch out for cars, for wild dogs, for bad boys, for bullies, has ever had this edge of hysteria to it.

No. No. No. Not only is "no" the twenty-four-hour song in *my* ears, but The Skaters hear it, the Girl Scouts hear it, the listeners to radio hear it. *"No"* is affixed to the sky above us like sky-writing. No wind blurs or blows it away.

Esther Tempkin, a fellow Girl Scout whose father is a doctor, distributes special cotton masks at our Girl Scout meeting and warns us to wear them if we have to go on the subway, the trolley or into crowded waiting rooms at the dentist's or doctor's office. Her father has seen "terrible cases" she warns us—at the first sign of a sore throat or a stiff neck, we must rush to the doctor. She waggles her tongue in her mouth and rolls her eyes in her head to show what it will be like if we don't take care. She's a beautiful girl: red-haired and luscious-looking, though not a tramp at all (The Bike-Riders and I have discussed this). She has "developed" but wears loose blouses and big sweaters. She has been the first in our troop to see blood—we regard her as a successful warrior queen. She has seen blood and she has survived.

After her demonstration about how we are to wear the cotton masks, she invites us all to her house Tuesday night to watch "The Milton Berle Show."

"Isn't that going into a crowd?" a Scout asks.

"People you are with regularly are not a threat," Esther says, quoting her father. "It's strangers! Watch out for strangers!"

* * *

Television, though we have all seen it, still seems a miracle. Milton Berle is a legend—a man who wears a dress and lipstick. Esther Tempkin has told us that at her house they have placed a magnifier over the screen to make the picture bigger. I know what that means: Dr. Tempkin is rich—all doctors are rich.

My mother says she could have married a doctor. She tells this to my father when they are arguing about whether or not I can go to Esther's house. My father thinks I should not go: the doctor has his office in the downstairs of the house—and is not a doctor's office the most dangerous place to go? But my mother says a doctor knows what precautions to take. She wants me to see what a doctor's house is like. She wants me to keep these matters in mind when it's time for me to marry.

She also reminds my father she could have married a lawyer. Before she met my father, when she worked as a legal secretary in Manhattan, she met "all kinds of important men who wanted to marry me." I don't know what she expects him to do when she says these things to him. What can he do? He isn't a doctor. He isn't a lawyer. Perhaps she is saying these things for my benefit: if she had married a doctor, then *I* would have a television. If she had married a doctor, then *I* would be the one giving out cotton masks and have special information to protect my friends from the red-eyed glare of the polio bug.

We are sitting on the new rattan furniture when my mother makes her "could have married a doctor" speech. I now think of the talks with my father as speeches because the two of them don't exchange words; she lectures, he listens.

The Screamer has other matters to attend to. She's much bigger now, The Screamer/my sister, with her straight, neat hair, always with her head down over some jigsaw puzzle or follow-the-dot book, or coloring book, or cut-out book. She's of no interest to me, I ignore her, or I blame her if I can, or I mess up her dolls-of-foreign-lands collection—I do whatever I can to make it hard for her. I would be happier without her, but she's here forever. I am trying to learn not to spend all my time trying to understand why what's here forever is here, or what's gone forever is gone—just as I don't think, if I can help it, about my grandmother. There are just certain rules that are permanent. You can't cry or whine to change them, you can't kick or hit, you can't beg or plead, you can't sulk or vomit. The things that won't change sit there like a brick wall: they don't hear you, they don't move, they don't go away, they don't change.

But my mother and father *do* change. Could they also go away? From each other? From me?

My mother has a new hairdo; though Gilda knows every style and how to make it, my mother announced that she was going to a beauty shop on Avenue P to have it done: an upsweep, with many hairpins to hold the hair, swirled into a roll, against her scalp. Without hair around her face, loose and white, she looks narrow and thin; her skin looks tight, as if hairpins are also holding it stretched. Her mouth stretches over her big, unreal teeth. She has new clothes now, too—I don't remember much about her old clothes, but the new ones are silky and fancy, pale gray with weeping willows imprinted on them, or white, with the silhouettes of black panthers standing out. She wears high heels and nylons these days because the decorator who came to do the house wore high heels and told my mother her legs would look good in them.

I have to be careful with the rattan furniture; if I am nervous, and pull at the splinters that stick out, I can bring the whole couch down to the floor. I am warned. My mother warns me every day. So instead of picking at the splinters, I pick at the dry skin of my lips. If I peel off one layer of my delicate flesh, very slowly, my lips turn red. They look as if they have lipstick on them. The main problem is drinking orange juice. Then my lips burn as if I am dipping them into liquid fire.

"I want Issa to see what a doctor's house has in it," my mother says. "I want her to see what kind of furniture they have, what kind of dishes they have, what kind of silverware they have. She has a right to know what's out there in the world."

My father, smoking his pipe, picks at rattan splinters at the edge of his chair. His curly dark hair has gone a little flat, and his thick, strong fingers are flat out on his thighs. My father seems flattened. It's strange, but there seems to be less of him, although he hasn't gotten thinner or smaller.

He works as hard as ever; longer hours, more days. The antique store is open on Saturdays, now. And he goes on calls to buy new antiques every night. The women at our house no longer worry at the window that—because he is late—someone has tried to rob him or murder him. There *are* no women anymore to stand at the window and watch for his car to pull up at the curb. My sister is busy with her puzzles and dolls, my mother is busy with her furniture catalogs and clothing magazines, Gilda is alone upstairs, and my grandmother is not at any window anywhere. Even I myself no longer worry about my father now. Some things can't be influenced, no matter what I do.

"So, *let* her go to see Milton Berle, *let* her go to see a doctor's house," my father says. He picks up the newspaper. My mother picks up her fashion magazine. My sister

moves her bride doll and her bridegroom doll into position on the living room floor for yet another of their wedding ceremonies.

* * *

Some of the Girl Scouts in my troop know by heart the
opening song of "The Milton Berle Show" sung by the
men who come out on stage in mechanics' uniforms:

> *We are the men of Texaco*
> *We work from Maine to Mexico,*
> *There's nothing like this Tex-a-co of ours . . .*
> *Our show tonight is powerful,*
> *We'll wow you with an hourful*
> *Of showers from a showerful of stars . . .*
> *We're the merry Tex-a-co men—*
> *Tonight we may be show-men—*
> *Tomorrow we'll be servicing your cars!*

I settle back against the soft cushions of the couch. So:
this is a doctor's house. It isn't so fancy. The medical
examining rooms are downstairs, and Dr. Tempkin and
his family live upstairs. He has a side door in the alley just
like Gilda's, with a side-stoop, and a separate doorbell.
It's true that in the center of his front garden—where, at
our house, we have only a lilac tree—the doctor has a
mirrored ball resting on a tall marble pillar. *That's* fancy.
But after all, his patients need to know how to find his
house. That mirrored ball must shine very brightly in the
sunshine. The sickest person in the world, rushing along
Ocean Parkway in pain, would see the rainbow beams
fired off that mirrored ball.

I try to observe the doctor's house the way my mother
would look at it. Our Girl Scout troop members are
sprawled on the furniture in a way that would not please
my mother—but Mrs. Tempkin seems not to mind. Esther
is a beautiful hostess, wearing a flower-barrette in her
brilliant red hair, wearing a flowered apron, helping her

mother pass around trays of brownies and special paper cups full of malted milkshakes. In the dimness of the kitchen lurks the famous doctor; he is short, bald, with glasses. His name is Dr. Ruby Tempkin. He has the name of a jewel.

I am grateful for the luxury of the paper cups: they are for safety from the polio germ.

Mrs. Gargano, one of our leaders, tells us not to be shocked if Milton Berle comes out on stage wearing a dress. "Men do that for a joke, you know," she says, and we all laugh nervously. My father would never wear a dress, not for a joke, not for any reason. I think of all the fathers of my friends that I know: they would not wear dresses, either. (But I am eager to wear boys' clothes. I already do, when I put on my dungarees. They have the zipper on the side, because no girl would wear pants with a fly, but from a distance they do look like boys' pants. They look tough. They look handsome.)

And suddenly, there he is, the famous Milton Berle, with a dress, lipstick, a curly wig, a cigar—what an imbecile. Everyone is laughing. I don't think it's funny, really— I think it's stupid. I look around at the lit up faces of my friends, my clubmates and my Girl Scout buddies. We are all watching a little round screen through a sheet of magnifying glass; we are all watching the figure of a man dressed like a woman, with his hairy legs showing, dancing around.

There's a sense of comfort in being in a big friendly crowd of people I know, a sense of safety and good cheer, but it also feels flat and unreal to me; something inside me withdraws, backs up like a turtle pulling deep into his shell, I can almost feel my skin telescoping like a turtle's neck. I go back to a place in my mind that is deeply familiar and most comfortable: to thoughts of the pile of books beside my bed I wish I were reading, to thoughts about my mother's new hairdo and what it means, to thoughts about Izzy and how I can't wait to see him again, and to thoughts about my grandmother, knotted in the trap of her wet sheets, helpless . . .

But laughter from the world recalls me, I force my tur-tle-head out of its shell. Reluctantly, I come back to the doctor's living room, I come back to Milton Berle telling a joke and pursing his lips, I come back to my milkshake, my brownie, to the vision of the little clump of blue flow-ers on the barrette in Esther's red hair.

* * *

As we are leaving, I see Mrs. Tempkin pursing her lips against Esther's forehead, a gesture I think is strange. *She's* not going anywhere, this is her home, why kiss her goodbye?

The rest of us circle about in a commotion of leaving, saying thank you, waving to one another, accepting an extra brownie to take home. As we go out into the night, I see the mirrored ball reflecting the moon, big and brilliant as the sun. And from behind it, or under it, or over it—it's hard to tell which—the mirror throws off dull bits of starlight, like chips of broken glass.

My mother wants me to look at what they have here, and so I do. It's true, we have no starry night in slivered glass at our house, we have nothing of this kind at all.

* * *

Two days later our troop leader calls to say that Esther is in an iron lung, a cocoon that breathes for her. That the fever and stiff neck struck her the night we saw Milton Berle, that her legs were paralyzed within a few hours. That she can't breathe by herself and can't move. That if we still have the brownie that was given to us to take home, we must flush it away.

My mother's voice when she sets down the phone is pure quivering panic. Not sympathy. Just fury and panic.

Without asking permission, without telling her where I'm going, I dash out front with my bicycle and ride down East 4th Street to the playground. The vast concrete city is deserted because children are forbidden to come here. I have the entire place to myself. I walk my bike from place to place, examining the silver spout of the drinking fountain, the seesaws (where strangers play), the monkey bars (where strangers climb), and even the spigots of the wading pool, though no spray is coming from them: the pool is dry.

I am looking for the enemy: the wide green bug with blinking red eyes.

An old woman in a black cape, carrying shopping bags from the shops on Avenue P comes walking through the playground very slowly. She doesn't know me, I am sure, but she walks right toward me. Her ankles are thick, her shoes are heavy and black, laced tight. She has a black babushka tied under her chin. She comes right toward me as if she were supposed to meet me here, and she says to me, "I have something for you." She takes an object tied on a string from around her neck and she comes right up to me and places the circle over my head like a necklace. The thing tied to the string smells like mothballs. My eyes burn as the fumes rise up.

"Wear it," she says. "Don't take it off till the winter. And go home from this place."

I ride home as fast as I can. I am shaking and my teeth are chattering. When I get in the door, my mother is holding the phone away from her body. She looks wild, almost insane.

"Esther is dead," she says to me. "And with a doctor right there."

CHAPTER

30

On my bed are two cushions Gilda has embroidered for me with famous sayings:

Be good, sweet maid, and let who will be clever.

Her voice was ever soft, gentle, and low,
An excellent thing in woman.

When Izzy and Iggy come to pick us up for a Dodgers game, they step into my front porch bedroom and Iggy lets out a howl.

"Who in holy heaven gave these to you?"

"Gilda made them."

"Hey, Gilda, come in here—do you want to ruin this kid?" she yells at Gilda, who is standing outside, waiting for us.

Gilda comes up the front steps and ventures into the house, but hesitantly. She never comes in without an invitation, but my mother and The Screamer aren't home—they have gone to buy my sister tap dance shoes. My father is at the store. My dog, forever banished from the house now that it's so elegantly furnished, howls his endless siren of neglect from the back porch.

Iggy tosses the pillows over so only their blank backs

show. "You have to give up this baloney," she says to Gilda. "If anything, you should be teaching Issa to be as clever as she can be! As loud as she has to be to make herself heard! Forget about being a lady in lace collars, sweet patootie. That's rule number one in our making you into a new woman."

This is not the first I have heard of this—their making Gilda into a new woman—and lately I have seen signs of it. Gilda has begun doing her fingernails with red polish instead of colorless. She has begun to wear various bright-colored silk flowers bobbie-pinned into her hair. She has abandoned all her solid laced-up beauty-parlor work shoes and is now wearing pointy-toed embossed leather pumps. Her clothes have changed, too: cotton house dresses and gray cardigans have made way for two-piece suits with peplum jackets and slits in the narrow skirts. Even today, Gilda is wearing to match her suit a large wavy-brimmed hat that covers half her face. Her lips are glowing red and shapely and the curve of her chin is graceful. Her skin is shadowed, blurred in its details, its scars almost unnoticeable.

Iggy says, "Next we'll remake Issa!"

"Issa is great the way she is," Izzy says. He looks me over and I'm ready for it. I'm wearing my dungarees and penny loafers and a red plaid man's shirt. If I keep my mouth shut and thus force my small teeth into the background, I look pretty impressive.

* * *

Iggy drives fast, with the top down, toward Ebbets Field. She makes one stop, at the rest home, so Gilda can drop off a jar of gefilte fish for someone to feed to my grandmother. Gilda teeters in on her delicate high heels, wearing her glamorous hat, and indicates by a wave she will be only a few seconds.

Iggy begins to sing: "Take me out to the ball game, take me out with the crowd, buy me some peanuts and *Cracker Jacks*, I don't care if I never get back . . ."

Izzy is doing something to me in the back seat; he's pretending to teach me how to crack my knuckles, but instead he's just folding my fingers back and forth, rolling them in a gentle, tender rhythm that relays itself in waves up my arm and in arrows of heat to the deep center of my body.

I don't care if we never get to the ball game. I don't know why the world loves baseball so much; especially men. (Iggy loves it like a man.) Teams playing against one another are like countries at war: they have to hate the others because they have to love themselves, and that's reason enough for them to want to wipe the others out, to kill. They do whatever they have to do to get the right feeling.

Gilda is taking a long, long time. Iggy gets tired of singing.

"Wait here, kids," she tells us. "I'll go get that slow poke out of there."

But she doesn't come out, either. It's getting hot with the top down, Izzy wants to go into the rest home to get them.

"Come on," he says. "Or we'll be late for the game."

"You don't want to go in there." A buzzing has started in my head and is growing louder, as if a swarm of bees is crawling in through my ears. "I can't go in." I have the oddest thought in my head: that if I wear my favorite clothes into that building, my dungarees and my man's shirt, and my best penny loafers, they will be ruined forever. I have such fear of what is inside those walls: I will see what is to become of me.

"Then I'll go myself," and, in a blink, Izzy is out of the car and up the steps of the rest home. He disappears inside. Now I am *really* afraid. I'm alone in a red convertible, and although I thought I was on my way to a great adventure, a long ball game, hours of sitting and letting Izzy play games with my fingers, I am now staring at the door of a house of skeletons.

I let out a single sob, a kind of practice cry for whatever is going on, the horror I will soon be shown.

* * *

I don't know if it's a half-hour or an hour later: I have been sitting at the wheel of the car and pretending to drive. I drive myself to Florida, it so happens, and I am back on the beach gathering coconuts. My mother is not with me, so the soldiers have only me to admire. Only me to give chocolate bars to, only me to applaud. This is a technique I learned in kindergarten: put yourself somewhere else when you don't want to be where you have to be. It's not easy, holding onto that wheel and keeping the car going to Florida when in truth you're bouncing over craters and caverns in the road and the wheel is being wrenched out of your hands. When in truth the front door of the rest home is waiting to suck you inside and throw you to the wild animals. *Look over here*, it keeps saying, but I won't. I'm going in another direction. To the sunshine, to the ocean, to the admiration of an army; if, in fact, not to the Dodgers game.

But louder than my thoughts is the siren of an ambulance. It's pulling up right behind me, a bulbous white truck with signs and symbols on it denoting the battle against death.

"Hey-Issa, Hey-Issa," is what I hear from the front porch of the rest home, the sound of a snake hissing my name, and there is Izzy, holding open the screen door of the building, and now here comes Iggy and Gilda, out the door while the ambulance men run in with their stretcher.

"It's your grandmother," Izzy says, letting go of the screen door and running to the car. He opens the driver's door and lets me out. "She was bleeding from the mouth."

No. I won't hear about it. I won't think about it. They can't make me take this in and picture it, feel it, remember it forever with all the other things I have had to bury under the sand, deep under, under sand that's wet and further buried under sand that's dry.

"Don't tell me, Izzy."

But he doesn't have to. Because now I see what I have avoided the sight of—for how many years? Now it's inescapable. She's coming out, feet first on the stretcher, a limp helpless lump of the human being I used to love, and blood is on her chin, on her gown, on her tangled sheets.

I don't want to see her face, but my eyes are drawn to it with an enormous force. I pray she won't be looking, that if she is, she can't see, that if she sees, she won't know me.

But she does. She knows me. Her eyes rivet themselves to mine and hold there as she is moved past me.

"Grandma!"

She cranes her neck to watch me as they carry her away, into the back of the ambulance. So she isn't unaware, she isn't unconscious, insane, gone out. She isn't—as I have fooled myself into believing—not there. The only truth is that she cannot move and she cannot talk. But she is there and she has been there every single day and night that I have *not* been there, she has been strapped into that bed for all the time I've been riding my bike, dreaming my dreams, kissing Beloved, playing stoop ball with Izzy, licking ice cream cones, watching Milton Berle. I have only had to wait a half-hour in a hot car in a state of fear and uncertainty, and she has been waiting for the torture to break and for the fear to relent for almost forever!

"Grandma!"

They are closing her into the ambulance and I am leaning against a square post on the porch of the rest home and sobbing. I am punching the wooden post with my fist, I am trying to bite the wooden post with my tiny, worthless, hideous, weak, ugly teeth.

"Take her home, Izzy," Iggy tells her son, and then they are gone, the ambulance is gone, and Iggy's red car, with Gilda in it, is following along behind.

We are only a few blocks from home. Izzy pulls me along. I see the sun glinting off the points of the gilded poles separating the bicycle path from the benches on Ocean Parkway. I want to fling myself on one of those golden spears. I want to, I will!

But Izzy keeps both arms around me, to hold me up, to keep me going. "She's old, Issa," he whispers. "You're not old."

"But I will be," I say. "And so will you. And you know it."

The Skaters who became The Bike-Riders have now become The Cookers/Sewers and I am one of them. A contest at P.S. 238 has pitted our homemaking class, led by Miss Thomas, against the class led by Mrs. Slutzkin. There will be two weeks of preparation of cooking and sewing at home and in school, at the end of which the two classes will present their delicacies to our principal, Mr. Hunt, for a taste-test, and our sewing creations to his wife, Mrs. Hunt, for a judgment by her expert eye.

I have been required to write down the Safety Rules of the Kitchen in my Homemaking Notebook, on whose brown cover some other rules are listed. Four boys on the cover (one of them a colored boy) stand behind a fence holding baseball bats and mitts. The words over their heads are, "What's his race or religion got to do with it . . . HE CAN *PITCH!*" Nailed to the fence is an admonition to me telling me what I can do:

1. ACCEPT or reject people on their *individual worth*.

2. SPEAK UP wherever we are, at home, in business, in our school, labor, church or social groups, *against* prejudice, *for* understanding.

3. DON'T LISTEN to, or spread, rumors against a race, or a religion. Remember—*that's being an American!*

Rules are overtaking me; we are bombarded with them,

must know them, be able to recite them, be ready to be tested on them, and the main way to guarantee this is to have us write them down. Our time in school is primarily spent writing down all the rules:

1. Each girl must have a potholder when handling hot pans and dishes.
2. Water spilt on the floor must be wiped up with newspaper.
3. Stools must be placed under the table or under the sink when not in use.
4. If you injure yourself in any way, tell Miss Thomas immediately.
5. Always be careful when striking matches.
6. Never light the gas without permission.
7. Long hair must be braided or tied back off the shoulders to prevent catching fire and for sanitary reasons.
8. Please do not wear sweaters or long sleeves for your own safety and comfort.

It seems to me that every one of those rules is just a result of common sense. Couldn't they trust me to figure it out for myself?

Miss Thomas's *essential* requirement for planning a meal is the writing down of all the details that have to be remembered and attended to:

1. Count up the number of people being served.
2. Write down each course of the menu in detail.
3. List the exact amount of food to be prepared.
4. Enumerate needs for table setting, including cups, sherbet glasses, water glasses, spoons, forks, knives, saucers, small plates, large plates, table decoration, napkins, tablecloth, doilies, salt, pepper.

I am against all this. The formalities sap my energies. Don't they know I have a brain and can remember that plates have to be set on the table before food can be served? That if I am cooking Stuffed Norwegian Prune Salad and Puffed Rice Balls, I will need to have prunes and puffed rice ready to use?

Still, recipes are dictated to us hour after hour, and we dutifully bend our heads and take them down. All across the home ec room I see a sea of heads with neat parts in their hair bending over their notebooks. I yawn and write, yawn and write: *wash prunes thoroughly, steam prunes until tender, remove the prune stones, fill the hollow prune with peanut butter, or other prunes. Press the prunes into shape and roll them in granulated sugar. Arrange prunes like a flower in plate. Place cream cheese into center prune and serve prunes proudly. Show that you are proud of your prunes.*

If this is what I will have to do when I get married, I am worried whether or not I will be able to bear marriage. Marriage to Izzy, as I imagine it, doesn't seem to include either prunes or dictation. What would we two do if married? Play Old Maid, crack our knuckles, play stoop ball, eat licorice whips and drink egg creams, touch each other (accidentally and on purpose), go to Coney Island and live in the fun house, travel on the bumper cars, ride the steeplechase, plunge from the parachute jump.

But we can't do any of this, even before we are married, because I am committed to the Homemaking Contest. I have to stay home and make vegetable chowder, baking powder biscuits, Spanish rice, scalloped fish, peanut brittle and cinnamon toast. I have to be prepared, if asked, to recite from memory all ingredients and methods of preparation. When I'm not cooking, I have to be sewing. Our teacher has taught us to perform the hemstitch on white muslin, overcasting on unbleached muslin, gathering on white cotton, tucking on a ruffle, darning on scrim, darning on cashmere, and darning on stockinet, catch stitching on flannel, overhand stitching on French linen, and slip stitching on silk. In my sewing notebook, called "Plain Sewing," I have pinned in little squares of material demonstrating each of these stitches, one to a page. If this is plain sewing, I wonder, then, what is *fancy* sewing?

At our house, my mother never sews, but Gilda is permitted to darn my father's socks. He goes upstairs once a month (I have to accompany him) and tries on all the socks she has mended for him. There is a ritual to this: my father and I sit on the couch and Gilda sits at her desk (its top is covered by a green paper blotter) under the light of a floor lamp, and she hands him each sock, one by one. He peels off one of the socks he is wearing, usually the one on his left foot, and pulls on the mended sock. If it is lumpy, he strips it off and hands it back to Gilda who slides it onto the smooth round surface of the wooden darning egg she holds by a graceful handle and pounds it with the pocked surface of her silver thimble. Then she hands it back to my father. He puts it back on his foot.

His toes are long and hairy; his big toe is enormous, and the others are fitted against one another as if they are paired for sleeping cuddled together. There are some blue veins on his ankles; without his sock on, his foot has the look of a pale, unprotected primitive animal.

Tonight there is a particularly lumpy bulge at the tip of the big toe where Gilda has darned a large hole. My father tries on the sock and takes it off several times, each time handing it to Gilda to pound it further. He begins to laugh as she taps her thimble fiercely on the darning egg; the wood of the egg is golden brown and smoother than marble. She looks up and laughs at what he must be seeing. She taps again, then hands the egg to my father so he can use his greater strength. She offers him the thimble, but he can't get it on—not even on his pinky. They are both laughing. She works on it further and then it's time for him to try the sock on again. When she hands the sock back to him, he looks helpless, so she gets down on her knees at his feet, props his foot on her thigh and slides the navy blue cloth gently on at the toes, then slowly smooths the cloth up over his heel and ankle. She pulls it halfway up his calf so that her hands disappear under his trousers.

"How's that?" she says, keeping her head bowed. Under the light of the floor lamp, her hair glows auburn, almost aflame.

My father wiggles his toes. "Still a little lumpy in there, I think." He holds out his foot to her, and she takes his big toe between her fingers. She massages his toe.

"That feels pretty smooth to me," she says.

"No, it's still got a ridge there."

"I never said I could make it perfect," Gilda says. "Maybe you'll just have to throw this sock out."

"That's what *she* says," my father says. "Throw them all out and buy new ones."

"You could," Gilda says.

"But then I couldn't come up here," my father says. They both look at me. Then he says, "Shouldn't you be downstairs cooking vanilla cornstarch pudding tonight for your contest?"

"No, candied sweet potatoes," I correct him.

"You better get busy."

As I get up to leave, my father rises also. Gilda goes down the hall and gets her coat from the hall closet.

"Do you want me to drive you to the hospital?" he asks. "She couldn't complain about that."

"That's okay, Iggy is picking me up."

* * *

I haven't asked and they haven't said anything about my grandmother. She's just in the hospital, she's been there for three weeks. They don't trouble me with news of her because they know I'm so busy cooking and sewing. I am sewing my public project for Mrs. Hunt to judge (it's an embroidered dishcloth) and a private project for myself (a satin brassiere, which I can't get right.) I have cut out two circles of pink satin, using my compass to guide me, but a circle is flat, and I don't know how to get the slight cupping I need for my nipples. That's all I have: nipples. And barely raised. Nothing else around them has grown and they, themselves, are infinitesimal, nearly invisible. But a flat circle won't do. (I sew this private part of my project carefully locked in the bathroom.)

* * *

All week long I am allowed to stay up late to plan my imaginary menu for the imaginary major dinner party that I am required to invent for my home economics notebook. Tonight they absolutely don't want me to stay up late: something strange is in the air. No one talks during dinner, except The Screamer, who babbles on about some nonsense, but my mother and father keep their heads down and eat their food without looking up. I wonder if they have had another fight. But I don't wonder long. I can't be bothered. I have myself to think about.

Once I get into bed, I carry a flashlight under my blanket so I can work on my project without waking The Screamer, who has fallen asleep while forcing her dolls to talk to one another. They both talk just like her, even the bridegroom.

I can see her neat straight hair on the pillow of the bed that is catty-cornered to mine. My eyes linger on her head for a few seconds, wondering who she is, what her life could possibly be like, how she came to be so closely associated with me when I don't know her or care about her at all.

I am restless: in my home ec notebook I write down tapioca pudding for dessert, and note beside it that "Tapioca is made from the juice of the cassava tree, which is one of several tropical-American shrubs or herbs of the spurge family." Is it a shrub or is it a herb? What is the spurge family? (The information is in my notebook, from something Miss Thomas said.)

Never mind the menu. I fish under my bed for my Slam Book, which is a secret book that I passed around in seventh grade to other girls, who write down secrets like their "Best Song," "Best Actress," "Best Friend," and most important, "Remarks and Comments." I read my last year's entry, which indicated that my favorite song was "Buttons and Bows," my favorite actress Esther Williams, my favorite movie *Luxury Liner*, my best friend: "There is no such thing as a true friend." (I probably hadn't met Izzy yet.)

I notice that I must have had my father fill out a page:

his best song was "I'm Looking Over a Four-Leaf Clover," his best actress was Bette Davis and worst actress Mae West, best actor Gary Cooper and worst actor Eddie Cantor, best movie *It Happened One Night*, and under comments he wrote, "Other good songs are 'Offen prepachick brent a fierl' and 'I Wish I Was in Dixie.'" Under best friend, he wrote, "Gilda," and added, "because she makes such good mandelbrot."

Burn this, I thought. If my mother ever sees it, she will go mad. Lately whenever my father praises Gilda for anything at all, even just for her good mending of his socks, my mother says, "She's got you completely fooled. She's evil. She's a cat with velvet claws."

I slip the Slam Book far and deep under my bed and switch off my flashlight.

Just as I am falling asleep, I hear a tapping at the window over my head. My heart nearly stops. The man who used to stare in my nine windows hasn't come for a very long time. I am afraid to look, afraid of what is there now, and whose face he wears.

I keep my neck rigid, I don't move at all. Fear again. Just when a moment arrives that I am almost able to bat fear away, ignore polio, ignore bombs, forget pain, concentrate on tapioca, a whirlwind of it takes me unaware and I feel the spin begin.

The tapping continues, turns into the tattoo of "Shave and a haircut, shampoo," and I leap up and see Izzy's face pressing against the glass. He must be standing on the bench in the front garden. He places his finger to his lips and points to the front door. Down beneath him, in the faint glow of moonlight, I see the outline of his bicycle.

Fear disappears. He has come to delight me. To challenge my adherence to rules. He wants me to forget rules. His tapping on the window is my invitation and my dare.

And so I do the forbidden thing: I unlock and unbolt and unchain the front door to my house and to my bedroom. In my nightclothes, with my hair wild from the pillow, I invite Izzy in.

CHAPTER
32

Being in a dark room with a man has its own essence; I am as electric as if a ball of lightning is in the room with us. Izzy and I cover our heads with my blanket, to cushion our whispers and to enhance the thrill of our collusion. (We have an enemy to watch out for; the sister/Screamer can't be trusted, though I know she tends to sleep heavily, stupidly, like the thick-skinned lump that she is.)

"What? What? Why are you here?" I demand of him. I think it's some great, wild idea he's had, sneaking out of his house, riding his bike over the bumps of the sidewalk in the dead of night, feeling his rubber tires knit the old, crooked cracks into a freeway of adventure.

"I have bad news," he whispers. "The worst."

"The *worst?*" The worst, as I understand it, is *dead*, but who could be dead? His worst would be his mother, my worst would be my dog. *"Who?"*

"Your grandmother!"

"My grandmother?"

"Dead," he says. "I saw her myself, in her coffin."

"You saw her?"

"This morning. In the funeral home."

I can't take this into my mind. Scenes of the day flash by and I find nothing out of the ordinary: my hours in school, coming home, Gilda upstairs, my mother downstairs, milk and cookies, my practicing the complicated performance of making Stuffed Norwegian Prune Salad, the oil burner man coming to fill the tank in the basement.

My mind circles these events—is this a "find the mistake in the picture" puzzle?—and comes to rest on the snake of the oilman's black rubber hose, as if it must contain the clue to Izzy's bombshell.

I see it, both in recent memory and in conjunction with all the years I have witnessed the ritual: the unwinding of the thick black snake from the coils rolled in the oil truck, the dragging of the great tube up the front walkway, the turn around the stoop as it's tugged and twisted into an unnatural right angle, the scraping-jerk of it up the long alley and into the opening of the low cellar window.

"You have to believe me. She's really dead," Izzy is pleading. "I saw her myself."

But I can't talk to him now, not while I'm following the progress of the hose as it's pushed into the slit of the cellar window; not while I'm feeling the uneasy thrill of witnessing this bizarre, allowable penetration into my house, the entry of this awesome object through the cellar window (also the place through which I imagine bad men must enter if they are to get to me, the way all nine men looking in all my nine windows will someday attack me).

The oil man is always ragged and smeared with black, his face is black, his hands are black, he's dirty, and smells of rancid oil, he's never the same man but always looks the same, and he pushes that huge black cylinder into the secret opening of my house and pumps the dangerous, flammable oil into the waiting mouth of the oil tank.

"She looked like a ghost," Izzy says.

The enormous oil tank rests like a submarine beside the green monster of the oil burner which, each morning, belches steam up from its pipes and rattles the bones of the house.

"There was white powder on her face," Izzy says, talking so close to my ear that he blows my hair deep into its opening and I shake with a chill. I fend him off for the

moment while I consider how *long* it takes for the oil to
be pumped in! How impressed I am by the simultaneous
emptying of one vessel and the filling of another. And
always, as accompaniment, I hear the steady whirring
noise, the low thrumming vibration traveling from the
truck at the curb along the length of the house, into the
window, down to the cellar floor, into the hole in the oil
tank.

Sometimes I watch from the alley, sometimes I go down
into the cellar to see the needle of the gauge rise from
Empty to Full, moving like the single hand of a clock that
travels from the start of the universe to the end of time.

The black hose pulses and shivers; if I touch it, the rubber is hot and moves like a stream of black lava under my
hand. The man with the black face stands holding the
hose at his pelvis, staring down into the cellar window to
see the gauge on the tank, and watching me, if I am down
there.

I was down there today, putting soap powder into the
Bendix for my mother, while the black thing unloaded its
stuff, jerked and convulsed and leaked a few drops of
thick oil under the tank.

"I actually touched her face," Izzy insists. "It was ice
cold."

"Nothing bad happened here today!" I blow the words
at him. He blinks his eyes at the blast. "No one died
today. Only the oil man came."

"Your mother didn't want anyone to tell you," Izzy
says to me. "I heard my mother talking on the phone to
Gilda about it. Your mother wants you to win some kind
of cooking contest at school and she didn't want this to
upset you. She warned Gilda not to tell you, *or else*. She
said it wasn't important enough."

"But prunes!" I say. "How important are prunes?"

"I told them you *have* to know. I told them at the
funeral home this morning. I told them you should be at
the funeral tomorrow, but they're going to send you to
school like today and go without you. That's why I came
over here tonight."

I consider Izzy now, under the blanket. Is he a liar? Is he an enemy? If he is not my enemy, then my family is the enemy.

"They would *never* not tell me!" I scream out suddenly. "She's MY GRANDMOTHER!"

My scream wakes The Screamer, who also screams, which is her automatic response to everything.

And then we hear the steps of my father approaching the bedroom, the steps of a giant who shakes the walls with the force of his heavy steps. He flicks on the switch and blasts our eyes open in a flare of orange light.

"What's going on here?" he roars as he takes in the scene before him: Issa, his daughter, in bed, under a blanket, with a man.

* * *

They try to explain it away: my mother and father babbling, outdoing each other in their desperation to make it seem fair, myself screaming back, Izzy defending himself and close to tears. Gilda running downstairs to see what's wrong. Izzy's mother is called to come and take him away, he is castigated and shouted down, *"You had no goddamn business telling her*, you little bastard,"—(my mother is not hoarding her bad words)— their miserable excuses are prying out my eyes, coming at me like arrows, *"We wanted to protect you, no need to disturb you, Grandma was old and wanted to die, she wouldn't have wanted to ruin your winning the cooking contest."* Prunes, they're talking about prunes, and they don't know in the slightest how happy I am, that Grandma can't shame me any more by a look from her eyes, that she is free of her tangled sheets and her twisted limbs, free of her pain and free of her brain that knew everything but could not get her any peace.

* * *

When I look into her coffin the next day at the funeral

parlor (I have screamed that I must see her or I will kill everyone), I assure myself that she is gone, that the life has been vacuumed out of her, that wherever she is, she's not in her ruined costume of a body. Then I run into the bathroom and kiss my own arms, from the wrists to the elbows, up and down, big wet kisses begging my body to keep me in it, that I have a long way to go, that I can't go anywhere without it.

And while I am kissing myself, I go into the toilet cubicle to pee, and I see my first blood. Oh good, it is a sign, I will get my life as promised, I have all those things to do ahead of me, a boyfriend and marriage and menus and table settings—a thousand years before I come to this moment in my own coffin that my grandmother is having in hers.

I come out, trying not to smile. Toilet paper is stuffed in my underpants, and I let them take me to the funeral, to the deadly digging of dirt and burial, to the boring drone of the Hebrew prayers said by an old and bearded creature of a synagogue, I let them comfort me and kiss my brow and smooth the hair out of my eyes, I let them think whatever they think about how my chances for the contest are ruined, but I am really so happy, I am free of my grandmother's heartbreaking glance forever, and I have blood in my pants, and Izzy is not my enemy, he is home with his mother who is taking care of The Screamer, and he is waiting for me.

CHAPTER

33

No sooner does one major event fade out behind me than another looms ahead. I mark my growing up by the dangerous adventures I have survived: the necessity of going to kindergarten, the irreversible arrival of The Screamer, the division of my house into two houses, the sinister ambush-plans of the polio bug, and, most recently, the putting underground of my grandmother. But now there is something unexpected and enormous raising its teeth at me: my mother wants to sell the house and take us away to Florida! (Gilda doesn't know yet and I am forbidden to tell her. We are to pretend that nothing is in the air; we are waiting for Florida newspapers to arrive that will tell us what houses cost in Miami Beach.)

I don't know what to make of this new development. No one asks my opinion. In some important way my life feels exactly like the song we sing in Scouts:

> *The bear went over the mountain*
> *The bear went over the mountain*
> *The bear went over the mountain*
> *And what do you think he saw?*
>
> *He saw another mountain*
> *He saw another mountain*

He saw another mountain
And what do you think he did?

He climbed the other mountain
He climbed the other mountain
He climbed the other mountain
And what do you think he saw?

He saw another mountain
He saw another mountain
He saw another mountain
And what do you think he did?

He climbed . . .

Up and down is all I do. As soon as I get calm from one
hair-raising close call, the next one starts. Is this the way
it's supposed to be? What if I want to sit somewhere on
the mountain and read a book and stare at the sky and
drink from the stream and never climb up to the next top,
never climb down to the next bottom, and, most of all,
never look over to what's coming next?

I need some *time*. Everything takes time to do, reading
a book, or steaming a pot of prunes, or getting expert at
playing jacks, and I can't always be climbing up and
climbing down and looking ahead and looking behind.

Izzy is on this mountain. The Skaters/Bikers/Cookers
are also on this mountain and we are all sewing our own
brassieres at club meetings and this will take *time*. My
Kingdom of Brooklyn is on this mountain—as are my
treasured provinces of Prospect Park and Coney Island
and Ocean Parkway and Ebbets Field (though I never saw
it, and no one has invited me to a ball game again).

And there are wonders on this mountain I haven't even
seen yet . . . like the train one can take into the great New
York City where everything is fancy and huge and crowded and amazing. Two of the Girl Scouts are already
allowed to go there—one to a real ballet school where she
takes lessons, and one to see a plastic surgeon who, as

soon as her nose stops growing, is going to do an opera-
tion on it to make it beautiful. (Could he do me, I wonder,
tug on my teeth to make them longer, and remove my
curls and replace them with straight hairs that fall in one
shining wave like a curtain, toppling this way and that as
I turn my head from side to side?)

There's not much else I want fixed: I have my regular
body that I live in that's looking pretty good these days
and is even learning to resist the birds that thump inside
my chest and the butterflies that churn in my stomach.
My body seems definitely more in harmony with me since
we—my baby-making machinery and I—have been
blessed with blood.

So I don't want to move to Florida! What's Florida got
to do with me? Besides, we already have rattan furniture.
We already have a Persian rug. Now we also have a Toast-
Tite sandwich maker that takes slices of white bread (but-
tered on the outside!) and presses them between two iron
disks on long handles, and makes magic sandwiches over
the stove flame. Toasty on the outside, melted and steaming on the inside. We put apples and butter and cinnamon
and sugar inside the bread, and we make little apple pies.
Food is not as bad as it used to be.

And even today, this very day, we are getting a new
Frigidaire with an electric motor on top of it. The old
refrigerator, the one I used to keep my used chewing gum
in, the one that has its motor in the basement, no longer
pleases my mother. "It has had its day," she announces.

"But if you talk about moving," my father says, baf-
fled, "why buy a new one? Why *now?*"

"One thing has nothing to do with another," she
answers. And to me she says, "Go down and do the buttons for defrosting. When the delivery man comes, we
must have it empty and dry so he can take it away."

* * *

The cellar—I never get over my fear of it. The rawness
of the cement walls on the way down is just the first hint

of the falling away of pretense. I descend on wooden steps
that have no backs (if I looked behind my heels, I could
see into the room with the oil burner), past the crude
splintery shelves that hold the flit gun and other poisons,
down and down to the two rooms under the house. There
is the room with green storage benches lining it (in which
my mother once played Ping-Pong with friends before she
married my father), there is the painting of the harlequin
figure on black velvet that my grandfather once bought
for my mother. (Did my mother ever *have* friends? I can't
imagine it, just as I wonder if she ever read any books.
I've never seen it happen. And did my grandfather ever
really live here, in this house, where I have been forever
but have never seen him? The same grandfather who
knew my mother had musical talent, but that Gilda
didn't?)

A bare bulb lights this green room, and at the far end of
it is the dreaded hole in the wall: just a hole to the place
under the sun porch which is my bedroom, just a hole
into a deeper, darker hole, where there is only dirt. Nothing else: dirt, no walls or floors, just the same kind of dirt
I saw piled on the hill beside my grandmother's grave.

I never go that way. The *other way* is the room with the
furnace, the oil tank, the Bendix, the washtub, and the
refrigerator motor. I hold my breath in that room, believing that if I don't breathe, time can't move forward and
nothing can change. The Bendix, with its foam-whirling
window, can't open and flood the room, and thus drown
me; the oil tank can't send spouts of oil through its round
entry hold and cover me with thick, black sludge; and the
furnace can't open its fiery mouth and suck me into its
hellish maw. I *never* breathe when I have to do my job
with the refrigerator motor.

And this is what I have to do: I have to face the metal
motor that vibrates the table it rests on, the floor I stand
on and my very teeth. There are gears and pulleys and
rubber belts on this machine, and they whirr and turn
until I do the necessary thing I have to do with the two
round rubber-tipped buttons. And this job I have to do is

the taking of them, these buttons, between the tips of my thumbs and forefingers, and—*at the same exact moment*—I have to pull them out of the holes they are pressed into.

All of this has to be done while I am not breathing. If I do it correctly, the motor will stop, the whirring will cease, the vibration will quiet to silence. And then I have to runupthestairsasfastasIcango.

The last time! This is the very last time. The new refrigerator will have its motor right on top of itself, right in the bright, busy, noisy, friendly kitchen. I will never have to come down into the cellar again! I give it my farewell glance—the low cobwebbed ceiling, the high window through which the oil burner man sticks his hose into the tank, the ugly tank itself, which even now has a thick black puddle of oil oozing out of its underparts, and the mystery of the furnace, with its cargo of power and flame.

I dash, I skid, I take the steps two at a time (backless and threatening as they are), my cheeks are bursting with my held breath till I pop into the kitchen like a red balloon, blasting out the bad air, sucking in the good.

"I did it!" I cry.

* * *

"You can't be serious about this," Gilda is saying to my mother. She has just come downstairs to admire the new Frigidaire, expressly at my mother's invitation, expressly for the amazing eating of ice cream *not* just bought five minutes ago from the ice cream man but ice cream simply taken out of a freezer, which will keep it frozen as long as we want it there.

I am proud, I can't help but feel our good luck, our advantage in life, our *superiority*. We are the winners. But to win over Gilda, is that good? To feel good while she feels bad—she has no freezer—isn't that bad? Still, I am bursting with delight over the knowledge that ice cream can now be mine, at any time, winter or summer.

This ice cream is my mother's favorite: chocolate.

Gilda's favorite, as I have witnessed and been told many times, is vanilla, which just shows—in my mother's view—how lacking Gilda is, how insensitive to what's really good, how dumb.

"We *are* serious," my mother says, licking the back of the teaspoon. She still wears her hair in the upsweep; she can do it herself without using a mirror, by holding hairpins in her mouth, their ends sticking out like fangs of wire, and then jabbing them, one by one, into her roll of twisted hair.

"But how can you do this to me?" Gilda asks. "Issa is my life."

Now I stop eating ice cream long enough to wonder what they could be talking about. Mostly I don't listen to adults talk anymore; my own thoughts are far more compelling; wherever they jump or land, I go with them to see what I think. I always amaze myself—by the distances I travel with a daydream, by the graphic scenes I imagine by following a floating thought here and there through a maze of *what-if-this?* and *what-if-that?* adventures. But Gilda has just said my name, said it like a cry!

"We wouldn't move right away," my mother says. "Not till the summer, probably." She rests her elbow on the kitchen table and her wrist is bent, her hand dangles limply, her gold lion bracelet gleams in the light. The lions have gold faces, gold manes, but their eyes glow with rubies and their nostrils are diamonds. When my father buys out an estate of antique jewelry, she takes her pick before she lets him sell any of it.

"But even so!" Gilda says. "Where would I go, what would I do?"

"You'll get part of the money from the sale of the house. We'll go to a lawyer and work out a fair arrangement."

"I don't want an arrangement. I want to live here! This is my home!"

My mother now addresses me, to give me the history of this house, which I've already heard a million times. "Think of it, Issa," she says. "When my father bought this house he paid $9,999 for it! With a four percent mortgage. Of course, when he died so young, I had to work to pay the bills and support Mama and Gilda till I married your father. Then *he* supported *all* of us!" She pauses and gives Gilda a look. "Of course, Gilda did what she could, giving a few haircuts, but how much could she really contribute?"

So? I am listening, but what does this mean to me? She's telling me this as if I haven't lived my entire life in this house, knowing everything about everything.

"And now," my mother says, "the house is worth much more, much more than we paid for it!"

This news causes Gilda to bow her head and begin to stir her ice cream in circles, mushing it down till the hill of chocolate melts to a runny brown mess.

My mother begins one of her lists, I see it coming, by her inhaling a deep breath, before she even begins.

"The winters are better in Florida, the weather is better in Florida, the antique business, we hear, is thriving in Florida, there's no reason to stay in this filthy, cold, stinking place."

Brooklyn? Is she talking about my Brooklyn?

"Except that you live here with me," Gilda says. "Except that you are my only family. You know the children are like my own."

"Only I am," I remind Gilda. "Not so much Blossom."

She smiles, so very sadly, and she takes my hand.

"Yes," she admits. "You are like my own child."

"It's never too late. You could still find someone to marry," my mother says. "And have your own children."

"It will never happen," Gilda says. "You took care of that very nicely, didn't you?"

"I had nothing to do with it," my mother says. "That Sam was a no-good bum."

"Maybe he wasn't perfect, but neither am I," Gilda says. "You know it was my only chance. You ruined it because you didn't want him living here."

"You can have anyone you want living here," my mother says, ". . . if you find someone to buy the house for you."

"You would really do that," Gilda says. "Take Issa away from me, just like that. Just disappear with her . . ."

Now I am really listening. Now I want to fling myself into Gilda's lap and wrap my arms around her neck. Now I want to promise, "I won't ever go, I won't ever leave you!"

"If you run around with that Iggy, you'll find some man or other," my mother says. "You probably can't help it, that dame has so many men after her, one of them might even settle for you."

I see it in her eyes, the cargo of bad words amassing there—they're gathering in her mind like an army getting ready to strike. Doesn't my mother know she has got to be careful? Gilda is like an eggshell. Gilda can't listen to this.

"Don't say any more," Gilda begs. "You'll be sorry for it!"

"I won't be sorry. What I'm sorry for is all the years I've wasted being your servant. What I'm sorry for is myself, and my children, who never had a natural family life! I'm sorry that my husband and I never had any privacy, not one stinking goddamn minute of privacy. I nearly killed myself, Gilda, working for you and Mama, and for what?" My mother's veins are standing out in her neck and in her forehead. She shakes her fist and rattles the heads of the lions on her bracelet, who have the same fierce expression she has. "So now we want to escape! To get out of this place. To go somewhere warm and beautiful and where you aren't always hanging on to me and my kids!"

"Oh!" Gilda says. The pits in her skin stand out dark and deep. They are like holes out of which her life will pour.

"But, Mommy!" I cry. "I don't want to leave Gilda!"

"Children don't decide these things!" my mother says, hitting her fist on the table. She shakes her head so that her cheeks flap. "You'll go where we say you'll go."

"But I *love* Gilda!" And this time I move, I leap into Gilda's lap and throw my arms around her, I wash her tears away with kisses, I kiss every place I can reach on the gravelly roughness of her skin.

"Fine, so you love her," my mother says. "And we won't be taking your dog with us," she adds in my direction. "Dogs die of the heat in Florida, so you'll have to give him away, Issa. We'll find a good home for him and that's that. And don't you dare talk back to me now."

34

The worst! Losing Beloved is the worst! Losing Gilda is terrible, losing Izzy is unimaginable, losing The Skaters/Bike-Riders/Cookers-Sewers is heartbreaking, but without Beloved I will surely die. *Don't you dare talk back to me now* is what she said. So I narrow my eyes and stare at her, stare at her with Chinese eyes, stare at her like a . . . Chink (oh yes) like a Chink staring at a . . . a . . . a Kike. What if I said that out loud? Would it shock her, jar her, astonish her, frighten her? Would she vomit from the shock?

I want to be so bad, I want to hurt her, I want to prove to her that she can't do this to me. *Children don't decide these things* is what she said. Well, why don't they? Why not? They have lives. Children count. Children matter. What they want matters as much as what she wants!

I don't want Florida. I don't need coconuts. I need *snow.* How could she ask me to live without snow, without that possibility of muted beauty, that screen of descending peace that lands on the curbs and cracked sidewalks as softly as falling flower petals? How could she pull me bodily out of my bed in the sunporch, away from my lilac tree, away from my Avenue O that I love, my Avenue P that I shop on, away from this entire world I am attached to by all the memories of all the days I have ever lived? I *need* Ocean Parkway, the street that has on one side the rest home (empty of my grandmother) and on the other side the mirrored ball on a pedestal in front of Dr. Ruby Tempkin's house (empty of my dead red-haired friend Esther Tempkin). I *need* Ocean Parkway to remind me that I am alive, that I am here and others are gone, to remind me that I am destined to go on and complete the work of my days.

What will *Florida* remind me of? Nothing much, nothing that matters. The things that matter to me are what turn the blur of my inattention to the sharpest awareness. Beloved, my soulmate, matters. I will chain myself to Beloved. They will never separate me from Beloved.

* * *

That night I sneak him out of his little doghouse on the back porch and into my bed. The Screamer says she will tell. I tell her, without raising my voice, that if she tells I will kill her.

She gets quiet. Maybe she loves Beloved, too. Maybe she is just convinced I will kill her. It doesn't matter how I get my way as long as I get it. I have learned this from my mother, who always gets her way. It's a marvel, isn't it, how you can hate what someone does, and then do things her way?

* * *

On Saturday, it is agreed that my father may take me to the antique shop; it is allowed that Beloved can go along since my mother can't stand his whining when I'm not at home to calm him. My reason for going with my father is that I have chosen to do a composition for my English teacher on "the beauty and value of antiques," and I need to examine certain ones in order to describe them in detail.

My mother, whose hopes were dashed when I was not in the class that won the home economics contest, now imagines that I will write the best composition and thus win the Excellence in Composition Medal when I graduate eighth grade in June. That's when the deadline looms: June, when I graduate. June when the house will be sold. June, which is the month of Gilda's birthday. We must move in June. We must go to Florida where dogs die in the heat and where I will start my new life in high school.

"Dogs don't *die* because it's too hot for them in Florida, Daddy," I tell him as we pull away from the curb. "I looked it up in the library. Dogs can live in any climate. They adapt. They can live in the North Pole."

"Whoever told you dogs can't live in Florida?"

"Mommy."

"Oh. Mommy."

"She says we can't take Spotty to Florida."

"She said that?"

"Why do we *have* to move to Florida?"

"She's hell bent," he says. "She thinks I can make more money there."

"Can you?"

"Who knows?" He glances over at me. "Don't worry, Issa. You won't ever have to give away this mutt." He reaches over and cuffs Beloved on the head. I glance at my father's foot on the gas pedal, and just there, where his pants ride up, I can see the line of stitches that match the ones on Beloved's torn and mangled ear.

"She said I can't talk back to her about it."

"I'll talk to her. I said don't worry." Now my father reaches over to ruffle my hair. On a crazy impulse, I whirl sideways and lay my head in his lap. He laughs while I watch the steering wheel turn just above my eyes.

"What's it like down there?"

"Well, let's see: there's sky and trees upside down, and lampposts, and traffic lights, and everything's spinning."

I feel the car turn; the universe reverses direction. Now I don't see lampposts anymore, or traffic lights, or apartment houses.

"Where are we?" I ask.

"Guess!" my father says.

"I can't. I'm too dizzy."

"We're going into Prospect Park!"

"Really?" I sit up, and he's right, we're not on Ocean Parkway or the big main highway that goes downtown to the antique store. We're on a curvy road, with hills and trees all around us.

"How about we take the day off, Issa? Let's go to the park and rent a paddleboat; we can have a picnic and we can go to the zoo. We'll play hooky."

"Mommy wouldn't like it. Mommy . . ."

"Forget Mommy for now," he says.

* * *

My father. The man who sat in the dark sunporch smoking a pipe while Gilda gave a party. My father, before he knew I would be his, sitting shyly in a corner in the dark, the bowl of his pipe flaring with each pull of his breath, waiting there for the shooting star of my mother to land in his lap. "He was so kind and decent," she told me once, when I asked why she married him. "He was so honest."

But his kindness and honesty have been the bone in her throat; he is not doing badly in business now, but she knows how weak he is in the area of ruthlessness. (I was with her in the antique store the day a young woman rushed in with her baby and begged my father to give her ten dollars for her gold wedding ring. He held the ring in the palm of his hand, as if weighing it, and then gave the girl twenty dollars. Then he reached for her hand and put the ring back on her finger. "Pay me back when you can," he said. I remember my mother's face, drawn to a point with anger. And not only *she* was angry: I did my own counting of how many things I could have bought in the toy store with that twenty dollars.)

If we play hooky today and he misses out on business (after all, he is having the beginnings of his "going out of business sale," for which he has placed a small ad in *The Brooklyn Eagle*), my mother will have another reason for fury. And what about my composition?

Besides, what *is* the "beauty and value of antiques"? I personally hate them. They're dusty, they're breakable, they're old and dirty, they come in ragged cartons wrapped in old newspaper whose ink gets on your fingers. If they're clocks, they don't tell time. If they're music boxes, they don't play. If they're pins, their clasps are broken. If they're necklaces, their chains are torn.

And if they're perfect, they are too valuable for me to touch, too expensive for us to take home, too delicate for me to hold. Who cares about antiques!

* * *

Ducks are on the lake, ducking their heads into the water and letting the sun stream in iridescent stripes down their backs. Oh sun! Oh water! My father has rented a paddleboat, two fishing poles, bought a jar of worms. We pedal and the paddles turn. We steer into the narrows of the lake, and pass under the low-hanging boughs of weeping trees. Beloved curls at our feet with his eyes bright, his tail wagging.

I hear everything: the lap of the water at the sides of the boat, the faint buzz of insects around my head, the shrill song of birds who chase one another from branch to branch of the trees on shore.

We maneuver into the shade of an umbrella-wide tree and toss our fishing rods into the lake. I can hear the tiny pull and rip of the nylon cord as it cuts gently through the still water as I thrust my rod one way and then another. I feel we are sitting under a magnifying glass, with everything bigger and closer and hotter.

My father smiles, puffs on his pipe, lets the caramel scent flavor the air.

Yes, he has told me before: the best things in life are free. The paddleboat and the worms aren't free, but still. The big things are: the sun, the water, the trees, the birds. Who made these things? Why do they delight me? Why do I forget my tight, hard, mean little worries when I see the flap of a jumping fish? The shimmer of a school of minnows hurrying by, as if they are connected by invisible webs?

Why don't we do this every day? It's so wonderful, so peaceful, so warm, so perfect. I lean down and kiss Beloved on the top of his head. I lean over and kiss my father on his cheek. He reaches into his pocket and hands me a stick of Black Jack chewing gum. Why can't I marry my father and just we two move to Florida?

* * *

I write my composition instead on "The Beauty of Nature." My mother has taught me that the first sentence of any piece of writing is the most important. When I had to do a report on Roman culture, she wrote the beginning words for me: "All roads lead to Rome."

I begin this one similarly, hoping to please her: "The best things in life are free."

My mother leans over my shoulder as I write at the kitchen table. She is angry that we spent the day in Prospect Park. She can't fix it, though; it's done. She reads my first sentence and she says, "Get that idea out of your head, Issa. The sooner the better."

CHAPTER
35

My father brings home an alligator purse in a white gift box. Bought at an estate sale, it rests in tissue paper, smelling of sanitized swamp and jungle. I am allowed to touch its scaly surface, run my fingers over the animal's woody head, touch its tiny sharp teeth protruding under the line of its upper jaw. Its sealed mouth is positioned just over the fastening snap. The alligator's eyes are stitched closed, its nostrils are sewn through with amber thread where its snout is attached to the body of the purse. The creature looks steamrollered onto its own skin: alligator hide comprises the entire square design of the purse, even as the alligator is overlaid upon the geometric arrangement of its scales. The back side of the purse shows his feet, with four perfect claws; his nails are splayed out as if he is trying to get a grip on a threatening surface and pull himself up to freedom.

"Look at the hand-stitching all around," my mother breathes in admiration. "It must be worth a fortune."

My father stands back proudly, glad to have been responsible for such a phenomenon.

"Let me show it to Gilda," I beg. "Let me call her."

By the time Gilda comes down, my mother is already modeling it, strutting back and forth through the living room with the varnished brown animal slung over her shoulder.

"Poor little fellow," Gilda says. "Killed for *that*."

"Oh, you make me sick," my mother says, but not unkindly, because she is so pleased with this present. "It's the sort of elegant thing one could wear to the opera." She looks at my father. "But never mind, you would never go to the opera."

"But *I'm* going to the opera," Gilda confesses with some shyness. "Maybe I could wear it."

Our heads pop up. "How come you're going?" my mother asks. I have the crazy thought that she has hunting-dog ears like Beloved, and they have just stiffened up to an alert position. My father is watching Gilda, too, but his head is tilted down, as if he isn't really watching.

"His name is Joe Boboli, I never met him, he's a friend of Iggy's. It's a blind date—she's arranged it."

"But how come the *opera*?" I ask.

"Well." Gilda seems embarrassed. "The fact is, he's Italian, and he wants to take me to a certain opera that has a character in it named Gilda."

My mother, in a sudden flurry of movement, rushes to open the piano bench and pull out a book of music called *Favorites of Opera Lovers*. She flings her fingers over the pages till she finds what she wants: then she lets the alligator purse slide gently down her arm and lays it on the side of the piano. She begins to play a song.

"This is an aria from *Rigoletto*, Gilda is his daughter . . ." she says over her shoulder to Gilda. "Not that you would know it. But she dies in the end, of course."

My mother plays on and on. We all stand around, getting tired, but no one sits down on the couch.

After we're sure she's not going to stop, my father makes a move: he reaches for the alligator purse, takes it in his big hands and holds it out to Gilda, careful to point its teeth downward. "Look, Gilda, take this if you want to wear it on a special night out, just take it, why don't you?"

"Oh no, you didn't get it for me," she says. My mother keeps playing, but I see her shoulders get stiff. She holds her head rigid, as if she is having trouble listening to the conversation above the noise she is making.

"It's quite a classy item," my father says. "You might as well take it if you have an opportunity to use it."

Gilda takes the purse in her hands and runs her fingers over it. "It is handsome," she says. "The poor thing. They've turned him into a work of art."

"Just keep it," my father insists, pressing his hand over her hand on the alligator's snout. "It's yours. I'll come across another someday."

Smash! My mother bangs her fists down on the piano keys and stands up. Her face is like a jigsaw puzzle fallen to pieces.

"It's mine! If you brought it home for me, it's mine! It isn't hers! It's mine, I own it, I need it, I deserve it." She lunges toward Gilda and rips the purse out of her hands. Then she cries out in pain, throwing the purse to the floor and holding up her index finger, which begins to ooze droplets of blood in a thin line. "Oh God damn it! You all hate me, don't you! You're all against me! I don't know why, no matter what I do, it's never enough. Never mind! Just go to hell, why don't you, every one of you!"

My mother stumbles, sobbing, to the bathroom, slams the door and locks herself in. Gilda runs upstairs. My father stares around the room, looks at me, and leaves. I hear his car drive away. I fling myself on the floor of the back porch and take Beloved in my lap. I rock with him against my heart.

Iodine, she is taking iodine, I know it. My eyes are filling with heavy fluid, tears that won't come out, salty tears that are flowing backwards, drowning me. *Why do these things happen?* How does a nice time transform itself into a nightmare so fast? How can people in a family be polite one minute, playing music, and admiring something wonderful, and the next minute there is cursing and screaming?

* * *

By afternoon, things look ordinary again. I am reading *Forever Amber* on the back porch. No one else is around—my father is at his store, The Screamer is still at someone's birthday party, Gilda is not stirring upstairs. My mother is back at the piano, playing "The Moonlight Sonata."

When I pass through the living room to my bedroom, I see her head bent over the keys. Her white hair is loose and hanging over her face. She rocks as if in pain on the piano bench and her fingers play the mournful, grieving notes without her seeming to know it. She isn't aware, she isn't looking at music. Her body quivers like a silk night-gown drying on the line. She lifts her head but doesn't see me. Her eyes seem sewn shut, like the alligator's. And then I see that her face is covered with tears, is slick and shining with them. They drip down, over her fingers, over the keys. On and on she plays.

* * *

Every day we get closer to my last day in Brooklyn. When I wake each morning, the day at first seems ordinary, one more day in the endless row of days that stretch into my life, but it isn't: It's more like a great truck bearing down on me, or like a boulder let loose on top of the mountain, far up there, but still—crashing its way down, aimed at my heart.

The house is going to be sold. Gilda is making inquiries about renting a room somewhere and then she will try to get a job as a beautician. My father is going to open an antique store in Florida. We might have another house, or we might not. I might make new friends or I might not. They tell me ways to think about it but I won't. I ignore the whole thing.

In the meantime, my father is packing his antiques, carton by carton, and bringing them home for putting in a trailer we will rent to attach to our car on the day we move; each day my mother takes strangers through our house, hoping they will want to buy it. I keep out of their way, hiding and reading books I still insist on taking out of the library. *Gone with the Wind* is my favorite now. Scarlett won't leave Tara; I don't blame her. It's the least you can do if you love your home.

* * *

Izzy and I plot and plan: he will make his mother move to Florida so he can be near me. If she won't move, then he'll come himself, as soon as he's old enough to drive. And we'll get married, of course. I'm guaranteed a husband, I will never have to be as lonely as Gilda. We kiss on the cellar steps, sitting very quietly with the light off so no one will discover us. If I look behind us, through the opening of the backless stair, I see the looming outlines of the oil tank and the furnace. Is it possible that I even love these monsters and want to be with them? At least I know them; I don't know the monsters in Florida.

The question in my mind is this: is this move really one of the things that can't be stopped? Some things, I know, can never be budged. But is this, does this *have* to be, one of them?

* * *

I don't know what happened to the alligator purse. The next weekend, when Gilda goes to the opera with Joe Boboli, she carries a white bag with blue and red and yellow wooden beads sewn all over it. She wears a white dress, a white hat with a big floppy brim, and white shoes with navy blue tips.

My father watches from my nine windows while she drives away in a new black Dodge car with Joe Boboli, who is shorter than Gilda and bald. My father sighs. Then he says, "I'm going into the cellar to mend a picture frame. Come down with me." He invites me, holding out his hand. "You can help me."

The cellar is looking more and more like a warehouse; the cartons of antiques he has brought home each day are piled like towers of blocks, one upon the other. These are the ones he will take to Florida, the ones with which he will open a new business. There are other piles of boxes, some to be given away, some to be thrown away. Soon all our furniture will have to be sold, even the rattan couch and chairs.

I don't think about it. I don't pack my things. I refuse to sort out my possessions. I won't throw away toys from my childhood, or books, I will never throw away books. There's no way I can pack my bike. I never did have skates. I hate this and I just won't do this. When the day comes, they'll have to drag me to the car. They can take my things or leave them. I don't care. I refuse to care. How can they do this to me? How can they make me throw away my entire life? When I think of Florida, I think of a big zero. Nothing, it's nothing. I don't want it. I won't have it. I will pull the coconuts off the trees there and kill my parents with them. There is nothing for me to hang onto. I feel like a zombie.

* * *

In the basement, my father sands the edges of a broken picture frame. "I'm fixing this painting for Gilda," my father explains. "You know it's her birthday coming up."

Of course I know. The painting is of a country girl wearing an apron and holding a pail, leading a cow through a meadow. "Gilda's always loved this since she first saw it in my store; now she's going to have it. She *should* have it." My father is now gluing the edges of the wooden frame together. He wants me to tighten the clamp while he presses the angled edges together. The fumes of the cement are strong; I turn my head away.

"Are you sure it's okay to give this to Gilda? Won't Mommy get mad?"

"Why should she?"

I'm astonished. Doesn't my father remember the alligator purse? Doesn't he ever learn *anything*? I begin to wonder if he understands what goes on here every day.

"Daddy, why can't Gilda move to Florida with us?" I ask him. It has been on my mind all along; with my grandmother dead, I can't see why we don't invite her.

"Well, she and your mother don't get along that well. Besides, she lives here, she's lived here all her life," he says. "This is her home."

"This is *my* home," I tell him.

"Well. Tell that to your mother."

I don't know if he's serious. Does he think my telling her would make any difference? Just then, we hear her opening the door at the top of the steps. She's coming down, her feet clumping in their loose slippers. She's bringing another load of laundry down to the Bendix.

"Tell her now," he says. "Maybe she'll change her mind. I'd be very happy if she changed her mind."

"Change my mind about what?" my mother says sharply.

"Issa wants to tell you something. Tell her, Issa."

I look at my mother holding the wicker basket full of dirty clothes: my clothes, The Screamer's clothes, my father's clothes. Since we have no maid now, she has to do hard things for us, we should be good to her.

"I don't want to move to Florida, Mommy," I say. "I want to stay in Brooklyn." I say it like a five-year-old, although I am now thirteen. Why don't I stand tall, right up to her? I am now her same height. "And Daddy doesn't want to move either."

"Is that so?" she says. She smiles, very slightly, with her mouth tightly closed as if something disgusting is trying to get into it. I realize that if I learn to smile the same way, I won't ever have to show my small teeth. It's amazing, how I learn things from her all the time.

"What's that doing here? Why isn't it packed in one of the cartons?" She lifts the toe of her floppy slipper toward the painting.

"It's the present for Gilda's birthday," I say as if we all know it already. "I think we should give her a party, too. We could invite Iggy and Izzy and Joe Boboli."

"An Italian!" my mother sneers. "Mama would turn

over in her grave."

"She's not marrying him," my father says.

My mother starts throwing the clothes into the Bendix. "That painting is going to Florida with us—we're not giving it away. It's valuable. It's an oil painting. It's by a known artist. We can sell it. We need stock for the new store."

"But Gilda has always admired it," my father says. "What can it hurt us to leave her something she loves? We're taking Issa."

"You gave away my purse to her. You give her too much money for her clothes. Now you want to give her this. The next thing you'll want to give her is my child! Don't you want to leave *anything for me*?"

Her voice rises up into that beginning of hysteria. Why must she do this? Why doesn't my father hit her? Why doesn't he stop her? How come she can get away with so much?

But I see by his face: even he is afraid of her. Like me, he's afraid she'll take iodine. *He's afraid we'll lose her forever.* Why else would he let her do this, let her start it and go all the way with it? What else could scare a grown man?

CHAPTER

36

Last things. There is a somberness to everything we do: the last visit to the library (we can't be having library books mixed up with our own books anymore, and, besides, my father has no time to take me and wait for me while I choose books), the last visit to Dr. Ellen for my teeth to be cleaned (thank heavens), the last visit to Irving's Delicatessen (Irving gives me a handful of Indian nuts as a going away present).

Gilda still presents me proudly to the storekeepers, but now it's the last act. "They're moving away," she tells everyone. "They're moving to Florida for the children's health." This is news to me. But it's the new reason: The Screamer has delicate lungs. She needs warm air. The freezing winters are dangerous for her. My sister's health seems a more decent reason to move than my mother's need for privacy. My mother seems to believe it: she starts treating The Screamer as if she is a true invalid. Now my sister gets even more attention, more dolls, more coddling.

Money is constantly under discussion. Division of everything. My mother has called a lawyer she used to work for and made an appointment with him. One day she and Gilda, dressed in city clothes, go away for the day and come back with their signed agreement: that Gilda will get only one quarter of the money from the sale of the house: she had to agree that she did not contribute as much as my mother and father did to the mortgage payments over the years. Even if my grandmother's death left the house to them equally, it is only fair this way. My mother made Gilda see it her way. But my mother assures us Gilda will have enough to live on, especially if she gets a job. Then she can rent a nice apartment, not just a room. And if she gets married—who knows? She could marry a millionaire! She could end up Queen of the May.

On our way to the vault on King's Highway (more legal matters have to be taken care of, Gilda has to put away this new written agreement) I ask Gilda about Joe Boboli. She shrugs her shoulders: Iggy meant well, but Joe Boboli turned out to be a disappointment: a loud mouth, a man in too much of a hurry for action. The opera wasn't bad, but it wasn't for her. "And I could never live with an Italian who has to sprinkle cheese on his spaghetti and meatballs," Gilda says. "Meat and cheese, it would turn my stomach."

We pass the suspicious eyes of the stern bank guards in uniform and we are back in the roomful of silver drawers. There's a fierce chill in here, as if the buried gold in this underground vault is encased in blocks of ice. How well I remember the ritual: Gilda puts her key in the lock of her drawer and the guard puts his key in the adjacent lock and together they turn their keys at the same moment. This unlocks the treasure.

We carry the metal box to the secret room. I feel the awesome power and hush of fortune; what treasures people own are as secret as what happens when men and women make babies together.

"There's no point my saving these for your wedding," Gilda says. "Who knows if I'll be there? Who knows what the future will bring?" and she plucks out of the tissue paper in the box the diamond earrings that belonged to my grandmother. She holds them before my eyes; they swing and sparkle.

"But didn't they get flushed away in the rest home?" I ask. I am truly astonished to see them again.

"They weren't the real ones," Gilda assures me. "How could we trust those colored girls with Mama's diamond earrings? But Mama wanted her earrings; she was so vain at the end, so vain! Your mother gets it from her, I think. So your father found some fake ones in his store that looked like the real thing. Mama never knew the difference." She dangles them again in front of me. "For you, Issa."

"For me?"

"Precious jewels for a precious girl."

"But what about Blossom? Doesn't she get half?"

"What good would one earring do her, tell me that! Besides, she never knew your grandmother like you did. No, these are yours, your heirloom from Grandma. Take care of them."

"Oh yes," I breathe, taking a pledge that is witnessed by the silver altars around us, "I will."

"Here, let me screw them on." The first earring pinches my earlobe as Gilda tightens the screw, then attaches the second one, but I don't even whimper. "What a beauty you are getting to be. In a few years, you'll drive the boys wild."

"Even with my silly little teeth?"

"Your teeth, Issa? What's wrong with your teeth? They're perfect! They're delicate and sharp, they're white and perfect."

"But my hair is wild and stupid."

"Your hair is magnificent," Gilda says. "Curly and thick and shining. What have you been thinking?"

"That I'm ugly."

"Oh sweetheart!" Gilda takes my face in her two hands and kisses my hair, my mouth. "You break my heart you are so beautiful."

"Gilda, I'll miss you so much. How can I live without you?"

"Don't," Gilda says. "I can't take that now. I won't be able to walk home on my two feet if you do that."

* * *

My last walk home from King's Highway, my last passing by this shoe store, this bakery, this drugstore. My last stepping down this curb, over this sewer grate . . . I decide I am carrying this too far and will be bored in a minute. Even moments this dramatic have their limitations. I swing my head carefully from side to side. My precious diamond earrings, tiny as they are, graze the skin of my neck. They tickle and thrill me.

We come in view of my house. How many more times will I see it like this, standing up like a dollhouse against the blue sky, its chimney straight as a soldier on guard, its lilac tree a factory of springtime perfume? How can I emboss these images on my memory so I am guaranteed to hold them forever?

I imagine we are all taking our last positions. My mother at the sink pouring grease out of a frying pan, my father in the easy chair puffing on his pipe, Gilda on a beach chair in the backyard, letting the sun bake her ragged skin, Beloved curled in a circle in his doghouse, head to tail, raising his eyes as I come into view.

A longing for Beloved tightens my throat like a thirst; I must drink him in right now! I run up the alley, up the three steps to the back porch and prepare to dangle my sparkling jewels for him.

The doghouse is dark inside, there's no splash of his white patch of fur, or the flip of his tail.

"Mommy," I call, the gong of alarm beginning to sound in my belly. "Mommy!"

She comes to the screen door but doesn't look at me.

"Where is Spotty?"

"I don't know, Issa. He got out."

"He got out? You mean he ran away?"

"Oh, look now," she says, "I told you what had to happen."

"*What?*"

"I told you we would find him a good home."

"He's gone?" I fall to my knees and put my forehead to the rough boards as if I will see him under the back porch, through the cracks. Then I leap up and shriek. "MA! MA! *What did you do?*"

"I don't like it when you carry on, Issa."

"*What did you DO? Daddy said we could take him with us. He promised!*"

"I never promised. They get ticks in the heat that suck your blood. They get fleas. Dogs are a health hazard."

"Gilda!" I scream at the top of my lungs for Gilda. "Come down. My dog is gone! She gave away my dog!" I know how to scream and be hysterical, too. I come by it naturally, I do this as well as she does it. "Gilda! Gilda! I'm going to die!"

"Oh shut up, Issa." My mother slaps my face and I do for the first time feel myself dying. This is dying. I can't have Beloved in my arms for the rest of time. This is death.

The rest is arguing and sobbing and denying and explaining and shouting and shrieking. The rest is done in the vacuum of my Beloved, in his absence, in a catalog of reasons and words that echo and bounce in my empty heart. My mother is saying the reason we can't sell the house is because he's been yapping whenever strangers come to see it; my mother is saying that she found him a perfectly good home with a farmer.

"I don't believe you," I scream. "There are no farms here!" and Gilda is smoothing my hair and saying, "She did this to me, too, darling, she did this to me and I lived through it. You'll live through it, too."

But I don't care to live. I might as well die right here, right now. Without Beloved, I don't even want my earrings. I don't want to get married someday, I don't want my life at all. Without Beloved, the future is a black pit. My mother is the cause of all this. My mother, who has done this to me, looks scared by what she has done. But it is done. I know it can't be undone. This is one of those brick walls.

She says, "After we move everything will be better. We'll be happier. I promise you. We'll all be happy in Florida, Issa. Where the sun shines all the time."

36

The house is sold to the Borocheks. They are just like us, a mother and father and two children downstairs, and an unmarried aunt and a grandmother upstairs. How amazing—as if, when we move away, ghosts of us will remain and continue living our lives there. I don't want to meet the children; I don't want there to be a girl my age who takes my place as one of The Skaters/Bike-Riders/Cookers, who will become Izzy's partner in playing Old Maid on the stairs. I want to get away as soon as possible.

The trailer is already rented for one month and is to be returned in Florida. My father loads it nightly, with his vases and lamps and statues and dishes and paintings and punch bowls. It's a big high thing, and it blocks my view of Avenue O, of the houses across the street. At night my father has to sleep in bed with me in order to watch the trailer; he spends half the night sitting up to look out one or another of the nine windows, to be sure no one is robbing him. I have the choice of staying in my narrow bed with him, or sleeping with The Screamer, or sharing the big bed with my mother. But I will not sleep with my mother; I will not let my skin touch her skin. I do not look at her or talk to her.

I still haven't packed. I won't do it and I have told them so. They'll have to do it for me if they want it done. I don't care if I have no clothes or books or games. I am dead, so why do I need them?

I go to school, I let my teachers say goodbye to me and wish me luck. They are all sure I will be a great success in my future. Apparently they can't tell I'm dead.

At the eighth grade graduation ceremony at the Avalon Theater, I win the Medal for Excellence in Composition; I hear the applause rise like a flock of seagulls flapping over my head. What do I care? I will never write another word in my life.

The Skaters/Bike-Riders/Cookers chip in to get me a going-away present, a mother-of-pearl pencil on a gold chain that snaps back into a pin I can wear on my chest. They hug and kiss me and tell me they can't live without me. It's fine, they think that's true, but things you can't live without really kill you if they're gone. I know it for a fact.

Everything moves along—the furniture is sold, Gilda finds a room to live in in the house of one of her old customers; the day after we leave she will supervise the moving out of the old furniture and the moving in of the Borochek's. The cellar is emptying out; there is nothing left down there but piles of old newspapers and empty cartons, and the oil painting of the milkmaid girl in the meadow with the cow. The mended frame has been drying down there all this time—and, although my mother thinks we will pack the painting in the trailer and take it to Florida, I know a secret. My father has shared this secret with me: we are giving the painting to Gilda at her birthday party. The birthday party is to be the night before we leave. He tells me he is sure my mother will have a change of heart; she will want to give her sister something fine and generous on the night before we move away. I don't think he knows much about sisters. I have a feeling of dread in me when I think about this last party for Gilda. We will light the candles, eat the cake, and then in the morning drive away to Florida. I see it in my mind like a dream. We drive away and disappear. And that is the end of that.

* * *

The birthday cake is from Ebinger's, layer cake with chocolate buttercream icing. The guests are Iggy and Izzy and the five of us. My mother is wearing a gray silk dress and black high heels; she is wearing her gold lion bracelet and a gold choker around her neck. I don't remember exactly seeing Izzy or Iggy; they are in the fuzzy edges of the room, they don't really belong here tonight because this is not the end of the world for them. Gilda is clear as crystal: in her white dress and her white hat and wearing dark glasses, she stands in the living room with her hand to her face. It is her birthday, she is being celebrated. We have candles already stuck in the cake, not lit yet, too many to count. We have paper cups and paper plates and wooden spoons (everything real is packed in the trailer). The Screamer has made Gilda a boat out of newspaper and she wants to put it on the cake in the middle of the candles. She doesn't understand what will happen if the flames touch the paper.

I am the one who is to bring the painting upstairs to give to Gilda. When my father gives me the sign, I will run down to the cellar and get it. I watch him for the sign. He is watching Gilda every second. His face is as white as Gilda's dress. Gilda leans against the table and says to everyone *Thank you for this party.* Because she leans so limply against the table, it's as if she has no spine in her body, or no body in her dress. I decide she looks like a ghost in her white dress, it's brilliantly white, it glows so that the edges of her entire form seem blurred.

I don't know what I'm doing, really. There are bottles of Coca-Cola on the table and I stick my finger into an open bottle and can't pull it out. *My mother gave Beloved to a farmer but there are no farms around here.* Could Beloved be running free in the hills right now, barking at squirrels and quivering in the joy of freedom? Could he be loping along beside a milkmaid who is holding a pail and leading a cow through the meadow?

My father gives me the sign, which is a nod and a wink. He says, "Gilda, we have a present for you for your birthday," and she says, "Oh really?" but her voice is muted.

"Issa will bring up your surprise from downstairs," he says. He laughs and adds, "It's an elephant." I don't know why he says that false thing: *It's an elephant.* I have to correct him, "It's a cow," I say.

My mother's face comes into my view now, her mouth drops open when I say it's a cow, her neck seems to swell so that the choker tightens and veins stand out on her forehead.

"It better not be the cow," she says. She is looking directly at my father, who has an odd crooked smile on his face. "It isn't the cow, is it?" she demands of him.

"It's the cow," he says.

"I forbid you to give that to her," my mother says. "I told you how I feel about that."

"The cow is for Gilda. She needs that cow. It belongs to her. I thought you'd see the sense of that."

"I'd sooner burn it than let her have it," my mother says, and with a sweep of her gold-braceleted arm, with the ruby glow of the lions' eyes making an arc across the table, she grabs the book of matches with which we are to light Gilda's birthday candles and she clatters in her high heels to the cellar steps. "I mean it," she calls back to us, "I'd sooner see it go up in flames."

We hear her making her way down the hollow, backless cellar steps. No one moves. Iggy's pink sweater glows brightly, Izzy says something about the buttercream icing beginning to melt, and Gilda and my father's eyes are locked together. Their gaze is like a steel band binding them together.

We wait. There is no sound from below, not even a shuffle or a bump.

"Should I cut the cake then?" Izzy offers. "And forget the candles?"

"We can light them with matches I have in my pocket," my father says. He fumbles first in one pocket of his jacket and then in the other. He hunts in the side pocket of his trousers. He finally discovers the matches in the last-chance pocket and holds them up like a prize for all of us to see. Then he tears a single match out of the book, strikes it on the cover and leans forward over the table to light Gilda's birthday candles.

Just as he lights the first one, a thunderous roar blasts up from below and the floor blows out from under us. The table with the cake on it falls through the hole into the cellar where there is a sea of fire burning and we hear my mother's screams.

Flames leap up and ignite my eyelashes; my father rushes to the cellar stairs but bellows, "They're gone! The stairs are gone!" Gilda begins to slide into the hole as more of the floor gives way, but Izzy takes hold of her by the waist and pulls her out the side door. Iggy grabs The Screamer and me from behind, and kicks us toward the front door using her knees to knock us along because we can't move by ourselves. The Screamer screams the whole time. How amazingly she screams, as if she has prepared for this from the day she was born.

While we stand outside, the fire bursts out of my nine windows at the same moment, in unison, like the flaming legs of Rockettes. My father comes hurtling out the front door, his clothes on fire. He burns in all directions until a man, leaping out of a car, knocks him to the ground and rolls him over and over like a rolling pin.

Neighbors are shouting, cars are stopping, and soon there are sirens. I don't blink. The heat is boiling my eyeballs. I watch my house burn down till someone pulls me back, wraps me in a blanket. I throw it off; it's summer, no one needs a blanket in June. I won't turn my head away from the light. I hold my elbow back, like knives; I will stab anyone who tries to deflect my attention from the spectacle. I have never seen anything like this in my life. In each burning window I see my mother, leaping, dancing, calling out to me. She disappears from one and appears in another. Her arms reach to hold me. She calls my name, "Issa, Issa"—or is it the sound of the water shooting from the hoses of the firemen? She dances away, deep into the house, upstairs, downstairs, she has it all to herself at last, she flies from room to room, she gazes at me from every window, flinging up the shades, letting in the night.

Sparks are shooting upward, great fountains of fire. The rising embers mix themselves with stars; they quiver and twinkle, flash and blink out. Walls of water are drowning the fire. Soon all the firelight begins to dim inside the skeleton of my house. I watch: from red to orange to a dusky glow . . . and then darkness reaches in. One by one the windows go dark.

I still watch the windows for a sign. No one is there for me. I watch and I watch. A long time later, when my house has burned to the ground, the firemen go in and find my mother. They carry her out and lay her body on the grass. Iggy lets go of my hand (has she been there all the time?) and walks to retrieve something that has fallen from my mother's burned arm. I see it as Iggy carries it back to me; my mother's charred bracelet. The lions' faces have melted into molten black lumps.

Just then one of the firemen notices my finger is swollen stuck in the Coca-Cola bottle. He goes to one of the six huge red fire engines churning in the street and gets a glass cutting saw which he uses to free me. Then he presses his sooty face against mine and kisses my cheek.

"You poor baby," he says. "You poor, lost baby."

* * *

I sleep in Izzy's bed that night. My sister sleeps with me while Izzy sleeps with his mother. Gilda and my father are somewhere, in the hospital, I think, although my father can walk, I saw him stand up, he isn't dead. He isn't even burned badly. But he couldn't talk to me. He could only look at the house, too, as if he couldn't believe it was gone. No one can believe a change like this. It happens too fast and there's nothing to hold on to, to get used to. One minute you have your life, the way it's always been, the way you're sure it always will be, and the next minute there's nothing there, you're leaning on the railing of a bridge and it gives way, and you fall straight down with nothing to hold onto, with no one to catch you.

* * *

They think my mother may have set the painting on fire while standing too close to the oil tank or the furnace—but she can't tell us, can she? Or maybe the newspapers or the rags down there might have—all by themselves—set an oil leak on fire, or the can of glue might have spilled and the fumes ignited, or the oil vapors took a spark. But how will we ever know? Maybe my mother just went down there at the wrong moment. Maybe she never even got to the painting. But now only Gilda and my father are left; the way I always wanted it to be. I think my mother's white hair had to have burned like a ball of lightning.

I want! I want! What I want is my mother.

CHAPTER
37

Oh, how I miss her. My days are like a cut-out book, with two white spaces on every page: my mother and Beloved, cut out and missing, only their ghostly outlines remaining to decorate the scene.

I live at Iggy's and play with cut-outs all day. Or with a jigsaw puzzle. Or with my sister's new doll house, moving the wrong furniture into the wrong rooms, putting the toilet and bathtub into the living room, putting the baby crib into the kitchen, putting the stove into the bedroom. Everything in the dollhouse is very small and my fingers are like giant-fingers. I knock furniture over, I jangle tiny vases to the floor, I overturn a grandfather's clock, a fireplace.

Izzy wants to play old Maid with me, or stoop ball, or even hopscotch; he tries to get me interested in anything, but I don't want to play with him.

"Leave her alone," Iggy says. "She'll get better soon."

My father has burns on his arms and the back of his neck, but they're healing. He sleeps on Iggy's couch and goes to work as soon as he can.

I heard all about the funeral for my mother, but I didn't go. I refused to go. I know about funerals and what they do there, what they did to my grandmother. I know about dirt and holes in the ground and old men who jabber prayers. I don't need to know any more about that.

What do I need? I need the person who knows about my life from the instant it started, even before I was born. I need the person who knows how to make me rhyme, how to make me use the dimples in my knees (I have them! I have them, too!), how to make me know how important I am, and how proud she will be when I get famous.

I never knew I wouldn't want to try if she weren't here with me. How could I have known I would feel this way? Why didn't she warn me?

* * *

We have a new apartment on Ocean Parkway now, overlooking the bicycle path and the bridle path. My father and Gilda sleep in separate bedrooms but soon they are going to marry and buy another house in Brooklyn. Gilda will be my legal stepmother. Now that I am almost truly hers we don't talk to each other very much. But that is because I am too busy. I am starting high school, soon I will be in college, and then married to someone, not likely Izzy, but I'm really all done with my childhood and mothers and fathers and aunts and grandmothers. They were important when I lived at 405 Avenue O in the Kingdom of Brooklyn when we were all subjects who kept watch over the house and the three playgrounds and Prospect Park and Coney Island, but those places can take care of themselves now.

From the window of my bedroom I can see the mirrored ball on the pedestal in Dr. Ruby Tempkin's front yard. The doctor and his wife don't live in that house anymore, they moved to Florida after Esther died, but they left the ball in the yard. The mirror has gone gray and flat looking, even on sunny days; it reminds me of the mercury that rolls out of a broken thermometer.

I sometimes think my mother is with Beloved and my grandmother, because why wouldn't they seek one another out in the land of the dead? Still, they might do better on little islands of their own, one with a piano, one with a doghouse, and one with a bubbling pot of chicken soup.

My sister doesn't scream at all lately; we share a big bed in our bedroom that overlooks Ocean Parkway. Sometimes she sobs very softly at night and I hug her. She isn't grown up enough to think about all the things that have happened.

I tell her someday we will forget the day of the fire, I am almost certain of it. All we need is time, like a fat pillow, to fill up the space between then and later on. I explain that I can hardly remember my grandmother's face, even the way she looked at me when they put her in the ambulance, which is proof we'll get better eventually—that's the way it works when you're alive. I promise my sister that I will always take care of her and that we will both live in wonderful houses someday.

Every night I read to her a few pages of *Katrinka, The Story of a Russian Child*. When Katrinka found her parents gone, she set out on a journey with her little brother. I tell my sister that when a house falls down, one way or another, and it can't take care of you, you might as well take a deep breath, pack a few provisions, and set out for the next one.

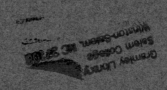